Dan Temianka

The Jack Vance Lexicon

Dan Temianka

The
Jack Vance
Lexicon

THE COINED WORDS
OF JACK VANCE:
FROM ABILOID TO ZYGAGE

Second Edition

Published by Spatterlight

Cover art by Howard Kistler

ISBN 978-1-61947-114-6

Amstelveen,
The Netherlands

www.jackvance.com

Contents

Foreword

AFTER THE PUBLICATION of The *Jack Vance Lexicon* by Underwood-Miller and Borgo Press, respectively, more than twenty years ago, Jack Vance wrote three additional novels: *Night Lamp, Ports of Call* and *Lurulu*. In those works he continued his incorrigible coining of neologisms, some 160 of them, which have been integrated into this second edition.

This volume would not have been possible without the dedication of these fine gentlemen, who are possessed of true *plambosh*:

Arjen Broeze

Wil Ceron

Patrick Dusoulier

Rob Friefeld

David A. Kennedy

Steve Sherman

John Vance

Koen Vyverman

Dave Worden

Richard K. Woodard

Dan Temianka
June 2015

INTRODUCTION

THE FORMATION OF LANGUAGE

> "Language has bloomed from the infinite fumblings
> of anonymous men."
>
> — *John Updike*

WE JABBER AND BABBLE ENDLESSLY, out loud and on paper. In the technical lingo of the electrical engineer or the mutterings of the wino, in comic strips, novels, graffiti, or the parlance of academic journals, we indulge in this frenetic process day and night, around the world. We humans are a huge orchestra, constantly "noodling" with those wonderful wind instruments, our mouths, and (in the case of sign language) with those faithful puppets, our hands and fingers.

We trowel nouns like adjectives, load and fire them as though they were verbs. We wrench our linguistic roots from the earth and clumsily graft suffixes, prefixes or spare-part slang onto them; we hurl grotesque linguistic hybrids about us with the insouciance of two-year-olds flinging their pablum.

Thus are new words born.

SOME DISTINGUISHED WORDSMITHS

But new language also blooms from the not-so-clumsy utterances of certain individual writers, particularly in the field of "speculative fiction". At least since Lewis Carroll intrigued his readers with "Jabberwocky", there have been writers — Robert Heinlein, Frank Herbert, Dr. Seuss and many others — who mint new words in addition to new concepts. Such writers are active volcanic vents, spewing out new words like fresh lava. In *A Clockwork Orange*[2], Anthony Burgess invented an entire dialect ("Nadsat, a Russified version of English") – "I could sort of slooshy myself making special sort of shoms and govoreeting slovos like 'Dear dead idlewilds, rot not in variform guises' and all that cal." This is fresh, serviceable language, not merely humdrum technical derivatives or the names of gadgets and aliens, and has certifiable potential to enter the English language. Frank Herbert was also no slouch at "wordvention": *chaumurky, sietch, filtplug, heighliner*, and the *ridulian crystals* are a few examples from *Dune*.

But for sheer variety, quantity, and above all, charm of his neologisms, I submit that none can compare with Jack Vance, a.k.a. John Holbrook Vance. As Jack Rawlins said, "...to make up words that carry just the right scent, that strike the reader as new and familiar simultaneously, is extremely challenging, and Vance is a master at it."[16] Such words can be found in virtually all of his hundreds of stories and novels, more so in those we call "science fantasy", or simply "fantasy", than in his "science fiction". (His mystery and detective works are, in this respect, staid.) It is not unusual for a single novel to have fifty or more newly created words; in *The Face* there are close to a hundred.

He created them with the instinct of a pack rat ferrying knickknacks. In *The Magnificent Showboats...*, Apollon Zamp advertises for musicians who "...play instruments of the following categories: Belphorn, screedle, cadenciver, variboom, elf-pipe, tympany, guitar, dulciole, heptagong, zinfonella." In *Galactic Effectuator*, Vance tosses off gangee, sprugge, cardenil bush, raptap and shatterbone in the space of two orgiastic paragraphs, in addition to half a dozen other species such as "antler fish" and "sea scrags", which, though novel enough, are not true neologisms. (This distinction can be maddeningly subtle, as we'll see later on.)

THE PERSONAL DICTIONARY

The invention of interesting new words in numbers sufficient to justify one's own dictionary is a remarkable achievement. G.T. McWhorter's *Burroughs Dictionary* is comparable, but consists primarily of characters and places from Edgar Rice Burrough's fiction, as its full title implies[12]; it is thus actually a concordance or encyclopedia rather than a true dictionary. And there is *The Dune Encyclopedia*[11], the extraordinarily detailed compendium of Herbertian lore, which includes many generic new words.

But the present work, like its predecessor *From Ahulph to Zipangote*, is perhaps the first true "personal dictionary" of one author's work. *From Abiloid to Zygage (second edition)* now includes some 1800 words drawn from all of his stories and novels.

This second edition is also informed by the *Vance Integral Edition* (VIE), a six-year worldwide effort by Vance's readers and admirers to produce a complete and corrected forty-four volume set of his works. These texts, now the definitive versions of Vance's oeuvre, are also available from Spatterlight Press. This edition of the *Lexicon* retains some more familiar but now obsolete titles, and indicates Vance's preferred title in the Abbreviations section.

A considerable amount of contextual information has been included in many entries. Can one define *dexax* as an explosive without mentioning Lens Larque's megalomaniacal scheme to carve out a lunar Mount Rushmore in his own image? Could the unique sports *hadaul* and *hussade* be explained without quoting extensively from Vance's vivid explanations? To Vance-lovers, the inclusion of such ancillary material requires no apology; they are in love. To those coming to Vance for the first time, it may add richness and depth.

SOME CATEGORIES

Vance's neologisms can be stratified according to several criteria. As parts of speech, most of them are nouns, and the majority of these are plants and animals and/or foods. Others designate musical instruments or weapons, define magical spells, crystallize cultural concepts or rituals, or encompass metaphors. Some, such as *skak* and *merrihew*, are footnoted with lengthy explanations about the sociology of magical creatures. Terms like *Monomantic Syntoraxis* and *Tempofluxion Dogma* reflect Vance's droll skepticism toward religion. Some are wonderfully playful, such as *pinky-panky-poo*, or simply wonderful, e.g. *scurch* and *dreuhwy* (the latter alleged by the author to have been drawn from the ancient Welsh).

The adjectives are always vivid: the colors *rawn* and *pallow* and *smaudre* (which also function as nouns), and *squalmaceous* or *halcositic*. He also gives us verbs (*disturgle, skirkling*), a few articles and cardinal numbers, and even a sprinkling of interjections and appellatives. In the latter case, Vance also sometimes includes the associated abbreviation, such as *Visfer* (contracted from *Viasvar* and abbreviated *Vv*).

Or the words may be categorized according to whether they are intended to be "English". Clearly most of them are; we are expected to read them without recoiling, though we may grope for a dictionary. Others are implicitly or expressly taken from an imaginary tongue, e.g. Paonese, or the idiom of the Dirdir, or that of the "Water-folk" (e.g. the shibbolethic *brga skth gz*). Both "English" and "non-English" neologisms are included herein.

But the most interesting way of analyzing Vance's neologisms is by guessing at their etymology.

A SPECULATIVE ETYMOLOGY

Vance's coined words fall into roughly seven categories, which shade into one another like colors in the spectrum. I list these divisions in order of decreasing distance from English.

1. Those which appear to have come into the world *de novo*, from stem to suffix. We can think of no corollary, and feel little or no resonance with known words. Examples: *dyssac* (an herb liquor), *thawn* (a bearded cave-dweller), *bgrassik* (translation uncertain).

2. Those that tantalize us with faint echoes of known words. The morphemes are rather familiar, but overall we cannot place them: *harquisade* (a variety of tree with glass foliage), *marathaxus* (a scale from the body of the demon Sadlark).

3. Words that are another neighborhood closer to reality. The echoes are louder, yet we yearn to hear them more clearly. These are "...hauntingly familiar growths, like catafalque trees and hangman trees", as Terry Dowling put it.[5] *Submulgery, ensqualm, bifaulgulate* — the reader runs to the dictionary and is surprised to find them absent. Some are so real-sounding that

they flit past like butterflies or called strikes, only to awaken us in the middle of the night with the realization that they cannot be. *Halcoid, subuculate, Chief Manciple.*

Close cousins of such words float unbidden into our consciousness. We think of "subterfuge" and "skulduggery" to explain *submulgery;* coaxed by *ensqualm,* we recall "ensnare", "qualm" and "squall"; for *bifaulgulate,* "ungulate" and a host of words beginning with the prefix "bi-" come to mind. We are crowded with conjecture.

4. Portmanteau words. This category is easily the most fascinating and treacherous; sometimes it is difficult to distinguish from the third group. Here the stems are reasonably certain, but they ignite an extended metaphor.

Thasdrubal's Laganetic Transfer was the spell used by Iucounu to banish Cugel on his search for the cusps of the Overworld. One might easily overlook the hidden word "lagan", a maritime term meaning "goods thrown into the sea with a buoy attached." This is certainly a reference to Firx, the painful parasite installed in Cugel's liver to keep his mind on his task. Moreover, the phrase is a reminder of Vance's love of sailing.

Another example is *gleft* — a kind of phantom, one of which stole part of Guyal's brain while his mother was in labor. Surely this word arose from "glia", a class of brain cells, and "theft".

An especially intriguing case is *pleurmalion,* the tube-shaped device used by Rhialto to discern the location of a precious textual prism, even from great distances in space and time. (That prism was known as the *Perciplex,* a word probably derived from "percipient" and "complex".) We cannot avoid recognition of the Latin *pleura,* meaning "side" or "rib". And mustn't the *-malion* fragment refer to Pygmalion, the legendary artist who fell in love with his sculpture of a woman and persuaded Aphrodite to bring it to life? We are struck by the insight that the *pleurmalion* relates to the lost prism as the biblical rib to a woman, bringing it (her) into view and thus to hand. They must be reunited.

Do these distinctions seem farfetched? Reflect that even the notion of far-fetchedness is germane to this point, for the *pleurmalion* was designed specifically to locate from afar! Such subtleties are uniquely Vance. Furthermore, any doubts that he actually thought along these lines are dispelled by a revealing footnote to the word *murst* in Chapter 16 of the last of the "Demon Princes" series: "The meaning of this word, like others in *The Book of Dreams* [Howard Alan Treesong's childhood notebook] can only be conjectured. (Must: urgency? With *verst*: in Old Russia, a league? Farfetched, but who knows?)"

5. In this group are words that draw clearly from identifiable roots and appendages and combine them according to traditional rules: *calligynics, malepsy, Gynodyne, photochrometz*. These are mix-'n'-match suits of clothes. The Latin, Greek or Old English roots are as readily discernible as the hem of a slip (though I cannot explain the *-etz* in the last case), and generate few if any metaphorical overtones.

Needless to say, the citation of Latin and Greek roots does not imply that they evolved as they do in real words, growing like trees through the generations. How could they, when Vance had just plucked them from his garden, as ingredients for his verbal stews? I have nonetheless included those components in the etymological portion of such entries because they often illustrate Vance's thinking. *Perrupter* (and later *Perrumpter*) is not merely a modification of "interrupter"; it displays the strength of the Latin *per*, meaning "through", and *rompere*, to break. A *perrupter* thus "breaks through" enemy lines. And perhaps Vance was even intrigued by the suggestion of the word "romp" when he was rummaging through his dictionary (which I believe he did with regularity).

Such shameless juggling of prefixes and suffixes, incidentally, was a habit of Vance's: *transpolation* (versus "extrapolation" or "transposition"), *subsede* (from "supersede" or "subsume"), and *pervulsion* ("perversion" and "convulsion"), to name only three.

Compounds. These are straightforward alloys of real words, sturdily welded or hyphenated: *sagmaw, trapperfish, sad-apple, bumbuster*, and the delightfully macabre *ghost-clutch*. He has even been known to do this in French: *garde-nez*, or "nose-protector", is a logical amalgam of *pince-nez* and *garder*, "to guard". ("An extravagant garde-nez of gold filigree clung to the ridge of his nose.")

Such compounds can seduce us into spurious assumptions. The term *elving-platform* — a birthing station for the species *hyrcan major* — implies the existence of the verb to *elve*, i.e. "to give birth to an elf"! Vance can indeed be master of the ridiculous. (Meanwhile we should not overlook that *hyrcan major* is also a fine portmanteau word, with its references to "Hyrcania", a province of the ancient Persian and Parthian empires, and "Ursa Major", the Great Bear constellation.)

6. Variant usages. These are existing words that Vance has used in such novel and intriguing ways that they should be considered neologisms: *lincture, darkling, deodand*. Or *bobadil* blossoms, woven by children into decorative ropes for the ship *Miraldra's Enchantment* in *The Magnificent Showboats…* : he has borrowed the name of Captain Bobadil, the character in Ben Jonson's *Every Man in His Humor*. Here Vance merely bent the law rather than breaking it outright. In some instances the true meaning of the variant usage is so esoteric that Vance may well not have been aware of it, e.g. *nene*. All the more credit to him.

Vance sometimes used this vehicle for satire, political or otherwise. In *The Anome*, a *syndic tree* is a unique species "…whose seeds sprouted legs and poisonous pincers. After walking to a satisfactory location, each seed roved within a ten-foot circle, poisoning all competing vegetation, then dug a hole and buried itself." In reality, a "syndic" is "a government official having different powers in different countries"!

Determining which of such terms to include in a dictionary is a subtle and vexing task. *Gruff* and *wobbly* are used so unexpectedly in *Wyst: Alastor 1716*, the meanings so removed from their customary ones, that I have included them as "variant usages". But "Brood" and "Wedge", two of the levels of achievement on the quest to immortality in *Clarges* (*To Live Forever*), seem somehow to lack the earmarks of new-wordhood. Their adopted meanings lie too close to their intrinsic ones. Novel concepts, yes; neologisms, no. If we open this door any further we are overwhelmed by a mob of cuddly puppies, and all our efforts at taxonomy fall into chaos: "pilgrim pod", "wambles", "antler fish", and on and on.

Vance also frequently misused words in ways that reflect a deep understanding of their origins. A "cornuter" is actually a cuckolder, i.e. one who "puts the horns" on someone; but in *The Face*, such an individual is an official blower of a brass horn. "Centaurium trioxide" is supposed to be a chemical in "The Sub-standard Sardines", but "centaurium" is in reality a genus of herbs. "Frivols, Flimsies, Flapdoodles" are fancy desserts listed on the menu of a ritzy restaurant (*The Face*). Most such subtly redirected words have been omitted from this book.

Vance's use of obsolete terms, such as "vellope" and "dominie", demands a passing comment. In *Cugel's Saga*, he refers to the great magician, Makke the Maugifer. Now, "mauger" means "ill-will" or "spite", and is listed only as a noun in modern dictionaries; one must go to the *Oxford English Dictionary* to find its listing as a transitive verb — (spelled "maugre"). Yet Vance not only uses it as a verb in various forms — "...he ruled the land with his mauging magic. He mauged east and he mauged west, north and south" — he also coins the terms *maugery* and *Maugifer*, "a maker of spite". Vance set no limits on what materials could be used as substrate for his verbal alchemy.

As implied at the beginning of this section, the origins of Vance's invented words are open to speculation. In many cases no etymological surmise came to mind, and the reader is invited to make his own. Ultimately a personal dictionary is no more objective or scientific than biography or history.

Regrettably, there are a few words which Vance used only once and left undefined either explicitly or by context, e.g. *isthiated* (a term which the sprite from the realm of Green Magic used in connection with two of the universal regions), or *squalings* in *Lyonesse*. These are hors d'oeuvres for the imagination.

The lovely Mrs. Vance was once kind enough to read some of the conjectures in this book to the author. "He found them amusing", she reported. "Many of the names no doubt were derived from subconscious association(s), and some even consciously, but others, like 'shamb' with 'shambling' have no connection whatever, according to Jack."

PROPER NAMES

Vance had an extraordinary ability to concoct names, and he produced them with the ease and incandescence of a comet spurting through the ether. Many are exquisitely amusing. It is with the greatest reluctance that this volume excludes such beauties as Throdorous Gassoon, Evulsifer, Sangreal Rubloon, Visbhume, Semm Voiderveg, Emacho Feroxibus, Schiafarilla, Uthaw, Yaa-Yimpe and a thousand others.

But moreover, where many other writers might merely invent something fanciful, many of Vance's proper nouns hint strongly at the existence of daily words, and some of these have been included: *Universal Pancomium* (a boat's name) suggests a more generalized category of "encomium"; the name of a spaceship, the *Dylas Extranuator*, compels us to ask what *extranuate* means — could it denote "to strain in wonder"? A building called the *Catademnon* — a wondrous gust of ancient Greek syllables! — is certainly not a mere confection, reminding us as it does of "condemn", "Agamemnon", and "Parthenon", all of which relate to the hero Emphyrio and his tragic fate. One senses that the word *Flamboyard* — "...a feathered two-legged fruit eater, the most gaudy and bizarre creature imaginable" — will someday lose its capitalization and refer generally to any outlandish figure.

A FEW POINTS OF ORDER

The index word and its definition are followed by the abbreviated title(s) and chapter(s) where it was found. A key to the abbreviations is appended at the end of this Introduction. Many words found such widespread or repeated usage that it was impossible to cite all their appearances; accordingly, the chapter references denote the first and/or most significant appearance(s). Where Vance footnoted a neologism with an explanation, I have so indicated by adding an asterisk (*) after the chapter number, and have reproduced his comment.

The entry word itself, and its appearance in any direct quotations from text, is italicized only if Vance did so. However, neologisms are always italicized when referred to in other discussions herein.

In formulating the definitions, I have tried to integrate descriptions and references which appear in various places throughout the pertinent text(s). I have taken the liberty of assuming that characteristics applied in a single instance were universal. For example, if an *olophar* tree is described as "thick-boled", I define the tree as generally having that characteristic, or at least specify that an *olophar* was "commonly thick-boled". Or if Vance referred to "a visp's melancholy call", I made the assumption that the voice of those creatures generally had such a timbre.

The etymological conjectures appear in brackets after the definitions. Variant usages are indicated as such; where the normal meaning of the variantly used word is not obvious, it is included in quotations.

Some of the imaginary words in Vance's *oeuvre* have undoubtedly been overlooked. Likewise some which have been included will be discovered to have already staked out their turf in a "real" dictionary somewhere, or perhaps in some obscure botanical or Welsh historical text. The righting of such wrongs is left to posterity.

A BRIEF CONCLUSION

Most neologisms remain in their literary greenhouses, to be enjoyed only by visitors. But some have escaped and spread like weeds to become part of the language: Heinlein's *grok*, for example. How many of Vance's mintings will infiltrate our daily gab? Will we send our enemies *skirkling*, or drink *skull-busters* at the corner bar? Will our windows be made of *translux*? Will some enterprising metallurgist name his new compound *herculoy*? But these questions are nuncupatory.

In *The Languages of Pao*, Vance explored the notion of using created languages as instruments of social engineering. Let us hope that his whimsical words — "Whimsicant" — are already doing just that.

REFERENCES

1. Bailey, L.H., Manual of Cultivated Plants, Macmillan, New York, 1949.

2. Burgess, Anthony, A Clockwork Orange, W.W. Norton & Co., New York, 1963.

3. Burgess, Anthony, Language Made Plain, Fontana Paperbacks, London, 1984.

4. Byrne, J. H., Mrs. Byrne's Dictionary, University Books, Secaucus, 1974.

5. Dowling, Terry, "The Art of Xenography: Jack Vance's 'General Culture' Novels", in Science Fiction: A Review of Speculative Literature, Vol. 1 no. 3, December, 1978.

6. Farb, Peter, Word Play, Alfred Knopf, New York, 1974.

7. Funk, Isaac K., Funk & Wagnalls New Standard Dictionary of the English Language, Funk & Wagnalls Press, New York and London, 1913.

8. Glare, P.G.W., Ed., The Oxford Latin Dictionary, Clarendon Press, Oxford, 1982.

9. Gove, Philip B., Ed., Webster's Third New International Dictionary, G. & C. Merriam Company, Springfield, 1968.

10. McKechnie, Jean L., Ed., Webster's New Universal Unabridged Dictionary, Simon & Schuster, New York, 1979.

11. McNelly, W.E., The Dune Encyclopedia, G.P. Putnam's Sons, New York, 1984.

12. McWhorter, George T., Burroughs Dictionary: An alphabetical list of proper names, words, phrases and concepts contained in the published works of Edgar Rice Burroughs, University Press, Lanham, MD, 1987.

13. Oxford University, The Compact Edition of the Oxford English Dictionary, Oxford University Press, Oxford, 1971.

14. Plowden, C. C., A Manual of Plant Names, Philosophical Library, New York, 1969.

15. Pukui, M.K. and Elbert S.H., Hawaiian Dictionary, U. of Hawaii Press, Honolulu, 1971.

16. Rawlins, Jack, Demon Prince: The Dissonant Worlds of Jack Vance, Borgo Press, San Bernardino, 1986.

17. Rebora, Piero, Cassell's Italian Dictionary, Funk & Wagnalls, New York, 1959.

18. Smith, A.W., and Stearn, William T., A Gardener's Dictionary of Plant Names, St. Martin's Press, New York, 1972.

19. Swartz, Delbert, The Collegiate Dictionary of Botany, Ronald Press Co., New York, 1971.

ABBREVIATIONS

AA   "The Augmented Agent" (a.k.a. "I-C-a-BeM")

AbS   "Abercrombie Station"

An   *The Anome* (a.k.a. *The Faceless Man*)

AOC   "Assault on a City" (VIE: "The Insufferable Red-Headed Daughter of Commander Tynnott O.T.E.")

ArS   *Araminta Station*

As   *The Asutra*

BD   *The Book of Dreams*

BE   *The Brains of Earth* (VIE: *Nopalgarth*)

BFM   *The Brave Free Men*

BG   "Brain of the Galaxy" (VIE: "The New Prime")

BP   *Big Planet*

BW   *Blue World*

CC   *City of the Chasch* (VIE: *The Chasch*)

CD   "Chateau d'If" (a.k.a. "New Bodies for Old")

ChC   "Cholwell's Chickens"

CI   "Cat Island" (a never-completed story outline published in Light from a Lone Star, NESFA Press, Cambridge, 1985)

CS   *Cugel's Saga* (VIE: *Cugel: The Skybreak Spatterlight*)

D   *The Dirdir*

DC   "I'll Build Your Dream Castle" (a.k.a. "Dream Castle")

DE   *The Dying Earth* (VIE: *Mazirian the Magician*)

DJ   "Dodkin's Job"

DM	*The Dragon Masters*
DSB	"The Devil on Salvation Bluff"
DTA	"The Dogtown Tourist Agency"
E	*Emphyrio*
EO	*The Eyes of the Overworld* (VIE: *Cugel the Clever*)
EOE	*Cadwal II: Ecce and Old Earth*
EP	"The Enchanted Princess" (a.k.a. "The Enchanted Princess and Roger Atkin" and "The Dreamer")
F	*The Face*
FHB	"Four Hundred Blackbirds"
FT	"Freitzke's Turn"
GG	"The Gift of Gab"
GI	*Gold and Iron* (a.k.a. *Planet of the Damned* and *Slaves of the Klau*)
GM	"Green Magic"
GP	*The Green Pearl*
GPr	*The Gray Prince* (VIE: *The Domains of Koryphon*)
HB	"The Howling Bounders"
HI	*The Houses of Iszm*
HLD	"Hard Luck Diggings"
ISV	International Scientific Vocabulary
KM	*The Killing Machine*
KT	"The King of Thieves"
KW	"The Kokod Warriors"
L	*Lyonesse I* (VIE: *Suldrun's Garden*)
LC	*The Last Castle*
LP	*The Languages of Pao*
Lu	*Lurulu*
M	*Madouc*
Ma	*Marune: Alastor 933*
MD	"Masquerade on Dicantropus"

MM   "The Moon Moth"

MMU   "Meet Miss Universe"

Mo   "Morreion"

MT   *Maske: Thaery*

MTB   "Men of the Ten Books" (VIE: "The Ten Books")

MW   "The Miracle Workers"

MZ   "The Man from Zodiac" (VIE: "Milton Hack from Zodiac")

NL   *Night Lamp*

OM   "Overlords of Maxus" (VIE: "Crusade to Maxus")

PBD   "Planet of the Black Dust" (a.k.a. "Planet of the Red Star")

PF   "Phalid's Fate"

PL   *The Palace of Love*

PM   "The Planet Machine" (a.k.a. "The Plagian Siphon". VIE: "The Uninhibited Robot")

Pn   *The Pnume*

PoC   *Ports of Call*

R   "Rumfuddle"

Rh   *Rhialto the Marvellous*

S   "The Secret"

S25   "Sail 25" (a.k.a. "Gateway to Strangeness" and "Dust of Far Suns")

SEB   "Seven Exits from Bocz"

ShW   *Showboat World* (VIE: *The Magnificent Showboats of the Lower Vissel River, Lune XXIII South, Big Planet*)

Sj   "Sjambak"

SK   *The Star King*

SO   *Space Opera*

SP   *The Space Pirate* (a.k.a. *The Five Gold Bands*. VIE : *The Rapparee*)

SpS   "The Spa of the Stars"

SSh   "Sanatoris Shortcut"

SSP	"Sabotage on Sulfur Planet"
SSt	"The Sub-standard Sardines"
ST	*Son of the Tree*
SU	"Shape-Up"
SvW	*Servants of the Wankh* (VIE: *The Wannek*)
T	"Telek"
TB	"To Be or Not To C or to D" (a.k.a. "Cosmic Hotfoot")
Th	*Throy*
TLF	*To Live Forever* (VIE: *Clarges*)
TLJ	"Three-Legged Joe"
ToH	"The Temple of Han" (VIE: "The God and the Temple Robber")
Tr	*Trullion: Alastor 2262*
UM	"The Unspeakable McInch"
UQ	"Ultimate Quest" (VIE: "Dead Ahead")
UR	"Ullward's Retreat"
W	*Wyst: Alastor 1716*
WB	"The World Between" (a.k.a. "Ecological Onslaught")
WFMR	"When the Five Moons Rise"
WHF	"Where Hesperus Falls"
WLA	"Winner Lose All" (VIE: "The Visitors")

THE JACK VANCE LEXICON

A

A ros ros ros
The battle cry of the carrier birds at Castle Hagedorn. [? from the German *heraus*, "out", and/or the Latin *rostrum*, "beak".] **LC** *II*

Abiloid
A slow explosive used by the Klau; it was manufactured in "canisters the size of apples", packed in crates, and detonated by means of thread-like fuses. Ten such crates were equal in power to a small cut of "Super", a high explosive which "... smashes. Abiloid pushes." See also *diambroid*. **GI** *XII*

Abracadabrist
A member of a mystical cult. [From "abracadabra".] **TLF** *XVII*

Acclaimander
A famous and important person: "... then along the wide boulevard of Acclaimanders, with its rows of monumental black iron statues to either side, each representing a grandee of substance and reputation ..." [From "acclaim".] **Th** *III*

accr
"... an atomic fuel, compressed electricity, solidified radiation." It was used in the Klau's air-cars, and proved identical to "Super", a high explosive. **GI** *XVI*

activant
1. Generally, any of a magician's potions or implements; the term

was used in reference to the possessions of Iucounu the Laughing Magician. (EO) 2. A knob or lever on the *Mechanismus* (q.v.) in the Museum of Man; its manipulation altered the image of the ghost Blikdak. (DE) [From "activate".] *EO I, DE VI*

Actuarian
The institution where the life-data of all citizens was processed for purposes of determining "slope", or progress towards eternal life. [From "actuary".] *TLF III*

adarak
A tall, commonly yellow-green tree resembling a poplar and having a fresh odor. *CC VI*

advouter
A proponent of the *Tempofluxion Dogma* (q.v.). [? combination of "advocate" and "devout".] *BP XII*

Aelsheur
"…literally: air-color", a delicate shade sometimes used in interior decoration. See also *Ael'skian*. *BFM V**

Ael'skian
"Color-lore. More exactly, the symbology of color and color-combinations; in Shant an intensely meaningful aspect of life, adding another dimension to perception." *BFM I**

aernid
An envelope; the *Aernid Koromatik* ("chromatic envelope") was a popular and comprehensive newspaper. *BFM II**

aerospore
An organic material used to pack pads for sleeping. [From the Greek *aer*, "air", and "spore".] *GPr VIII*

aersk
"Untranslatable. Loosely, a fearless nobleman of the high crags, whose first needs are space, sunlight and storms." *As VI**

afflock

"…that implement with the pronged ball at the end of an elastic thong"; it was used in the combat sport *hadaul* (q.v.). **F** *XI*

agrix

A terminal kink of one of the *veruli*, or fibers, on the body of Miss Aries 44R951, an extraterrestrial participant in the Miss Universe contest; related terms are *clavon*, *gadel*, *orgote* and *therulta* (q.v.). **MMU** *IV*

ahagaree

A spice derived from bog-algae on Dar Sai and served as a staple; it was advertised as "fine Darsh provender" at Tintle's Shade. Its taste, however, was "ferocious", no doubt owing to its being seasoned with sulfur, iodine and sometimes red-oil. To the Darsh it was "…as valuable by weight as good black *duodecimate* [q.v.]." A milder preparation was available for tourists, "modified to suit the off-world taste." **F** *III**

ah-oo-cha

A meaningless ritual call: "At sundown face the east and utter a loud cry: 'Ah-oo-cha!' No one knows what it means but that is the Seraf way." **D** *II*

ahulph

"A half-intelligent biped autochthonous to Durdane, ranging wild in the backlands and wildernesses, on occasion tamed, bred and crossbred for a variety of uses, from unskilled labor and portage to house pets. When sick, the ahulph exudes a detestable odor that excites even itself to complaint" (An); the animal could control four odors as a means of communication. It was also used as a bloodhound, and its hide was tanned for leather. See also *chumpa*. **An** *I**, **As** *III*, **BFM** *II*

ai

The number one in the Paonese language. **LP** *X*

Ain

On Cadwal, "this day of", a term used in combination with the word for each of seven metals to represent the days of the week. "As the root language became archaic and was superseded, the *Ain* was lost and the days were designated simply by the metal names alone." See also *glimmet, ing, milden, ort, smollen, tzein* and *verd*. [Variant usage.] **ArS** I

aine
The number one in the Dirdir language. **D** X

aiole
A food additive used in the preparation of *percebs* (q.v.). **W** XII*

air-swish
A conductor's baton, as translated from the language of the Water-folk. [Compound.] **SO** VIII

air-weft
A flying conveyance. [Compound.] **E** I

a-kao-ut
The Pherasic word meaning "swift flyer"; Paddy Blackthorne used it as a euphemistic translation for "rascal". **SP** V

allombrosa
A forest tree, commonly dark blue. **ArS** V

almack
A riparian tree with a silver trunk and silver-purple fronds. **As** III

almirantes
A variety of tree, often cultivated in lush gardens. **Th** IV

Altengelb
A drink that Hilyer and Althea Fath, Jaro's adoptive parents, reserve for special occasions. "Althea jumped to her feet and poured three small glasses of the special Altengelb and gave one to Jaro. This was the wine of occasion, and Jaro sensed that something significant was afoot." [Compound; from the German *alt*, "old", and *gelb*, "yellow", referring probably to its age and color.] **NL** IV-1

alume

1. A semi-precious stone. (CS) 2. A common savanna plant. (Pn) **CS V-1, Pn X**

alyptus

A variety of tree, often black. [By shortening of "eucalyptus".] **As III**

amloid

A distorted, half-human rock-goblin; they had "…peaking scalps and neckless heads, so that their mouths opened directly into their upper torsos." **CS IV-2**

amphire

A type of wood, not described; it was delivered by caravan along with aromatics and essences. **CC VI**

amphruscule

One of "the enameled tablets forming the shoulder insignia and chest medallion of a Trelancthian knight." **BD XIV**

Anathresis

One of the "Natural Doctrines" taught at the Monomantic seminary of the Zubenites, along with *Thresis* and *Syntoraxis* (q.v.). [? humorous take on the Hegelian *thesis*, *antithesis*, and *synthesis*.] **ArS VIII**

anathrodetic

Uncertain; see *malleator*. **PoC VI-1**

andelwipe

A pejorative and probably vulgar term. [? euphemism for "ass-wipe".] **CS III-1**

andoril

Any of a group of "…large vicious *andromorphs* [q.v.]. Because of the difficulties of research, their habits remain obscure." One of them "… must have been twelve feet tall, with curving black shoulder horns and a crest of five bones. I knew he would like nothing better than to eat me, and he knew that I knew."

On Shattorak, "Certain varieties of andorils used a spoken language which, try as they might, linguists were unable to interpret."

And: "Perched in one of the branches [of a dead tree] was a disconsolate mud-walker: a gangling half-simian andoril eight feet tall, all bony arms and legs and tall narrow head. Tufts of white hair surrounded a visage formed of twisted cartilage and plaques of horn, with a pair of ocular stalks and a proboscis on its spindly chest." The proboscis was capable of emitting repellant fluids in self-defense. Further: "Coming upon large predators they showed what seemed reckless audacity, throwing branches, prodding the creature with their lances, then darting aside from its lunges on great high-legged jumps, sometimes even running up and down a massive back, shrilling and chittering in glee, until the beleaguered creature submerged in the river or the slime, or fled pounding into the jungle."

On Throop's Heath (Th) they sometimes "played their odd version of bowls." **ArS** III*, **EOE** Precursory, **Th** VIII

andromorph

A man-like creature. See also *andoril*. [From the Greek *andros*, "man", and *morphe*, "form".] **E** I, **ArS** III* et al., **EOE** VIII

andrope

A dumb, possibly man-like creature: "Even andropes can be guided." [? from "android".] **F** VIII

Anfangel dongobel

See *sphincter-clasp*. **CS** I-2

angbut

A food eaten by the Green Chasch, possibly fish. **CC** VI

angelesine

A type of floss used to make carpeting. [? from "angel" or "Los Angeles".] **OM** III

anissus

A sweet tree indigenous to the Darsh "shades", or oases covered with giant parasols. **F** VII

ankhe

"Malaise [is] a loose rendering of the word *ankhe*: futility, depression, discouragement." [? by association with the German *angst*, "anxiety".] *MT XV**

annel
A bush whose leaves were rubbed on the skin as an astringent, or chewed to disguise the breath. *CC X, E VI*

anome
A nameless traveler: "And I said, no, it is just another of the anomes who creep into Travelers' Inn for a sight of their own kind." [? from "anomia", the inability to name objects, or "anomie", a state of disorientation or anxiety.] *SvW IV*

Anome, The
The anonymous supreme governor of Shant, its "administrant of ultimate justice". He exercised power by means of the "torc", or explosive collar, which every citizen was required to wear around his neck and which he could activate from any distance. Also known as the Faceless Man, the *Anome* proved to be Sajarano of Sershan. *An I*

anthion
A species of aromatic plant. [From the Greek *anthos*, "flower".] *Ma VIII*

anthrocore
An anthropomorphic creature. [From the Greek *anthropos*, "man".] *OM IX*

anthrophib
A primordial ancestor of the race indigenous to Iszm: "...Diun, the primordial anthrophib, crawled out of the ocean. With saltwater still draining from his gills he took refuge in a pod." [From the Greek *anthropos*, "man", and *amphibios*, "amphibious".] *HI III*

anti-heptant
See *heptant*. *TLF VII*

apar
A variety of tree. [Variant usage: "the three-banded armadillo".] *An I*

Appodex
A high ecclesiastical title, often prefaced by "Holy". *F XV*

aquaclave
A musical instrument, not described, used in "the old Poly-Pacific Empire". [From the Latin *aqua*, "water", and *clavis*, "key".] **WHF**

aquastel
A chemical sometimes used in wizard's potions. [From the Latin *aqua*, "water".] *EO VII*

aquefact
An artist who created "intricate constructions of congealed water" displayed on pedestals; also, the sculpture itself. The artwork was produced in the gravity-free environment of space, and solidified with a mesongun. [From the Latin *aqua*, "water", and *facere*, "to do".] **TLF** *III*

arafin
A material used to fabricate tubing and roofing for the giant parasols covering the Darsh desert oases, or "shades". *F IX*

aratin
A potent poison which made the "face yellow, eyes and tongue hanging loose." It caused the brain to bubble "…like a pot of hot mush." Also used as a verb, to *aratinize*. **SSP** *II*

archveult
A species of tall, powerful magician with blue-scaled skin and a plumed headdress. [? from the Greek *archos*, "ruler", and ?]. **Rh** *I*

arcoid
Of or like an arc; see *Clincture*. [From "arc" and the Greek *oïdes*, "resembling".] **L** *XV*

Arenasaur
A denizen of Mars. [From the Latin *arena*, "sand", and *saurus*, "lizard".] **MMU** *I*

argove

A variety of arbor tree. **BFM** *XIV*

ariactin

A potent drug used illicitly to enrage a *bunter* (q.v.). **ArS** *V*

Aroisus

An exclamatory magical term having the power to transform a square of pink and white silk into a secure pavilion; the device was given to Madouc by her mother, the fairy Twisk, and reverted to the form of a handkerchief when its owner shouted "Deplectus". **M** *VIII*

arthrodine

A gentle stimulant, administered parenterally. **PF** *I*

arusch'thain

"The language of Shant discriminates between various types of sunsets. Hence: [*arusch'thain* is] a violet sunset with horizontal apple-green clouds." See also *feovhre, gorusjurhe, heizhen* and *shergorszhe*. **BFM** *V**

arzack

An aromatic wood used for carving; the tree was common in the woods back of Perdue, and seldom grew to a thickness of more than three feet. **E** *III*

asi achih

A Darsh expletive of fatalistic acceptance meaning, "And so it went", or, "That's the way it goes." **F** *IX**

asm

A dangerous, intelligent animal haunting the Plain of Standing Stones; it had eight fangs, a black forehead and bristling antennae, and spoke in a soft blurred voice. **CS** *V-2*

asofa

A plant whose roots were desirable as barter. **D** *II*

aspergantium

A bitter liquid; for philosophical reasons, Gaulph Rabi used a few drops to make his wine less palatable. [From *"aspergillum"*, a perforated globe for sprinkling holy water.] **CS** *IV-2*

asponistra
A variety of tree. **SvW** *XVI*

astinche
An agile *andromorph* (q.v.) unique to the Bethune Preserve: "…a local evolutionary development. The genus is especially rich on Shanar and in this particular neighborhood." It had a face "…formed of mottled red and blue cartilage", a glossy black pelt, and a crest "…like a small black hat." The creature's breeding habits, development and body chemistry were mysteries. Several varieties were known: a small one was known as the "puppet mandarin", while another could grow as tall as thirty feet. **BD** *XVIII*

asutra
An intelligent, parasitic creature which "…resembled a large insect, eight inches long and four inches in thickness: a hybrid of ant and tarantula, mingled with something unimaginable. Six arms, each terminating in three clever palps, depended from the torso. At one end ridges of purple-brown chitin protected the optical process: three oil-black balls in shallow cavities tufted with hair. Below trembled feeder mechanisms and a cluster of mandibles." (As)

"The creature was gnarled and convoluted like a small brown brain; eight jointed legs left the underside of the body, each terminating in three strong little palps. The long fibers or nerves extended from one end through a cluster of sensory organs." (BFM) It implanted itself into the chest and neck of its host, which it then controlled to its own ends. **As** *I*, **BFM** *XVI*

atomite
1. A form of atomic explosive; it was used in combination with "centaurium" to alter the course of the black star Noir. (TB) 2. A powerful fuel used in cutting torches. (MD) [From "atom".] **TB, MD**

atrachid
A mammoth creature indigenous to the Didion Swamp. **AOC** *II*

attander

A feared creature inhabiting swale-shadows. **CC II**

aud

"On Marune, day and night do not alternate as is the case with most planets. Instead, there are varying conditions of light, depending upon which sun or suns rule the sky; and these periods are designated by a specific nomenclature. Aud, isp, red rowan, green rowan, and umber are the ordinary gradations. Night occurs at intervals regulated by a complex pattern, on the average about once every thirty days." See also *chill isp*. **Ma III**

audiarium

A lecture, particularly that given by Kerlin, the Curator at the Museum of Man. [From the Latin *audire*, "to hear", and *arius*, "a connected thing or place".] **DE VI**

aurau

"Untranslatable; said of a tribesman afflicted with revulsion against civilized restrictions, and sometimes of a caged animal yearning for freedom." **GPr II***

autoflex

A medical computer. **NL III-3**

autolume

An illuminating device. [From the Greek *auto-*, "self", and the Latin *lumen*, "light".] **HB**

averroi

A grandee: "The Methlen term *averroi* signifies a status considerably more elevated than that connoted by the term 'gentleman'. *Averroi* implies dignity, punctilio, exclusivity, social poise and an unthinking mastery of Methlen etiquette. The Methlen give lip service to the fiction that any Methlen ranks on even terms with any other; hence they use a single honorific, here rendered by 'the Gentle'. In actual fact social distinctions are very real, reflecting factors far too numerous and subtle to be considered here." **F VIII***

avistioi
"The constabulary of the Aesthetic Corporation." (An)
"Discriminator: in the language of Shant ... literally, 'nice
discriminator'. The *avistioi* originally were inspectors hired by the
Garwiy Aesthetes, and only gradually assumed the function of the
cantonal police." (As) ***An X*, As II*, BFM I****

avness
"...the name of that pale hour immediately before sunset: a sad quiet
time when all color seemed to have drained from the world, and
the landscape revealed no dimensions other than those suggested
by receding planes of ever paler haze. Avness, like dawn, was a time
unsympathetic to the Trill temperament; the Trills had no taste for
melancholy reverie." During avness, the sky became "suffused with the
color of watered milk." ***Tr V***

awaile
A form of aberrant behavior similar to running amok: "The afflicted
person — one who feels shame — kills as many persons as he is able,
of any sex, age, or degree of relationship. Then, when he is able to
kill no more, he submits and becomes apathetic. His punishment is
dreadful and highly dramatic, and enlightens the entire population,
who crowd the place of punishment. Each execution has its particular
flavor and style and is essentially a dramatic pageant of pain, possibly
enjoyed even by the victim. The institution permeates the life of Cath.
The Dirdir on this basis consider all sub-men mad." ***SvW III***

ay caray
An ejaculation, akin to "ai caramba!". ***Th VIII***

Azday
A day of the week. ***SvW VII***

B

backwad
"Slang of the period: an ill-favored or otherwise repulsive woman. Etymology uncertain." One of them was described: "Face like a plateful of boiled pig's feet. She's not wearing a sweater; that's the hair on her arms." [Compound.] *AOC**

baicha
A species of tree; the smoke from its burning roots was inhaled by the Trevanyi "Grotesques" (seers) to induce an oracular state of mind, while others performed "bounding mood-dances". *Tr XIX*

baldama
A variety of tall forest tree. *EO V*

ballygagger
A word of insult. "Then you're going with this ballygagger to the recital?" [Portmanteau of "bally", and "lallygagger", meaning "dawdler".] *NL IX-4*

balt-ape
"…a white-sided creature splotched with black fur", indigenous to the Bethune Preserve. Its head was "half-bear, half-insect". The *balt-ape* was often twenty feet tall and moved with a "shambling trot". *BD XVIII*

balticon
A type of precious mineral found on Mars. *CD II*

balwoon
A variety of bush. *ArS V*

bandock
A variety of flatland plant, commonly rich green and "…raising a single pale blue spine that flicked at passing insects." *An VIII*

bane-bug
A species of noisome insect indigenous to Trans-Iskana.
[Compound.] **BD** IX

bangleberry
A fruit from which a type of rum was distilled. [Compound.] **F** XII

bangle-blossom
A tree on Fader. "There, with the pedicure salon to one side and a
great black bangle-blossom tree to the other, you will find the IPCC."
[Compound.] **NL** XIII-10

banice
A species of forest tree. **Ma** VI

banion
A variety of tree, commonly purple and found alongside rivers. [?
variant of "banyan".] **E** IV

banjee
"One of the many varieties of mandoril [q.v.] indigenous to Cadwal.
The usual banjee is a massive two-legged creature, somewhat
andromorphic, if grotesquely so. The banjee is sheathed in chitin,
black in the mature male, which stands eight to nine feet tall. The
head is covered with stiff black hair except for the frontal visage of
naked bone.

"The banjees are remarkable in many ways. They begin life as
neuters, become female at the age of six years, metamorphose to
males at the age of sixteen, growing each year thereafter in size, mass
and ferocity, until they are eventually killed in battle.

"Banjees communicate in a language impervious to the most subtle
analytical methods of the Gaean linguists. The banjees construct tools
and weapons, and exhibit what seems to be the glimmerings of an
aesthetic sense, which, like the language, evades the understanding of
the human mind.

"Banjees are intractable and while ferocious are not actively
aggressive under ordinary conditions. They are well aware of the
tourists who crowd the terrace at Mad Mountain Lodge to watch

them pass, but pay no heed. Reckless persons sometimes approach the marching hordes or even the battles in order to secure dramatic photographs. Emboldened by the apparent indifference of the banjees, they venture a step or two closer, then another step, which takes them past some imperceptible boundary in the banjees' 'zone of reaction', and then they are killed." They were also known to manufacture magic stone spheres and tablets. [? corruption of banshee.] *ArS V*, EOE III, Th I*

banner-bush
A common species of plant. [Compound.] *BW XII*

bant-iron
A type of stoneworker's tool. [Compound.] *EO III*

bantock
A variety of cultivated plant. *W IV*

barchnut
A type of nut gathered by the Trevanyi. *Tr IV*

bardicant
A large wild animal having a skewer-like tail which it used in defense. "…a heavy-headed beast with a lithe slate-gray body", indigenous to Deucas. It "…devoured anything which came its way with undiscriminating voracity." *ArS V, EOE II*

bargoon
A type of garment for the upper body: "There were shirts and pleated bargoons of fine white silk." *M IV*

batasta
See *busta batasta*. *M IX*

batracher
A variety of frog, often pickled for food. [From "*Batrachia*", the class Amphibia.] *W IV*

batrachies
Comestible served at the Three Feathers Inn on Fluter. They go with

vinegar, and the patrons call for more! [From "*Batrachia*", the family of frogs and salamanders.] *Lu II-2*

battarache
A form of high explosive. *D II*

batter-brain
A variety of plant "…with branches terminating in clublike knots." [Compound.] *ArS VII*

battern
A platter or portion, as of *twirps* (q.v.). *BD VIII*

bauk
An animal whose leather was used for boots. *CS III-1*

bawberry
A dark plant growing in groves. *An VIII*

bazil
A vile monster which, according to the casebook of the mad wizard Follinense (EO), was a hybrid of "felinodore, man, (wasp?)". It appeared in the form of a chimera as Nissifer: "…a burly black creature of hybrid character, half sime and half bazil, with a bristle of black fur between the eyes. From a rusty black thorax depended the segmented abdomen of a wasp; down the back hung sheaths of black chitin-like wing-cases. Four thin black arms ended in long thin human hands; thin shanks of black chitin and peculiar padded feet supported the thorax with the abdomen hanging between." [See Kevin Johnson's picture on the front jacket of the Timescape edition of *Cugel's Saga*, Simon and Schuster, New York, 1983.] *EO V, CS IV-2*

bear-fungus
A pleasantly pungent, olive-drab growth indigenous to tundras. [Compound.] *ChC III*

belchberry
A variety of berry from which a beverage called *belchberry sprig* was made. [Compound.] *BD XII*

belch-wort

A bitter plant from which, together with *nuxium*, Faucelme prepared a noxious, beer-like tea for a group of importunate *mermelants* (q.v.). [Compound.] *CS III-2*

bell-bug

A small insect which produced a tinkling sound. [Compound.] *An I*

bellegarde

A common herb having a pleasant odor. [From the French *belle*, "beautiful", and *garder*, "to keep".] *DM I*

belphorn

A popular wind instrument. *ShW V*, *Lu II-3*

belsifer

A legume whose roots were sometimes made into dumplings and garnished with saffron. *F XII*

Benchmaster

The title of a magistrate. "The Lord High Benchmaster no longer rode to the bench in a chair carried by four blind virgins, but the bench itself — the 'Balance' — still rested upon a wedge-shaped fulcrum, even though most progressive Benchmasters stipulated stabilizing struts to dampen the quivering Needle of Justice." Further, "The Benchmaster who rode the Balance so rigidly that the needle showed no motion, in the sly vernacular of the courtroom, was said to be 'stiff of arse', while a more restless official, under whose shifts and shrugs the needle swung back and forth, might become known as 'old flitter-britches'." [Compound.] *F IV**

bereglo

"...a word typically Paonese, applied to an unskillful slaughter-house worker, or a creature which worries and gnaws its victim." *LP V*

berl

A lithe, brown, predatory, boar-headed creature with long arms emanating from its neck. *CC II*

bewalkus
The arse: "…that's the very chair where he planted his bewalkus." **BD** *XII*

bezander
A type of piece in the chess-like game played by Vus and Vuwas, the two *gryphs* (griffins) which guarded the portal to Murgen's castle; other such pieces included the *darkdog*, the *mordyke* and the *reignet*. **M** *V*

Bezzler
A member of an aloof caste on Blue World. [By shortening of "embezzler".] **BW** *I*

bgrassik
A word in the language of the Water-folk, of uncertain translation: "Whatever it means it's something the singers do incorrectly when attempting to — another unfamiliar phrase: *thelu gy shlrama* during orchestral implications, which result in faulty *ghark jissu*, whatever that is." See also *brga skth gz*. **SO** *VIII*

bice
A small unit of currency, possibly equivalent to a penny: "I don't care a bice for your life." (SvW) "Are you the sort to go hungry because you begrudge the outlay of a few bice?" (Pn) [Variant usage: "a blue or green pigment"; and by association with "trice".] **SvW** *X*, **Pn** *VI*, **D** *XXII*, **E** *XVI*

bidechtil
The class or genus of fish or crustaceans to which the *spraling* (q.v.) belonged. **CS** *II-2*

Bidrachate Dendicap
A creature native to Capella's fourth planet: "…rather decent creatures, about five feet tall, with a heavy black fur. They have two little legs, and what's under the fur is anybody's guess." The *Dendicaps*, referred to colloquially as " 'caps", relished sulfur "like salt"; and though they loved music, they "…wouldn't know a concerto from a punch in the nose." **SO** *I*

bifaulgulate

A characteristic of certain *sandestins* (q.v.), not specified. [? by association with "ungulate".] **Rh** *II*

biffle

A nonsense term from a piece of doggerel sung at Tintle's Shade: "With her biffle belly, monstrous arse and gibble-gobble face." **F** *VI*

bilibob

A variety of yellow flower. Also *bilbob* (Th IV). See also *chulastic* and *thrum-tree*. **EO** *VII*

biloa

A species of grazing bird eaten as fowl; it sometimes attacked men when aroused. **E** *VII*

Binadary

See *Pan-Djan Binadary*. **MT** *Intro.*

bindlebane

A common species of plant which gave off a cloudy blue seepage; the leaves were used to form polished buttons for the uniforms of the Exemplars, and, more importantly, proved to be a source of iron. [Compound.] **BW** *XII*

birkwood

A type of wood used to make swords. [Compound.] **BP** *III*

blackbirk

A rare variety of wood used to make the *khitan* (q.v.). [Compound.] **BFM** *II*

black-tox

A form of poison. [From "black" and "toxin".] **PL** *II*

bladder-buggy

A type of omnibus — "a bumping thudding platform supported by rolling air-cushions." [Compound.] **PL** *X*

bladder-bush

A common plant. [Compound.] **D** *V*

bladder-sting
A medical instrument used to administer *hyperas* (q.v.). [Compound.] **MT** VI

blastiff
An unspecified creature: "...touchy as a blastiff with boils." [? from "blast" and "mastiff".] **F** IV

blinko
A child's game. **M** II

blister-bush
A moderately noxious plant. [Compound.] **CS** IV-1

bloorcock
A species of game fowl. [From "cock".] **E** IV

blue-baise
A variety of valley tree. [Compound; from the French *baiser*, "to kiss".] **GPr** X

blusk
A biochemical component of vegetation on some alien planets: "No chlorophyll, haemaphyll, blusk, or petradine absorption ...in short — no native vegetation." **WB** I

bluskin
A hand-weapon, worn on the hip. **W** VII

bobadil
A variety of blossom; it was woven by children into decorative ropes for the ship *Miraldra's Enchantment*. [Variant usage: Captain Bobadil was a character in Ben Jonson's *Every Man in His Humor*.] **ShW** III

bobbet
A knickknack. [? from "bauble" and "trinket".] **PM** I

bode-bird
A species of bird common to chasms and probably signifying an omen. [Compound.] **D** II

bogadil
A tailed animal, not described. **Rh** *II*

boligam
A variety of wood used for carving. **E** *III*

bombah
"Arrabin slang for a wealthy off-worlder: by extension a tourist. Loud Bombah: an important and powerful off-worlder. Loudest Bombah: the *Connatic* [q.v.]." [? by amalgamation of "bombast" and "poobah".] **W** *VI**

bong-bird
A long-legged yellow bird indigenous to the savannahs of Shadow Valley Ranch. It grazed in herds. [Compound.] **Th** *IV*

bonter
Natural food, as distinguished from *gruff*, *deedle* and *wobbly* (q.v.); it was virtually unknown on Arrabus, Wyst. A *bonterfest* was a party at which *bonter* was served. **W** *I*

booble
A beverage. "…a potion brewed from secret recipes but always more or less the same." **NL** *VIII-2*

boodlesnatch
A pilferer. [Compound.] **AOC**

borlock
A kind of delicacy, not described. **W** *VII*

borse
A marine creature preyed upon by the *gaid* (q.v.). **BD** *V*

boser
Slang for a woman; the louts in the hamlet of Poldoolie demanded books with pictures of "Bosers — with the wide arses and no clothes on." **BD** *VIII*

bournade
A common herb, sometimes used in wizard's potions. **EO** *VII*

bouschterness
"…untranslatable, is roughly equivalent to 'conspicuous vulgarity', or 'obviously absurd and unsuitable display', such as wearing an expensive garment at an inappropriate occasion, or flaunting extravagant ornaments." Further, "The affluent could be picked out only by the most subtle of indications, and great skill was used in demonstrating one's position in life while carefully avoiding 'bouschterness'." **Th** *Glossary**

bowner
A nonsense term in the ditty sung by Mikelaus the circus performer. **M** *VIII*

brach
The small upper appendage of a dragon. [By shortening of the Latin *brachium*, "arm".] **DM** *III*

brain-eggs
See *IOUN stones*. [Compound.] **Mo**

Breakness
The language spoken at the Institute on the planet Breakness, Palafox's home. In modified form it was introduced on Pao as *Cogitant* (q.v.). **LP** *XIII*

brga skth gz
A phrase of uncertain translation from the language of the Water-folk; it was part of their criticism of the performance of *The Barber of Seville* by Dame Isabel's space-traveling opera company. "The original antiphony was incomplete. The *thakal skth hg* were too close to the *brga skth gz*, and neither were of standard texture." See also *bgrassik*. **SO** *VIII*

brontotaubus
A large animal, not described. Vance notes, however, that its droppings would be "…a matter of prime significance to a dung-beetle." [? from "brontosaurus".] **Rh** *II*

brouha

In the Dinton Forest, a species of tree which commonly grew seven hundred feet tall. Its wood was used for interior paneling. [? from "brouhaha".] *Th IV*

bruehorn

A type of ceremonial wind instrument. "The Rhunes produce no true music and are incapable of thinking in musical terms. Their fanfares and clamors are controlled by mathematical progressions, and must achieve a mathematical symmetry. The exercise is intellectual rather than emotional." [From "bruit", a loud noise, and "horn".] *Ma XI*

bsg rgassik

In the language of the Water-folk, one of the instruments in an orchestra; the Water-folk representative, or "monitor", said, "I would recommend that those musicians entrusted with the *bsg rgassik* listen for the introductory *slfks* from the air-swish [conductor's baton]." *SO VIII*

buder

A nonsense term in the ditty sung by Mikelaus the circus performer. *M VIII*

buiskid

The dregs of Lokhar society. "You are buiskid, the lowest of the low! You must carry water and clean slops!" *NL XIII-9*

bulditch

A nonsense term in the ditty sung by Mikelaus the circus performer. *M VIII*

bull-thorn

A large bush. [Compound.] *CS I-1*

bulrastia

A native cultivated plant. *BD III*

bulwig

A small squat creature, not described. [? from "bull" and "earwig".] *ShW I*

bumbleyap

Nonsense. "Stuff and bumbleyap!" [Compound of bumble, "to speak confusingly", and "yap".] *NL XVII-3*

bumbuster

A flying omnibus; the implication is that its cushions were hard. [Compound.] *W VII**

bump-ball

A popular sport: "Five men lying prone in eight-foot red torpedoes competed against five men in blue torpedoes, each team trying to bump a floating three-foot ball into the opposition goal. The game was lightning swift, apparently dangerous." [Compound.] *T VIII*

bundle-fungus

A common savanna plant. [Compound.] *Pn X*

bunter

"... an ugly beast that can be ridden if it is suitably prepared. It must be fed and soothed and put in a placid mood or it becomes quite unpleasant ..."

"Their sheer bulk was daunting in itself. Each stood six feet high, on six splayed legs, to the serrated upper edge of its dorsal ridge, and measured from eleven to twelve feet in length, exclusive of its tail: a linkage of bony nodules seven feet long. The dorsal ridge at the front terminated in a head of naked bony segments from which depended a flexible proboscis, of an unpleasant pale blue color. Optic stalks lifted from tufts of black fur; these were now covered over by leather cup-shaped blinders. The skin, mottled liver red, gray and purple, hung in flaps and folds and gave off an unpleasant musty odor.

"The bunter is pacified by a curious procedure. The Yip stablemen feed the bunter well, then tease it with sticks until the bunter is beside itself with rage. At this point the stablemen throw out a straw puppet dressed in a black hat, white coat, black breeches and a red sash — the riding habit. The bunter savages the puppet, stomping and kicking, tossing it in the air, and finally, when the puppet is thoroughly trounced, the bunter tucks it up on its back, to be eaten later, since it is not now hungry.

"The bunter's rage is discharged and it becomes relatively docile. The Yips drop blinders over its eyes; the rider takes the place of the puppet, lifts the blinders and rides away in comfort.

"To dismount, the rider must drop the blinders, otherwise the bunter thinks its victim is escaping and kills it again. So: if you ride a bunter, remember! Never dismount without dropping the blinders." [Variant usage.] *ArS V*

busta batasta
An expletive. *M IX*

buttle-fish
A large edible fish, often served poached. [Compound.] *MT VI*

bylo-by
A type of powerful hand weapon: "He carries a bylo-by. Had you touched his ores he would have blown away your head and ears." *BD VIII*

byzantaur
One of a race of creatures indigenous to Sirius Planet, and having "... four arms and four legs, and what appear to be two heads, but these latter simply contain the sense organs, as the brain is in the body itself. In spite of their nightmarish appearance they are responsive creatures, quite ready to adopt those human manners, methods, and institutions which seem useful to them. This is especially true of the Royal Giants of the Trapezus [a volcanic formation], who have a settled existence in their caves. They derive their livelihood by a kind of agriculture, and their lichen terraces are extremely interesting. They are a gentle folk, and arouse themselves only against the rogues and outcasts [of their species]." The *byzantaurs* understood pidgin English, wore clothing "woven of rock fiber", and were referred to colloquially as " 'zants". [? by combination of "Byzantine" and "centaur".] *SO V*

Bza
An untranslatable word referring to the Phalids' governing principle; approximately, "... custom, order, regulation, usual practice ... ancient manners." *PF II*

C

cabinche
An ingredient of a popular punch, "...a greenish yellow mixture which Hetzel found pleasantly astringent." **FT** IX

cackshaw
A species of loud bird. [? from "cackle" and "kickshaw", a trifle or toy.] **W** I

cadenciver
A popular musical instrument played aboard the ship *Miraldra's Enchantment*. [From "cadence".] **ShW** IX

cadensis
A type of stringed musical instrument; in the house of Murgen the magician Shimrod found "...a small six-stringed cadensis of unusual shape which, almost of its own accord, produced lively tunes." **L** XV

Cagliostro
A gambling game (unspecified) in which Moncrief the Mouse-rider "dispassionately vanquished Schwatzendale", "mulcting him to the amount of forty-seven sols and sixty dinkets." [Reference to Count Cagliostro, medieval adventurer and magician, with a suggestion of Byzantine cunning and treachery.] **PoC** VIII-1

calculite
A type of computational device. [From "calculate".] **KM** VI

calisthene
A hair dressing, applied as a tincture. [From the Greek *kalos*, "beautiful", and *sthenos*, "strength".] **ArS** VII

calligynics
The science of female beauty; Rhialto had expertise in this field. [From the Greek *kalos*, "beautiful", and *gyne*, "woman".] **Rh** I

cambent

A material or characteristic of a box found by Doctor Lalanke. **CS** *IV-2*

camfer

A rare wood; it was used in the construction of Doctor Lalanke's manse. **CS** *IV-2*

canchineel

A variety of rose-colored plum. **GPr** *X*

candole

A forest plant. [? by contraction of "Candollea", an evergreen flowering shrub.] **Rh** *I*

cang

"Indigenous stinging insect, reaching a length of four inches." **BD** *XII**

canker-wort

A common blue shrub. [Compound.] **W** *IV*

cantabulations

Uncertain; calculations? Recitations? " 'Now then,' said Doskoy, 'we shall proceed. In the envelope is my wager and the name of the girl I shall designate after you complete your cantabulations.'" [By association with "confabulation" and "tabulation".] **PoC** *VIII-2*

cany-flake

A species of long-stemmed flower. [Compound.] **CS** *VI-2*

Caraz

1. "A color, mottled, of black, maroon, plum, with a dusting or sheen of silver-gray; symbolic of chaos and pain, macabre events in general." 2. The largest of Durdane's three continents. **An** *II**

carbade

A kind of foodstuff. **CS** *I-2*

carbolon

A synthetic construction material used for framing poles. [From

"carbon" and/or "Carboloy", trade name of a kind of carbon alloy.]
DC

Carcery
A jail. [From the Latin *carcer*, "prison".] **KM III, F II**

cardenil
A common littoral plant. **FT IX**

carpet wole
A placid, eight-legged running creature with a long, flat back, ridden for transportation. **GP XV**

casammon
A species of giant tree having twisted branches. **Tr IX**

cassander
A variety of poisonous bush with purple foliage. **GPr IV**

cassas
A common herb, sometimes used in wizard's potions. **EO VII**

Catademnon
A temple-like structure whose crypt contained the remains of the tortured hero, Emphyrio. [From the Greek *kata*, "down", and "condemn"; the word also alludes to "Agamemnon" and "Parthenon".] **E XXII**

Cataxis
On Camberwell, a boys' activity. "They wore black felt scuttle-hats, with tufts of auburn hair protruding through holes above the ears, tight trousers and brown coats: proud formal garments, suitable for the weekly Cataxis, which was their immediate destination." [Related to "cathexis", concentration on one particular idea (to an unhealthy degree).] **NL I-4**

catrape
"Offensive epithet signifying bedragglement, offensive odor and vulgarity of manner." [? from "cantrap".] **W VII***

catto

Slang for a person who was "subject to the catatonic-manic syndrome". In its frantic quest for immortality, the population was particularly susceptible to this psychotic condition. [Contraction and corruption of "catatonic".] *TLF I**

cauch

"An aphrodisiac drug derived from the spore of a mountain mold and used by Trills to a greater or lesser extent. Some retreated so far into erotic fantasy as to become irresponsible, and thus the subject of mild ridicule." *Tr I**

cavout

A small animal kept for meat. *Tr VIII*

cazaldo

A kind of husked, edible fruit. *Tr IX*

ceegee eggs

"100 kg. candied ceegee eggs" were listed among the provisions for the animals in Magnus Ridolph's zoo. They sold for 80 munits per kilo, according to the invoice from Vanguard Organic Supply of Starport. *TB*

centim

A unit of money, one hundredth of a Standard Value Unit (SVU). [From "*centime*".] *F VI*

cephaloscope

A device similar in concept and purpose to a lie detector, though more advanced. However, "...cephaloscope evidence can not be introduced in court to prove guilt — only to prove innocence." [From the Greek *kephale*, "head", and *skopein*, "to view".] *HI II*

cerebrologist

A scientist of mentality. [From the Greek *kara*, "head", and *logos*, "reason".] *DE VI*

Chade

A rank of stoneworker, probably similar to foreman. *EO IV*

Chalcorex
A kind of feed given to a ship's giant propulsive worms. **CS** *II-1*

chancodilla grubs
One of the foodstuffs required by the animals in Magnus Ridolph's zoo. They were available from Vanguard Organic Supply of Starport, and sold for 4,235 munits per ton. See also *ceegee eggs*. **TB**

chanterbell
A variety of bush, commonly white. **MT** *III*

charnay
"…a purple fruit with rough skin. Inside, rough tubes full of poison run along the husk. The fruit itself is said to be delicious." Howard Alan Treesong used *charnay* to poison all the guests at his banquet. **BD** *V*

chastity-plant
A variety of large plant; Gilgad's pet simiode was chained between two of them. [Compound.] **Rh** *II*

chatowsies
A staple food, served at Tintle's Shade and elsewhere; though advertised as "fine Darsh provender", it was fetid. **F** *III*

chelt
"A young girl. After adolescence and until she grows her facial mustache, usually after six to eight years, she is a 'kitchet'. Thereafter she may incur any number of epithets, usually derogatory. The women use an equivalent set of terms in reference to the men." **F** *VI**

chichala
"An indelicate term. In the present context [Tintle's Shade, a dingy inn] the word metaphorically connotes food prepared for and served to men." **F** *III**

Chicken-thief's Trot
"[A] long loping prance, with body leaning far backwards and legs kicking out high to the front," danced by the Magistrate who gave Hilmar Krim a kick at Owlswyck Inn. [Compound]. **Lu** *Intro*

Chief Manciple

A high administrative title on the floats of Blue World, second only to that of Supreme Presiding Intercessor. [Variant usage: a purveyor or steward, esp. of a monastery or college.] *BW XIV*

chife

A particularly foul odor. "Everywhere across the Gaean Reach, when knowledgeable talk turned to the subject of bad smells and intolerable stinks, someone would insist that the Big Chife of Yipton must be numbered among the contenders. A recipe for the Big Chife had been proposed in a semifacetious paper written on the subject by a savant in residence at Vagabond House." The recipe included "... human exudations ... smoke and charred bones ... fish, rotting ... decaying coral (very bad) ... canal stink ... complex cacodyls ... [and] unguessable (bad)." Also, "The influence permeates your clothes and lingers, finally attenuating to an almost pleasant musky intimation. This can be considered another souvenir of Yipton. Unlike almost everything else, it is free." (ArS). *ArS II, D IV, GP XIV, M V, Rh II, Th Glossary*

chill isp

A gradation of light on Marune. "Chill isp inspires the Rhune with a thrilling ascetic exultation, which completely supersedes lesser emotions of love, hate, jealousy, greed. Conversation occurs in a hushed archaic dialect; brave ventures are planned; gallant resolves sworn; schemes of glory proposed and ratified, and many of these projects become fact, and go into the Book of Deeds." See also *aud. Ma IV*

chinklepin

A type of clattering percussion instrument. [Compound.] *F III*

chipe

A delicate foodstuff often served with "black sauce"; chipes were served at the Black Barn. *F XV*

chir

A potent hormone: "The Gomaz were monosexual and reproduced by implanting zygotes in the bodies of vanquished enemies, apparently to their mutual exaltation, which the victor augmented by eating a nubbin of a gland at the back of the vanquished warrior's neck. This gland yielded the hormone *chir* which stimulated growth in the bantlings and martial zeal in the adult warrior. The thought of *chir* dominated the lives of the Gomaz. The bantlings in their mock battles ingested the *chir* of those they had bested and killed; in the adult battles the warriors performed the same act and were thereby exalted, strengthened, and endowed with a mysterious *mana*; *chir* conceivably fertilized the zygotes." See also *mana*. **DTA** *III*

chirret
"A very nice damson [plum] cider and not at all strong." Chirret was served at the Black Barn. **F** *XV*

chister
A tool used by a *worminger* (q.v.) to maintain the flukes of giant worms. [? from "chisel" or the Spanish "*chistera*", a wicker scoop used in jai alai.] **CS** *II-2*

chitumih
Infested or parasitized by a *nopal* (q.v.); see also *tauptu*. **BE** *VII*

chob-chow
A kind of delicacy, not described. **W** *VII*

chorasm
"*Sebalism* [sexuality; q.v.] carried to a remarkable degree"; adj. *chorastic*. **Ma** *V**

chorastic
See *chorasm*. **Ma** *V**

chotz
"Personal music [would be] a limping and inadequate translation of the term *chotz*: that music with which an Eisel surrounds himself, to project his mood or to present an ideal version of his personality. It is interesting to note that the Eisels are uninterested in the composition or rendition of music; they rarely sing or whistle, although

occasionally they jerk their fingers or tap their feet in reflex reaction to the rhythm. The ability to play a musical instrument is so rare as to be considered a freakish eccentricity. The 'personal music' is produced by an ingenious mechanism programmed, not by musicians, but by musicologists." A mechanism, worn on the shoulder and controlled by a selector, produced an assortment of themes such as *Stately Mien, Joviality, Pensive Dreams, Skylark Song, Receptiveness to Novel Ideas, Condolences*, etc. **MT X***

choundril
A species of rock-dwelling, taloned beast. **WFMR**

chraus
Lazy or dishonorable; see *Yellow*. **MT** *Glossary*

chromatil
A recreational coloring device. [From the Greek *chroma*, "color".] **KM** *VIII*

chronoplex
The temporal continuum. [From the Greek *chronos*, "time", and Latin *plectere*, "to braid".] **Rh** *II*

chronotope
An artist who used time as his medium. [From the Greek *chronos*, "time".] **TLF** *III*

chrysospine
A precious mineral which "... grows only in the Black Zone, which is to say, the Carabas, where uranium compounds occur in the soil. A full node yields two hundred and eighty-two sequins, of one or another color." The sequins were used as money. [From the Greek *chrysos*, "gold", and the Latin *spina*, "thorn".] **D** *I*

chsein
1. Conditioned recoil from a forbidden thought. 2. Blindness or obliviousness to the actuality of unfamiliar, forbidden, or unorthodox circumstances. **An I***

chug

"A semi-intelligent sub-type of *sandestin* [q.v.], which by a system too intricate to be presently detailed, works to control the sandestins. Even use of the word 'chug' is repellent to the sandestin." A snake-like, black- and red-striped chug resided in Rhialto's work-room, and was in charge of the sandestin Sarsem. *Rh II**

chulastic

A species of tree: "…dense forests of featherwoods, bilbobs, chulastics and thrums which covered the landscape with an intricately detailed carpet of black, brown and tan foliage." See also *bilibob* and *thrum-tree*. *Th IV*

chulka

A species of very tall tree cultivated on ranches on Rosalia. "Blue mahogany is blue; black chulka is black." See also *pinkum*. *Th II*

chumpa

"A large, indigenous animal similar to the quasi-biped ahulphs but less intelligent and characterized by a ferocious disposition." (As) "Amphibious creatures of the Salt Bog, cousin to the ahulph, but larger, hairless, and somewhat more sluggish of habit. The chumpa, combining the subtlety and malice of the ahulph with a hysterical obstinacy, were proof against domestication." (BFM) The *chumpa's* hide was used to make leather. See also *ahulph*. *As III*, BFM IV**

chut

Slang: a lout or urchin. *BD VIII*

chwig

"Reference to a peculiar vice associated with food, encountered almost exclusively on Wyst." A *chwig* was a person overly fond of natural food, or *bonter* (q.v.). *W III**

chymax

A variety of tree, commonly tall and black. *D III*

cimiter

A type of herb; it was used by Dr. Fidelius in his medicines. *L XXV*

cinctor

A belt-shaped design or device carved in stone. [From the Latin *cinctura*, "girdle".] *EO IV*

cinniborine

A species of tree. *Ma II*

Clam Muffin

On Gallingale, a club at the very apex of the status pyramid, one of the three Sempiternals, which were unique in that their members enjoyed hereditary privileges denied the common ruck. "I am Skirl Hutsenreiter, and a Clam Muffin; I am nothing else." [Compound; humorous take on "stud muffin".] *NL II-2*

clarensia

A variety of massive tree. *ArS III*

clavon

An anatomic structure on the body of Miss Aries 44R951, an extraterrestrial participant in the Miss Universe contest; related terms were *agrix, gadel, orgote, therulta* and *veruli* (q.v.). *MMU IV*

cleanorator

A personal hygienic appliance. [From "clean" and the Latin *operatus*, "worked".] *KT*

cleanotis

A cultivated plant having a pleasant fragrance. *L XXIV*

cleax

A tough, transparent material used to make window panes. [From "clear" and ? "Plexiglas".] *LP IV*

Clincture

An axiom or principle; the *Doctrine of Arcoid Clincture* was one of the "competing religions" subscribed to by the animate mountains in the realm of Irerly. *L XV*

clob-boot

A variety of heavy work boot. [From "clobber" and "boot".] *GI XVIII*

cloche
"Close-fitting casque or bonnet, of leather or felt, with a pointed crown and earflaps; an article worn by Glint mountaineers." See also *quat* and *katch*. [Variant usage: "a type of woman's hat".] **MT XII***

clote
An anatomic part of a ship's giant propulsive worm, probably an organ of excretion; it was wont to become impacted. [Variant usage: a "species of burdock plant".] **CS II-1**

cloudtrees
A famous feature of Taubry: "...enormous masses of billowing gray foam clutched in black tendrils, towering high into the air like small thunderheads." [Compound.] **PoC III-1, Lu Intro**

Clover-leaf Femurial
A scale from the demon Sadlark's disintegrated corpus; its value was ten terces. See also *Interlocking Sequalion, Malar Astrangal, marathaxus, Pectoral Skybreak Spatterlight* and *protonastic centrum*. [From "femur", the largest bone in the leg.] **CS I-1**

cluthe
A form of deadly poison commonly used by a Sarkoy *venefice* (q.v.); Kirth Gersen used it to kill Lens Larque. **F XVI, SK V**

Cmodor
A musical mode of the Lekthwan race, "...in which a group of notes· start in the distance, approach, certain notes advancing, then falling back, and all meeting at a core." See also *Liddrsk* and *Lyzg*. **GI V**

code-sono
An automatic device which activated circuits in response to voiced commands. [From "code" and the Latin *sonus*, "sound".] **WLA**

codorfin
A species of sea-monster. **CS II-3**

cogence
"...that fervent erudition and virtuosity of the Rhunes." [From the Latin *cogere*, "to compel".] **Ma VI***

Cogitant

One of the three new languages deliberately introduced into Paonese culture by Palafox for purposes of social engineering. (The others were *Valiant* and *Technicant*.) Cogitant was equivalent to the language of Breakness, "…modified considerably against the solipsism latent in the original tongue." [From the Latin *cogere*, "to compel".] **LP XII**

coigel

Meaning uncertain: "…you'd look a silly jape with the *prut* [a type of hat; q.v.] hanging past your cheek like a spent coigel." **BD VIII**

Colloquary

The Roum seat of government. "Public policy was controlled by a council of grandees, sitting at the Colloquary." [Corruption of "colloquy".] **NL XIII-7**

coluca

A variety of tree indigenous to Rosalia. **Th IV**

colucoid creeper

A plant whose pods were harvested as "the source of a peculiarly rich red dye." **Ma I**

commu

An electronic audiovisual communications device. [By shortening of "communicator".] **TLF II**

comporture

A person's status on Gallingale was determined by the prestige of his club and by his comporture: that dynamic surge which generated upward thrust, and was similar to the concept of 'mana'. [From "comport".] **NL I-2**

condaptery

"From the Gaean *condaptriol*: the science of information management, which includes the more restricted field of cybernetics." **W II***

condosiir

The Shaul word derived from the old Tuscan *condottiere*, and meaning a freelance soldier; Paddy Blackthorne used it as a euphemistic translation of "rascal". *SP V*

Connatic
The supreme master of Alastor Cluster. He "...wears a severe black uniform with a black casque, in order to project an image of inflexible authority. After an ancient tradition he roams anonymously about the cluster." He was also known as the "Loudest *Bombah*" (q.v.). *Tr Preface*

coppola
See *double coppola*. *CS I-2*

copriote
A nonsense term in the ditty sung by Mikelaus the circus performer. *M VIII*

cor
An animal, often red in color, found under rocks in the chasms on Tschai. [Variant usage: "the heart" (hence the color red).] *D II*

corbalbird
A species of predatory bird. *ArS V*

corfume
A material used in the ancient city Chelopsik for making utensils; Nisbet possessed a salver made of *corfume* and inlaid with petrified fire-flies. *CS III-1*

coriolus
A halo, as of hair. [By amalgamation of "corolla" and "coriolis".] *GP VI*

corpentine
A type of foodstuff, not described. *E VII*

corolopsis
One of the ancient sciences and secret lores known to Rogol Domedonfors; others included *metathasm* and *superphysic numeration*. *DE V*

corroboratic index
"In rough terms, it's the average area of the integral under a series of probability curves, each given the proper weighting." [From "corroborate".] *UQ*

cosmoscope
A device which projects a cosmic image for group inspection. [Compound of *"cosmos"* and *"scope"*.] *ToH*

cottrell
A type of game food; cutlets of *cottrell* were served at the Black Barn. *F XV*

counterwink
To contradict or violate, e.g. religious teachings. [Compound.] *BD XII*

crackleberry
A bush, commonly russet in color and cultivated as a hedge. [Compound.] *F VIII*

crebarin
A Sirenese musical instrument, possibly the water-lute. *MM*

cripthorn
A thorny plant common to the chasms on Tschai. [? from "cripple" and "thorn".] *D III*

criptid
"A long, low, pad-footed variant of the terrestrial horse. The Uldras of the Retent disdain criptids as mounts fit only for wittols [q.v.], sexual deviates, and women." *GPr IV**

croque-couvert
A person who is mentally ill. "Ha hah! Perhaps you are crazy, after all … what the trade calls a 'croque-couvert'." [A combination of two French words which might be read as "one who munches the table setting", undoubtedly a symptom of mental problems. By association with "croque-monsieur".] *NL V-1*

cryptorrhoid

Metaphysically hidden; the sorcerer Pharesm referred to *Kratinjae's Second Law of Cryptorrhoid Affinities*, according to which TOTALITY must necessarily attach itself to NULLITY. [From the Greek *kryptos*, "hidden", and *rhein*, "to flow".] *EO IV*

crystorrhoid

Having metaphysical, crystal-like properties; the term was applied by the sorcerer Pharesm to the whorl induced by his elaborate rock-carving. [From the Greek *krystallos*, "ice", and *rhein*, "to flow".] *EO IV*

cudger gun

A six-pound hand-weapon. *MT XI, W VII*

culbrass

"Personal emblems, ornaments, tablets, and other insignia of ilk or caste." *Culbrass* was sometimes worn on a type of tall hat known as a *dath* (q.v.). *MT I**

cursar

"The Connatic's local representative, usually based in an enclave known as 'Alastor Centrality'." See also *Connatic*. [? from "bursar", influenced by *Connatic*.] *W I**

curset

"A crab-like sea insect." *Tr XV**

cyclodon

A large land-dwelling creature, not described. [? by association with *mastodon*.] *CC VIII*

cycloprodacterol phosphate

An artificial flavoring used in soda pop. [Corruption of ISV.] *UR*

D

daban

A variety of wood used in carving. *E VII*

dadu

"A language of finger signs and the syllables *da, de, di, do, du*." *An III**

daggeret

A small dagger. ["Dagger" plus the diminutive suffix "-et".] *PoC VI*

daihak

A class of fractious creatures including demons and gods, capable of being controlled by a spell; see also *sandestin*. *Rh Foreword*

dako

A species of burled tree. *Tr IX*

daldank

A species of shade tree. *MT IV*

dammel-ray

A somewhat bulky handgun; it could be fitted into one's body. *SU*

daobado

A characteristic forest tree: "...a rounded massy construction of heavy gnarled branches, these a burnished russet bronze, clumped with dark balls of foliage." [? from "dao", a large Philippine tree.] *DE VI, EO VII*

daraba

A variety of rainforest tree, often shaped like a parasol. *An V, BFM XIII*

darabence

A musical instrument sometimes having a green jade fingerplate. *BFM V*

darango
A five-horned animal whose meat, served as "prime cutlets", was a delicacy. *F XII*

darkdog
A type of piece in the chess-like game played by Vus and Vuwas, the two *gryphs* (griffins) which guarded the portal to Murgen's castle: "... you would push my reignet into limbo and baffle my darkdog into the corner." Other such pieces included the *bezander*, the *mordyke* and the *reignet*. [Compound.] *M V*

darkling
A category of supernatural creature distinguished from fairies and certain other halflings: "In a third class are merrihews, willawen and hyslop, and also, by some reckonings, quists and darklings. (...) ... darklings prefer only to hint of their presence." See also *skak*. [Variant usage.] *L X**

Dassawary
A type of tea having a sharp taste and sometimes added in small amounts to other varieties. *F IV*

dath
"A tall hat, in the shape of a truncated cone, from six inches to as much as twenty-four inches in height. The article, when worn by women, is often enlivened by flowers nested in the crown, or a spray of dyed *eph-plumes* [q.v.], or a flurry of ribbons. The male dath is ordinarily unadorned, except occasionally for a trifle of silver *culbrass* [q.v.]." It was commonly black. See also *katch* and *quat* (other forms of hats). *MT III**

de-da pidgin
A primitive language. *As V*

dedactor
A type of handgun: "He jerked his left biceps and displayed that complicated weapon known as a dedactor. It discharges three sorts of glass needles. The mildest causes a maddening itch of three weeks' duration." *BD VIII*

deed-debtor

See *smaidair*. [Compound.] **MT V***

deedle

A nutritious, manufactured, viscous white liquid having a tart, faintly astringent taste, and constituting one of the three staple foods of Arrabus, on Wyst. See also *bonter, gruff, sturge* and *wobbly*. **W I**

degurgle

A nonsense verb used in a bit of doggerel concerning "Tim R. Mortiss" (the latter a play on the Latin words *timor mortis*, "fear of death"). It was written by the mad poet Navarth. **PL V**

dek

See *dekabrach*. **GG**

dekabrach

An intelligent sea creature vaguely resembling a seal and capable of organized self-defense. Its head had a "…pink-golden cluster of arms, radiating like the arms of a starfish, the black patch at their core which might be an eye"; its sleek, seal-like body terminated in "three propulsive vanes". Its skeleton "…was based on an anterior dome of bone with three flexible cartilaginous vertebrae."

The dekabrachs "…appear to belong in the Sabrian Class A group, the silico-carbo-nitride phase, although they deviate in important respects." The men on Sabria referred to them casually as "deks". [From the Greek *deka*, "ten", and the Latin *brachium*, "arm".] **GG**

delp

A species of dog; one vicious black variety were known as "mouthers" and kept as watchdogs. **W IV**

demosophist

Not defined; the term suggests an advocate of specious populism. [From the Greek *demos*, "populace", and *sophos*, "wise".] **Ma II**

Dendicap

See *Bidrachate Dendicap*. **SO I**

dendifer
A common vine. **MT** *VIII*

denopalization
The agonizing removal of a *nopal* (q.v.) from a host's psyche by means of an electrically charged grill. **BE** *VI*

deodand
A species of flesh-eating, forest-dwelling monster; it was larger than a man and "...black as midnight except for shining white eyes, white teeth and claws." The one encountered by Cugel was "...wearing straps of leather to support a green velvet shirt." According to the casebook of the mad wizard Follinense, the deodand was a hybrid of "wolverine, basilisk, man". [Variant usage: "a thing forfeited to the crown for causing a person's death".] **EO** *III*

depilatorium
A commercial establishment for the removal of body hair: a barber shop. [From the Latin *pilus*, "hair", and *-orius*, "a place for".] **Pn** *VII*

Deplectus
See *Aroisus*. **M** *VIII*

descensor
An elevator. [From the Latin *descendere*, "to climb down".] **W** *VIII*

desqualmate
See *ensqualm*. **Rh** *I*

detensifier
A device conjectured to have been used by Reinhold Biebursson for the creation of his *aquefacts* (q.v.). [From the Latin *tendere*, "to stretch".] **TLF** *XI*

detervan
A tough material used for the shields of a type of military ship known as a *scape* (q.v.). [From "deter" and ? "impervious".] **MT** *XIII*

deucas

"The [second] cardinal number in the language of Ancient Etruria."
*ArS I**

Devariant

An adherent of a heretical sect. [From the Latin *varius*, "diverse".] **F**
XV

Deweaseling Brigade

"The single interworld organization of Beyond, existing to identify
and destroy agents of the IPCC [Interworld Police Coordination
Company]. The IPCC, accepting a contract to locate and destroy
a malefactor who had fled the Oikumene, could implement its
commitments only by sending one or more agents Beyond,
where they were known as weasels and considered fair game." The
Deweaselers interrogated visitors with the aid of truth machines. Also
Deweaseling Corps. [From "weasel".] **KM I***, **PL III***

Dexad

The Fellows of ranks 101 through 109 (the 110th being traditionally
empty) in the "Institute". [From the Greek *deka*, "ten".] **BD VII***

dexax

An explosive used in bombs, grenades, the tips of arrows and pikes,
and in the "torc", a computer-controlled device worn by every citizen
of Shant around his neck as a means of subjugation (BFM). It was
also used in the needles fired from handguns (GPr), and figured in
Lens Larque's elaborate scheme to engineer his image, à la Mount
Rushmore, on the moon Shanitra (F). It was a black, soft material
(An). *An VIII*, **BFM V**, **F XIV**, **GPr X**

dexode

An electronic part used in air-cars, probably analogous to a diode. [?
from the Greek *deka*, "ten", and "diode".] **GPr III**

diakapre

A type of forest tree. **MT I**

diambroid
A form of high explosive. *CS VI-1*

dibbet
A type of coin. *GP XVI*

difono
See *gauze difono*. *CS IV-2*

Digitalia
The active, presumably finger-like elements in *Arnhoult's Sequestrous Digitalia*, a spell of material acquisition. *CS VI-1*

diko
A "…sweet-salt wafer which served as a relish to the otherwise bland food" of the Pnumekin (humans who had taken on the attributes of the Pnume); it contained a drug which suppressed sexual maturation. *Pn IV*

dilly-bug
A species of insect; it made a characteristic twittering sound. [Compound.] *W II*

dimble-flower
A wildflower, commonly white and growing in thickets. [Compound.] *L XVIII*

dimple-horn
A musical instrument; it was played by one of the "Seven Barnswallows" at the Black Barn. [Compound.] *F XV*

dinket
"A coin worth the tenth part of an *ozol* [q.v.]." (W) [? from "dinky" and/or "trinket".] *ArS VI, BD II, PoC V-1, Th I, W XII**

diper
A nonsense term in the ditty sung by Mikelaus the circus performer. *M VIII*

diphany

A precious metal formed from bloom on the face of the High Disk and collected in ingots; it comprised part of Uthaw's treasure. **CS V-2**

diplonet

A wind instrument used for ceremonial fanfares. [? from the Greek *di-*, "double", and "coronet".] **LP VII**

displasm

A discomfiting spell or phantom, as in *Panguire's Triumphant Displasms*. [From the Latin *dis-*, "apart", and "plasm".] **CS VI-1**

distemporize

A euphemism meaning to kill; to "transition" was also used in this sense. [From the Latin *tempus*, "time".] **TLF VIII**

disturgle

A nonsense verb used in a bit of doggerel concerning "Tim R. Mortiss" (the latter a play on the Latin words *timor mortis*, "fear of death"). It was written by the mad poet Navarth. **PL V**

dnazd

A horrid creature inhabiting the mountains to the north of Misk, on the planet Thamber; it resembled a giant centipede, had large mandibles with poison-tipped prongs, and produced a wild, whistling scream when enraged. **KM IX**

Dog-beard

"Dog-beards are no-hopers — beach folk." They lived mostly at one end of the Torpeltine Islands. Dr. Dacre was rumored to have set up "...a secret laboratory up the coast at Tinkum's Bar, where he conducted odd experiments and tried to cross a Dog-beard with a *Flamboyard* [q.v.]." [Compound.] **FT IX**

doghole

A hole dug into the ground and enclosed by bars weighted with rocks, and used as an oubliette for solitary confinement. [Compound.] **EOE II**

dog's-breath
A species of noisome herb. [Compound; by association with "baby's breath".] *ShW III*

dogs-body
A menial position: "This post does not include the offices of valet, scullion, porter, dogs-body and general roustabout." [Variant usage.] *CS I-1*

Dombrillion
The senior prom of Gallingale. "The most important social event of the year, the Dombrillion, a grand ball for the graduating class, would take place a week before Commencement. The Dombrillion, an official school function, disregarded social difference." [By association with "cotillion" and perhaps "dominion".] *NL IX-4*

Domine
One of the "...two most common appellatives of the Gaean Reach which may properly be applied to all persons of distinguished or exalted station." It was abbreviated Dm. See also *Viasvar*. [From the Latin *dominus*, "lord or master".] *GPr II**

doodle-whisker
Nonsense. "Skirlet laughed scornfully. 'That's sheer doodle-whisker! Have you forgotten? I am a Clam Muffin; I plan no career! The idea is a vulgarity.'" [Compound.] *NL V-1*

double coppola
A form of popular dance. *CS I-2*

double-kamanthil
"An instrument similar to the *ganga*, except the tones are produced by twisting and inclining a disk of resined leather against one or more of the forty-six strings." It was used on ceremonial occasions. *MM**

double-moko
A lively game of cards practiced (for small stakes at first) by the pilgrims on board the *Glicca*. Schwatzendale reveals himself a master of the game, and the pilgrims are left sol-less. "The pilgrims, ever more

impatient, soothed themselves with endless games of double-moko, pounding the table with their fists and pulling at their beards when their scumbles went awry, and their gallant rambles-from-hell were ambushed and sent reeling." [Compound; from the Maori "*moko*", a form of tattoo.] **PoC V-4**

dounge

A stable-animal, described only in its form as a hybrid with the *felukhary*: "…a large dun-colored beast with powerful hind legs and a tufted tail … it moves with an easy stride; it feeds upon inexpensive wastes, and is notorious for its stubborn loyalty." **CS V-2**

dragon-bats

Flying creatures living in the region of the Gaspard Peaks, on the world Mariah's fourth continent, Gamma. They "measure as much as forty feet from wingtip to wingtip." A strange people, the Arcts, are "rumored to ride from peak to peak on their backs." In fact, they do more than that: "A related folk, the Yeltings, live in the stony fastness at the base of the Gaspards, notably among the Balch Rocks. Yelting women are the prey of Arct warriors. The *dragon-bats* swoop down; the women flee in panic, but they are often seized and carried aloft to the Arct eyries. When they no longer produce children, they work the crops in the high yards." [Compound.] **PoC XII-2**

draygosser

A type of tradesman. [? from "drayage".] **TLF I**

dreuhwy

"From the ancient Welsh and untranslatable; approximately: a self-induced mood of morose extra-human intensity, in which any grotesque excess of conduct is possible; full identification of self with the afflatus which drives the eerie, the weird, the terrible. The adepts of the so-called 'Ninth Power' conceived of 'dreuhwy' as a condition of liberation, in which their force reached its culmination." **GP VIII***

drist

A food used to make porridge. **CS II-3**

drivet
Salary for labor, or drudge (q.v.); ten tokens were paid for each hour worked. Five hundred such tokens equaled only about one *ozol* (q.v.). **W** *III*

drogbattie
A pejorative term applied to a woman, probably equivalent to "old bat" or "dingbat". **FT** *IX*

drogger
A squat, heavy-legged creature with long, slender ears; it was used to draw the carriages in Pompodouros. [? by association with "drogher", a barge or clumsy cargo boat, and/or "drag".] **CS** *II-2*

drona
The number six in the Paonese language. **LP** *X*

dros
The number three in the Dirdir language. **D** *X*

drot
A dolt. **F** *VI*

dr'ssa
Dirdir: to call "*dr'ssa dr'ssa, dr'ssa*" invokes an obligation to arbitration. **D** *XX*

drudge
A citizen's brief weekly work period on Arrabus, Wyst. [Variant usage.] **W** *I*

druithine
A type of musician, e.g. Dystar (An, As, BFM). He was "…one who does not go with a troupe. He wanders by himself; he carries a khitan …or perhaps a gastaing; thus he is able to impart his wisdom and the circumstances of his life." (An) *Druithines* were lumped with "wandering minstrels, scholar-poets, bards, scops and troubadours", and were accorded safe passage across dangerous lands (SvW); however, they did not sing.

"Druithines, unlike the troupes, never advertised their comings and goings; after an unheralded, almost furtive arrival at some locality, the druithine would visit one of the taverns and order a repast, sumptuous or frugal, according to his whim or personal flair. Then, he would bring forth his khitan and play but would not eat until someone in the audience had paid for his meal. The 'uneaten meal', indeed, was a common jocular reference. Druithines in decline reputedly employed a person to make ostentatious payment for the meal as soon as it was set forth. After the meal the druithine's further income depended on gratuities, gifts from the tavern-keeper, engagements and private parties or in the manor houses of aristocrats. A *druithine* of talent might become wealthy, as he had few expenses." (An)

See also *gastaing* and *khitan*. [? by association with "druid".] *An I, An VI*, As XI, BFM V, EOE X, M VII, SvW VII*

duddle

A fuddy-duddy (?): "...he's tight as a constipated duddle on a cheese diet." *BD XII*

Dulcidrome

A famous, spacious sweetshop on Gara. [From the Latin *dulcis*, "sweet", and the Greek *dromos*, "racecourse".] *F II*

Dulcinato

A category of sweet beverages, e.g. "Ysander's Quality Cordial". [From the Latin *dulc(is)* meaning "sweet".] *ShW VI*

dulciole

A popular musical instrument played aboard the ship *Miraldra's Enchantment*. [? from "dulcimer".] *ShW IX*

dumble

The Darsh residence within their giant desert "shades", consisting of "...a confusion of small heavy-walled concrete domes: low, high, large and small; domes piled on domes, domes impinging upon or growing out of other domes; domes in clusters of three, four, five, or six ... an architecture at once heavy, vital and appropriate to the environment, like the Darsh themselves. Vegetation surrounded and overhung each dumble." *F VII*

duodecimate
Any of "Those stable transuranic elements of atomic number in the 120's and beyond. Duodecimate Black is an unrefined sand consisting of various duodecimate sulfides, oxides and similar compounds, with a specific gravity here stipulated as 'SG-22'." *Duodecimates* were mined on Dar Sai. Vance adds that the term was "a misnomer, which nevertheless has achieved wide popular usage." [From the Latin *duodecimus*, "twelve".] *F III*, F VII**

durastrang
A very hard protective material. [From the Latin *durus*, "hard".] *ArS IX*

durible
A substance used in the construction of machinery. [From the Latin *durus*, "hard".] *SP I*

DxDx
A type of control button; one was present on the back of the neck of Milton Hack's air-car pilot. *MZ II*

dyan
A variety of enormous tree. *D V, Pn V*

Dylas Extranuator
The proper name of a spaceship; the existence of the verb *extranuate* is implied, though not defined. *Ma III*

dymphne
A glade-dwelling plant, commonly white. *Rh II*

dympnet
A type of sequin, probably geological in origin; its uses included the making of protective vests. *F XI*

dyssac
A type of liquor distilled from herbs. *CS VI-1*

dyvolt
A flying, sky-ruling creature resembling the *pelgrane* (q.v.); it had "...a long nasal horn and uses the common language." *Rh II*

E

ear-amulets
Stereophonic radar units, worn at the ears, which guide the user in the dark and offer a short warning of sudden movement. [Compound.] *AA*

easil
A variety of bush whose leaves were dried to produce *galga* (q.v.). *An I**

ebane
A species of forest tree, sometimes planted along boulevards. *MT II*

ecce
"The first … cardinal number in the language of Ancient Etruria." [? from the Latin *ecce*, "behold".] *ArS I**

ectreen
A type of musical instrument with a bright tone, often played in the Carnevalle. *TLF I*

edel
A variety of table wine. [? from "edelweiss", a white herb.] *E VII*

eel-vine
A species of plant found in the jungle outside Brinktown. [Compound.] *SK II*

eer-light
Eerie light. *DE VI*

effectuary
Generally, a magical device. [From the Latin *effectus*, "effect".] *L XIII*

effectuator
A combination of detective and special agent. "Very well. You're an

effectuator. Effect an investigation." [From "effectuate", to cause to happen, to accomplish.] **NL** *X-4*, **DTA** *II*, **FT** *I*

egalism
The egalitarian philosophy prevailing on Wyst. [From "egal", meaning "equal".] **W** *I*

eidolology
The study of ideas or culture. [From "*eidos*", meaning "the cognitive part of cultural structure".] **F** *XV*

eiodark
The third highest rank among the Rhune hierarchy of aristocrats (the others being *kaiark* and *kang*). See also *lissolet*. **Ma** *III*

eirmelrath
"A malicious ghost of Canton Green Stone". **BFM** *VI**

elanthis
A species of flower. **ShW** *III*

elderkin
A senior *falloy* (q.v.); the magician Tamurello sometimes appeared disguised as an *elderkin* with white hair, silver-pale skin and green eyes. **L** *XXVII*

electromorphic
Based on or deriving from electricity; "*electromorphic action*" was conjectured to be the cause of corrosion in the engine of Adam Reith's sky-raft. [From the Latin *electrum*, "amber", and the Greek *morphe*, "form".] **SvW** *I*

elethea
A cultivated plant having a pleasant fragrance. **L** *XXIV*

elf-pipe
A popular musical instrument played aboard the ship *Miraldra's Enchantment*. [Compound.] **ShW** *IX*

eljus
A nonsense term in the ditty sung by Mikelaus the circus performer.
M VIII

eluctance
A bursting forth. [From the Latin *eluctari*, "to struggle out".] *EO VII*

elving-platform
The birthing site of a *hyrcan major* (q.v.). [Compound; from "elf".]
PL I

emalque extract
An ingredient of *schmeer* (q.v.). *Lu V-1*

emblance
"...warm propulsive immediacy", a quality possessed by the finest
sheirls (q.v.). [? from "emblem" and "ambience".] *Tr XIV*

Emosynary
A member of the Order of Solar Emosynaries, who were charged with
stimulating the vitality of the dying sun by means of fire-projecting
devices. [Possibly by association with "eleemosynary", meaning
"related to charity".] *CS V-1*

empharism
A dull sheen. *Mo*

eng'sharatz
"No satisfactory equivalent for the word *eng'sharatz* (literally: the
revered master of a large domain) exists. 'Baron' or 'lord' implies a
formal aristocracy; a 'squire' is master of a small property; 'rancher'
implies emphasis upon agricultural activity. 'Land baron' is awkward
and somewhat labored but is perhaps closer to the sense of *eng'sharatz*
than any other term." *GPr Prologue**

enser
The number four in the Dirdir language. *D X*

ensqualm
To feminize or emasculate, as by action of the Murthe (a powerful,

witch-like woman). "In the final stages the evidence is obvious: the victim becomes a woman. An early mannerism is the habit of darting the tongue rapidly in and out of the mouth." Related terms: *desqualmate, squalm, squalmaceous* and *squalmation*. [? from "squaw", "squall", "qualm" and/or "ensnare".] *Rh I*

Entercationer
A traveling entertainer, as in *Framtree's Peripatezic Entercationers*. [? by combination of "entertainer" and "vacation".] *E II*

epaing
A court game played with pink and gray balls. *ArS I*

eph-plume
A dyed plume used to adorn a *dath* (q.v.), a type of tall hat. *MT III**

Epidrome
A public house of entertainment and gambling. [From the Greek *epi*, "upon", and *dromos*, "racecourse".] *AOC*

epignotic
Hyper-knowledgeable; the *Epignotic Cultural Calculation* was a method of determining the dates and origin of a people. [From the Greek *epi*, "upon", and *gnosis*, "knowledge".] *GI VII*

erb
A dangerous, prowling, forest-dwelling creature with four legs, a distinctive odor and a powerful sense of smell. According to the casebook of the mad wizard Follinense, the erb was a hybrid of "bear, man, lank-lizard, demon" (EO). Erbs were responsible for the death of Florejin the Dream-builder and the destruction of his bubbles (DE). [? acronym for "Edgar Rice Burroughs".] *CS I-2, DE III, EO I*

ercycle
A personal conveyance, commonly single-wheeled. [From the Greek *kyklos*, "ring".] *MT II*

Erdenfreude
"A mysterious and intimate emotion which dilates blood vessels, slides chills along the subcutaneous nerves, arouses qualms of

apprehension and excitement like those infecting a girl at her first ball. *Erdenfreude* typically attacks the outworld man approaching Earth for the first time. Only the dull, the insensitive, are immune. The excitable have been known to suffer near-fatal palpitations.

"The cause is the subject of learned dispute. Neurologists describe the condition as anticipatory adjustment of the organism to absolute normality of all the sensory modes: color recognition, sonic perception, coriolis force and gravitational equilibrium. The psychologists differ; *Erdenfreude*, they state, is the flux of a hundred thousand racial memories boiling up almost to the level of consciousness. Geneticists speak of RNA; metaphysicians refer to the soul; parapsychologists make the possibly irrelevant observation that haunted houses are to be found on Earth alone." [From the German *Erde*, "earth", and *Freude*, "joy".] *PL IV*

erflatus
A variety of noisome herb. *ShW III*

ergothermic
Related to heat energy: "…the castle was adequately heated by ergothermic mechanisms." [From the Greek *ergon*, "work", and *thermos*, "warm".] *EOE VI*

erjin
A member of a telepathic, brutish, quasi-intelligent race on Koryphon, but later found to be off-world in origin. An erjin "… stood seven feet tall, with massive arms banded with stripes of black and yellow fur. Tufts of stiff golden fiber [conjectured to be telepathic receptors] stood above the head; folds of gun-metal cartilage almost concealed the four small eyes in the neck under the jutting frontal bone." Ridges of cartilage shielded its optical processes, and its shoulders were plated with bone. Deadly talons were extended when it balled the six palps of its hand into a fist. Despite their ferocity, some *erjins* were domesticated. See also *morphote*. *GPr Prologue*

ermink
An animal eaten for food; not described. *As IV*

ernice
A flavoring used in gourmet foods. **BFM** *V*

Erythrist
A medicament that was "…useless, especially against Soumian itch."
ArS VI

escalabra
A directional device used for marine navigation. **CS** *II-3*

esgracio
A nonsense term in the ditty sung by Mikelaus the circus performer.
M VIII

esmeric
"…derives from a dialect of old Caraz and means the association or
atmosphere clinging to a place: the unseen ghosts, the dissipated
sounds, the suffused glory, music, tragedy, exultation, grief, and terror,
which according to Kreposkin never dissipates." **As** *III*

esper
An evil spirit or monster: "Were her rank less exalted, one could
almost think her controlled by a cacodaemon, or an esper or some
other malignant entity!" **M** *II*

esperge
A popular food item, often served in spice sauce. [From the French
asperge, meaning "asparagus".] **E** *VIII*

estaphract
Probably an equestrian soldier; see also *sanque*. [? from "estafette", a
mounted courier, and "cataphract", a suit of armor.] **W** *XI**

Ettaday
A day of the week, possibly equivalent to Saturday. **BFM** *X*

Ettilia Gargantyr
The name of a rocketship; the existence of a creature called a
gargantyr may be implied. [By amalgamation of "gargantuan" and
"tyrant".] **F** *IV*

exotracking

The process by which citizens' whereabouts were followed using *televection* (q.v.). [From the Greek *exo*, "outside of", and "track".] *TLF XIII*

Exprescience

See *Vital Exprescience*. *ST II*

extin

A powerful poison derived from *mepothanax* (q.v.). *LP III*

extranuate

See *Dylas Extranuator*. *Ma III*

extuition

Probably a sort of divination or fortune telling. "Moncrief the Mage. Purportments! Extuitions! Great and good fortunes." [From "intuition", as an opposite.] *PoC VIII-1*

F

fabricoid
A material used in the making of Kyash rugs. [From "fabric" and the Greek *oïdes*, "resembling".] **MT** *XI*

faiole
A material, commonly white, used to carve such items as chairs. [? from "faience".] **MT** *XIX*

falloy
"A variety of halfling, much like a fairy, but larger and far more gentle of disposition." (GP) "A slender halfling akin to fairies, but larger, less antic and lacking deft control of magic; creatures ever more rare in the Elder Isles." (L) Some *falloys* had silver skins. See also *skak*. **GP** *VI*, **L** *X**, **L** *XXVI**

falorial
A species of thin, poisonous, carnivorous, phosphorescent silver fish, about four inches long and moving in cloud-like schools. **ArS** *VI*

faniche
"A fairy fabric woven from dandelion silk." **L** *XXVI**

fanique
A variety of dark brown, burled wood used for interior paneling. **Th** *VIII*

fankle
A nonsense word from a bit of doggerel sung at Tintle's Shade: "Tinkle tankle winkle wankle finkle fankle fime, All the aeons gone before are simply wasted time." **F** *VI*

Fanscher
A participant in *Fanscherade* (q.v.). **Tr** *V*

Fanscherade

An anti-social but altruistic creed or movement: "…one single outcry of wild despair, the loneliness of a single man lost among an infinity of infinities. Through Fanscherade the one man defies and rejects anonymity; he insists upon his personal magnificence. One might remark, parenthetically, that the only truly fulfilled Fanscher is the *Connatic* [q.v.] …The name derives from old Glottisch: *Fan* is a corybantic celebration of glory." *Tr V*

fanticule

A creature with a deadly sting; a blue *fanticule* was responsible for the death of Nisbet's wife. *CS III-1*

fanzaneel

An enormous tree having "shaggy pompoms". *Tr I*

farlock

A bulky animal used for drayage. *CS IV-2*

farraw

A free-for-all; a fiasco. *EOE V*

farvoyer

A device in the form of a polished tabouret for visualizing distant events. [From "far" and a deviation from the French *voyeur*, "watcher".] *Rh I*

farynx

A species of small wild animal, not described; its natural enemy was the *corbalbird* (q.v.). "Farynxes live up the mountain. They hunt in a most ingenious fashion. One hides in the bushes; the other lies on its back and exudes the odor of carrion which presently attracts a scavenger bird. The hidden farynx makes a quick leap and both dine on fowl." *ArS V*

fausicle

An anatomic part of a ship's giant propulsive worm. [? from "fauces", the passage from the soft palate to the base of the tongue.] *CS II-1*

faylet
A small flying creature in the fairy world, commonly having gauzy wings. *M VIII*

featherfern
A type of flora on Ushant. "Clusters of pink, black and orange featherferns shuddered in the breeze, emitting puffs of sweet-scented spores which, when collected and compressed, yielded a confection much enjoyed by local folk." [Compound.] *NL XI-1*

feeler-plane
The prehensile extension of a device which produced a *tri-type* (q.v.), or holographic image, of a subject person. [Compound.] *HI I*

felinodore
A possibly magical and/or cat-like creature which, according to the casebook of the mad wizard Follinense, was combined with man and wasp to form the *bazil* (q.v.). [? from "feline".] *EO V*

felukhary
See *dounge*. *CS V-2*

Femurial
See *Clover-leaf Femurial*. *CS I-1*

feovhre
"The language of Shant discriminates between various types of sunsets. Hence: [*feovhre* is] a calm, cloudless violet sunset." See also *arusch'thain*, *gorusjurhe*, *heizhen* and *shergorszhe*. *BFM V**

fer
A species of wild animal having a squat habitus; its image was used as one of the five iron emblems of the Servants. [From "feral", meaning "wild", and the French *fer*, "iron".] *MT III*

ferberator
Unspecified part of a Flitterwing spaceship. "They'll muck up your ferberator crystals and pour stale dog-piss into your air intakes." [? from "ferberite", a valuable form of ferrous tungstate, and ? "reverberate".] *BD VIII*

fere

A species of dangerous creature, not described, which inhabited the gulches on Tschai. [Variant usage: "sound, strong".] *D II*

fermin

A dangerous wild creature, not described. [? by association with "vermin".] *CS V-2*

ferris

A wild brown grain whose flour was used to make bread. [Variant usage: from "Ferris wheel".] *GPr I*

fester-shrub

A bush of the rocky hills, growing in thickets of blue and dark orange, from which the ancient ahulphs had cut their weapons. [Compound.] *An IV*

fex

A nonsense word from a bit of doggerel sung at Tintle's Shade; see *fankle.* *F VI*

fial

A variety of blue-green tree. *Tr XIX*

fiap

A talisman, protective sign or other magical device widely used to safeguard persons and property: "The black, green and white fiap will guard ... against vengeance, malice and *ghost-clutch* [q.v.]." *GPr VII*

fiddity-didjet

A careless or lackadaisical worker. [By association with "flibbertigibbet".] *L XXII*

fidget-ribbon

A bit of sartorial trimming, commonly black and worn affixed to trousers. [Compound.] *MT X*

fime

A nonsense word from a bit of doggerel sung at Tintle's Shade; see *fankle.* *F VI*

finberry
An edible berry. [Compound.] *W XIII*

finkle
A nonsense word from a bit of doggerel sung at Tintle's Shade; see *fankle*. *F VI*

fire-folk
Creatures living within stars; see *IOUN stones*. [Compound.] *Mo*

flactomies
That malady to which the ingestion of meats and wines gave rise, according to Madame Milgrim. *CS III-2*

Flam
See *Flamboyard*. *FT IX*

flamboy
1. A variety of tree in Maunish. (BD) 2. A torch. (GP) [By shortening of "flamboyant".] *BD XI, GP*

Flamboyard
The most important indigene of the Torpeltine Islands: "...feathered two-legged fruit eaters, the most gaudy and bizarre creatures imaginable. They have pink and purple plumes and orange fluff balls and golden horns." Further, "Each showed a pointed parchment-white visage surmounted first by a pair of twisted gilded horns, then a crest of scarlet, gray, and orange plumes. Under the head a collar of black hair hung over the heavy thorax, while the occipital crest continued down the back." They stood a foot taller than Miro Hetzel, and were casually referred to as *Flams*. See also *sarcenel*. [From "flamboyant".] *FT IX*

flantic
"A winged creature with a grotesque man-like head; precursor of the pelgrane [q.v.]." It was black, long-necked, clawed, articulate, and lived in the forest. *Rh II**

flashaway
A type of personal weapon. [Compound.] *PoC V-1*

flatsoon

A musical instrument; it was played by a member of the group "Denzel and his Seven Barnswallows" at the Black Barn. [From "flat" and "bassoon".] *F XV*

flax-whisk

A material used to weave light, decorative ropes. [Compound.] *ShW XIII*

fleshmolt

A species of jungle plant, commonly blue-white and growing in thick banks. [Compound.] *BFM IV*

flexite

A flexible material from which the "torc" was fashioned, an explosive collar worn by every citizen of Shant as a means of subjugation. [From "flexible" and the Latin *-ites*, "a substance".] *An IV*

flibbet

A scatterbrained person: "Where is that flibbet of a maid?" [By contraction of "flibbertigibbet".] *L VII*

flibbit

A carry-all air-car. [? from the British "flivver", a small car.] *W VII*

flip-flap

A variety of tree often found in beer gardens on the planet Dar Sai. [Compound.] *F X*

flitter-britches

A sly, vernacular term for an ambivalent or capricious magistrate; see *Benchmaster*. [Compound.] *F IV*

flitterfly

A capricious insect: "You are as mutable as a flitterfly." [Compound.] *MT IX*

flitterway

An aerial corridor in an imaginary realm discussed by two creatures controlled by the magician Shimrod. [Compound.] *M VII*

florarium

A large structure for the cultivation and display of flowers. [From the Latin *flor*, "flower", and *arius*, "a connected thing or place".] *LP VII*

fluke-fish

An edible species of fish, not otherwise described. [Compound.] *CC VI*

Foodarium

A restaurant in which patrons were "... served by a three-tier display of food moving slowly under a transparent case." [From "food" and the Latin *arius*, "a connected thing or place".] *T V*

foom

A nonsense word from a bit of doggerel sung at Tintle's Shade: "Tinkle tankle winkle wankle finkle fankle foom, Serene and bland, I walked the sand to meet an awful doom." *F VI*

forlostwenna

"A word from the Trevanyi jargon — an urgent mood compelling departure; more immediate than the general term 'wanderlust'." *Tr IV**

fortress-fish

A dangerous species of ocean fish: "One of the creatures drifted to within a hundred feet of the *Clanche*, its dorsal turrets, each equipped with an eye and harpoon, rearing six feet above the boat's gunwales." [Compound.] *MT XV*

Foundance

The building where dead Roum are disposed of. "When a Seishanee servant reaches a certain age ... the grichkins take the used Seishanee to the Foundance and slide him into the corpse bin, where he is processed and mixed into the slurry. When a Roum dies ... the grichkins carry the corpse to the Foundance and slide him into the bin, and he joins the slurry." [By association with "foundry".] *NL XIII-8*

four-twanger

A musical instrument. According to the expert opinion of Althea

Fath, it is "a far gentler instrument" than the *froghorn* (q.v.).
[Compound suggesting a set of four Jew's harps, probably of different
sizes and pitches.] **NL** *III-3*

foxen

Fox-like: "Impudence again? Condescension from a foxen fluff of a
girl!" [From "fox".] **M** *VI*

frack

A type of high explosive with industrial applications. [? from
"fracture".] **W** *X*, **F** *VI*

Fraze

"...a heavy sour-sweet liquor reputed to include among its
constituents a subtle hallucinizer." **SK** *I*

freaklet

A puny freak; pejorative. [From "freak" and "-let", diminutive suffix.]
An *I*

fringers

"...a human sub-class impossible to define exactly. 'Misanthropic
vagabonds' has been proposed as an acceptable approximation."
[From "fringe", as in the fringes of society.] **NL** *I-1**

frippet

A contemptible tart: "...teasing coquetry, as might be practiced
by some paltry little frippet, all paste and perfume and amorous
contortion." [From "frippery" and "snippet".] **M** *II*

frit

A frightful creature. [Variant usage: in dialect English, the past tense
of "frightened".] **DE** *V*

froggo

Slang for a resident of Frog Junction. [Corruption of "frog".] **SSh**

froghorn

A musical instrument comprising a mouthpiece fitted to a *plench-box*
(q.v.), tubes and valves, a central 'mixing pot', a *screedle flute* (q.v.)

nose piece, a big-bellied horn and an air-bladder. "Tawn Maihac performed 'The Bad Ladies of Antarbus', which went thusly: 'Teedle-deedle-eedle teedle a-boigle oigle a-boigle moan moan da-boigle-oigle moan teedle-eedle moan teedle-eedle-eedle a-boigle a-boigle-oigle moan moan teedle-eedle teedle da-boigle.'" [Compound.] *NL III-2*

frook
A slender black native tree, commonly a hundred feet tall and planted along boulevards. *ArS VII*

Froust
A type of magical spell; *Tinkler's Old-fashioned Froust* was one of the spells listed in *Killiclaw's Primer of Practical Magic.* [From "frowst", meaning "a stale and stuffy atmosphere".] *Rh Foreword*

fructance
A fruit drink, possibly liqueur. [From the Latin *fructus*, "fruit".] *BD XVII*

frunz
A variety of bush indigenous to Iszm. *HI III*

funella
A variety of bush. *LP II*

Fuolghan, the
"A religious ceremony with dancing [...]. It took place along the Sky-level, of course. And the music was different — the sound of metal wheels, and gongs of frozen hydrogen." *GI V*

furux
A poison derived from the *meng* (q.v.); when ingested, "...the interskeletal cartilage is dissolved so that the frame goes limp." The same substance could also be sold and used as *ulgar* (q.v.), with different effects. *PL II*

fusk-ivory
A tawny ivory color. [Probably from "fuscous".] *CS IV-2*

G

---

gaddle-stem
A meadow plant. *MT IV*

gadel
An anatomic structure on the body of Miss Aries 44R951, an
extraterrestrial participant in the Miss Universe contest; related terms
were *agrix, clavon, orgote, therulta* and *veruli* (q.v.). *MMU IV*

gadroon
A slender black-green tree, common to the Fairy Forest; its wood was
used in the construction of houses (GPr). It was (presumably) the
source of Black Gadroon rum (F). *F VII, GPr IV*

gaid
Vance quotes the following descriptive passage from *"Fauna of the
Vegan Worlds*, Volume III: *The Fish of Aloysius*, by Rapunzel K. Funk":

"... also known as *The Night-train*: this is a splendid fish of a
lustrous black color, often reaching a length of twenty feet. The body
is exceptionally well-shaped, with an almost round cross section. The
head is large and blunt with a single visual bulb, an aural pod and
a wide mouth, which when open displays an impressive dentition.
Immediately behind the head and almost to the tail grows a row of
dorsal spines, to the number of fifty-one, each tipped with a luminifer
[q.v.] which at night emits a bright blue light.

"By day the gaid swims beneath the surface, where it feeds upon
wracken, borse and similar creatures. At sundown the night-train rises
to the surface and cruises steadily with all lights aglow.

"The pelagic voyages of the night-train remain a mystery; the fish
peregrinates on a direct course, as if to a specified destination. This
may be a cape or an island or perhaps an unmarked station in the
middle of the ocean. Upon reaching its destination, the night-train
halts, floats quietly for half an hour, as if discharging cargo, or taking
on passengers, or awaiting orders; then it swings about with majestic

and ponderous deliberation. It hears a signal and sets off once more to its next destination, which well may be five thousand miles distant.

"To come upon this noble fish by night, as it cleaves the black waters of the Aloysian oceans, is a stirring experience indeed." **BD** *V*

gak
An insulting term. "I call him a cad, a gak and a peeker, and if he starts smelling around you, I'll be forced to teach him his piddles and squeaks." *NL VIII-2*

gakko
An oceanic creature found in the waters of Songerl Bay, on the world Mariah, "...with heads like little sponges. If the sponges touch you, a green fester appears, which kills you if it is not cut away." As Moncrief admonishes his companions: "Songerl Bay is not a favored venue for aquatic sports." [? by association with "gekko".] **PoC** *X-2*

galardinet
Descriptive of a particular shop manager on Mirsten who is exacting and unsympathetic but otherwise fair in her dealings. "Yonder shop is directed by a true galardinet named Dame Florice." [Portmanteau word, from the French *gaillarde*, a sprightly, strapping girl; and *martinet*, one who stubbornly adheres to methods or rules.] **Lu** *IX-2*

galga
"Dried leaves of the easil bush, pulverized, bound with easil gum and ahulph blood; an important adjunct to the spasmic Chilite worship of Galexis." When burned it gave off a sweet-acrid smoke. See also *ahulph* and *easil*. **An** *I**

gambril
A species of dangerous, giant, night-flying animal. **ArS** *II*

gandle-wood
A variety of wood used to make splints which were fired from a crossbow. **BFM** *IV*

ganga
A zither-like instrument not much larger than one's hand. It was

used "… for conversation between intimates or one a trifle lower than yourself in *strakh* [q.v.]." ***MM***

gangaree
An herb, minced and served as a sauce. ***ArS*** *VII*

gangee
A species of wild littoral shrub, often purple and mauve. ***FT*** *IX*

ganion
An edible plant. ***CS*** *V-2*

ganthar
A variety of wood used for centuries in construction. ***BD*** *II*

gant-hook
An instrument used by a *worminger* (q.v.). [Compound.] ***CS*** *II-1*

gargan
A creature taken as game, probably a bird. [? from "garganey", a European teal.] ***Pn*** *I**

Gargantyr
See *Ettilia Gargantyr*. ***F*** *IV*

gargus
A contraption. ***SP*** *I*

garom
A common farm tree. ***BD*** *XII*

gart
A form of vegetation commonly found on seaside dunes. ***W*** *XII*

gart-furze
A variety of dark green shrub among which the Green Chasch became all but invisible. ***CC*** *XII*

garvet
A variety of hedge. ***MT*** *XIII*

garwort
A plant whose fronds were used for thatch. **BW** *XIII*

gastaing
A musical instrument "…of deeper tone than the *khitan* [q.v.], with a plangent resonance which must remain under the control of the damping sleeve if the harmony were not to be overwhelmed." Various tonal subtleties could be achieved by "expert tilting and sliding of the sleeve." (BFM) **An** *I*, **BFM** *VII*

gaunch
A mysterious forest monster. "The witches know [what it is] but they say nothing, not even to each other." **W** *X*

gautch
A gratuity or payment. **BD** *VIII*

gauze difono
A rare wood; it was used in the construction of Doctor Lalanke's manse. **CS** *IV-2*

geisling
"Tower" is "…a drab translation of the word *geisling*, which carries warmer and dearer connotations." Such towers served as dwelling places, and one of them, of "stupendous dimensions", was home to the *Connatic* (q.v.). **Ma** *II**

geltner
A nonsense term in the ditty sung by Mikelaus the circus performer. **M** *VIII*

genified
Genetically identified as a criminal. "The noun is *gene-classification*, thence to adjective *gene-classified* abbreviated to *genified*." **SK** *III**

gergoid
A hybrid creature, "half-rat, half-scorpion", incorrectly rumored to be the predecessor of the *erjin* (q.v.); it lived in the mountains. **GPr** *VII*

ghark
A dangerous night creature, extant during *mirk* (q.v.). *Ma VII*

ghark jissu
A phrase in the language of the Water-folk, of uncertain translation but concerning some aspect of musical criticism; see also *bgrassik* and *brga skth gz*. *SO VIII*

ghaun
"A wild region exposed to wind and weather. In the special usage of the Pnume: the surface of Tschai, with emphasized connotations of exposure, oppressive emptiness, desolation." *Pn II**

gher
A colossal, para-cosmic entity which was the natural enemy of the *nopal* (q.v.): "...a colossal shape crouching in an indefinable mid-region, a black corpulence in which floated half-unseen a golden nucleus, like the moon behind clouds. From the dark shape issued a billion flagellae, white as new corn-silk, streaming and waving, reaching into every corner of this complicated space. At the end of certain strands Burke sensed dangling shapes, like puppets on a string, like plump rotten fruit, like hanged men on a rope." *BE X*

ghian
"An inhabitant of the *ghaun* [q.v.]: a surface-dweller." *Pn II**

ghisim
"...an alloy of silver, platinum, tin, and copper, forged and hardened by a secret process." It was used to make the Sorukh scimitars. *As IV*

ghost-apple
A variety of white fruit tree. [Compound.] *Pn X*

ghost-chaser
Unspecified protective structure seen at the village of Pengelly on Fluter. "The Iron Crow Inn ... a massive two-story structure built of antique timber and stone under a crotchety slate roof with ghost-chasers protecting the ridges." [Compound; by association with scarecrow.] *PoC VII-1, Lu III-5, L XIII*

ghost-clutch
The grip of a ghost: "The black, green and white *fiap* [q.v.; a magical amulet] will guard … against vengeance, malice and ghost-clutch." [Compound.] *GPr VII*

gialospan
"Literally, girl-denuders, in reference to the anticipated plight of the enemy *sheirl* [q.v.]." See *hussade*. *Tr VI**

gibble-gobble
A nonsense term from a piece of doggerel sung at Tintle's Shade: "With her biffle belly, monstrous arse and gibble-gobble face." [Echoic of "gobble".] *F VI*

gid
A dangerous wild animal: the *gids* "… leapt twenty feet across the turf and clasped themselves to their victims." According to the casebook of the mad wizard Follinense (EO), the *gid* was a "hybrid of man, gargoyle, whorl, leaping insect." *CS III-2, DE III, EO III*

Gihilite Perpatuaries
"Gihilites: a sect of mystics based in the Uirbach Region at the far side of the continent [on Gallingale]. The Perpatuaries were roving missionaries who purportedly stole children and conveyed them back to Uirbach for unpleasant purposes." [By association with "Carmelite" and "peripatetic".] *NL VI-1**

gilgaw
A species of obstreperous animal, probably a bird. "They strut; they posture; they clamor like gilgaws, but in the end they trot meekly off to their quarters." [By association with "gewgaw".] *PoC IX-1*

gilly-flower
A sweet flower having "an absurd smell" (W); it was common to the Appalachias (CD). [Compound.] *CD IX, W V*

ginger-tuft
A form of vegetation common to the seashore. [Compound.] *W XII*

gingle-berry
A berry from which juice was derived. *CS III-2*

ginsap
A variety of tree. [Compound.] *BD XI*

givim
A nonsense term in the ditty sung by Mikelaus the circus performer.
M VIII

glark
"A person not participating in the Fair-Play scheme [for advancement
to immortality] — roughly a fifth of the population." See also *phyle.*
[Etymology uncertain; perhaps from "gay lark".] *TLF I**

glass-fish
A genitophagous fish of the River Suametta on Fluter. "...you will lose
your private parts to the glass-fish within the minute. Swimming is a
poor economy." [Compound.] *Lu III-5*

glat
A heavy, dangerous species of jungle creature on Shattorak, which "...
merge[s] with the shadows and one never knows they are near until
it's too late." *EOE II*

glaywood
A variety of hardwood used to fashion swords. *BFM IX*

gleft
A kind of phantom; one of them stole part of Guyal's brain while
his mother was in labor. [? from "glia", a category of brain cells, and
"theft".] *DE V*

glemma
The antidote to *nyene,* a poison given off by *trapperfish* (q.v.). *Glemma*
was produced by the fish which ate trapperfish; when ingested by a
human it acted as a mild tranquilizer. *ArS VII*

glimmet
On Cadwal, the metal tin; when capitalized, the term also referred

to Thursday. "Using a nomenclature based on the so-called Metallic Schedule avoids the ear-grinding incongruity of contemporary equivalents (i.e. 'Monday', 'Tuesday', et cetera). Linguistic note: Originally, each term was preceded by the denominator *Ain* (literally: 'this day of'), so that the first workday of the week was 'Ain-Ort', or 'this day of iron'. As the root language became archaic and was superseded, the *Ain* was lost and the days were designated simply by the metal names alone." See also *ing, milden, ort, smollen, tzein* and *verd*. [Variant usage.] *ArS I*

glimmister
A shining, spangling silver powder provided by Faucelme to perfect the edge of Cugel's sword. [From "glimmer" and "glister".] *CS III-2*

Glint
"In Glentlin ['... a spare and stony peninsula west of Thaery'] the company of the thirteenth ship, adapting to their harsh environment, isolated themselves from the Thariots, and became the Glints. Each saw the other in terms of caricature. In Thaery, 'Glint' became synonymous with 'boorish', 'crude', 'boisterous', while for a Glint 'Thariot' meant 'devious', 'secretive', 'oversubtle'." [Variant usage.] *MT Intro.*

gliry
A sentiment encountered by Shimrod in the realm of Irerly; it "... chafed against his flesh." *L XV*

glochrome
A metal which turned blue-hot when electrified; Magnus Ridolph used wires of this substance to sever attacking tree-roots. [From "glow" and the Greek *chroma*, "color".] *HLD*

glossolary
An automatic language-translating device acquired by Vermoulian the Dream-walker. [By amalgamation of "glossary" and "glossolalia" ("speaking in tongues", a phenomenon which is also "automatic").] *Rh II*

glossold

A material, probably metallic, from which certain antique utensils were fabricated. [? from reversal of "old gloss".] **CS III-1**

gluco-fructoid nectar

A refreshing beverage served in globes. [From "glucose" and "fructose", and the Greek *oïdes*, "resembling".] **UR**

glunk

A part of Garlet's diet as prisoner. "It is not yet time for your glunk; you are far too avid for your luxuries, but then, who can blame you, since it is all so good! Ah, the tasty gruel!" [From "gunk" or "junk" and possibly "glue".] **NL XVIII-1**

glyd

"...a fermented pulp consumed almost exclusively by races of Hyarnimmic extraction, such as the Overmen, the Clas of Jena, the Luchistains." **OM III**

glyptus

A species of shade tree. **Tr XIX**

gnaw-bug

A species of annoying insect. [Compound.] **F VIII**

goana-nut

A common variety of nut, sometimes used for carving simple jewelry. **S**

gobboon

A big shot or mucky-muck. **BD I**

gobbulch

A species of edible fish found in lagoons. **Pn V**

Godogma

"The Great God of Destiny, who carries a flower and a flail, and walks on wheels." *Godogma* was the ruler of the Sarkoy pantheon. [From "god" and "dogma".] **PL, SK VIII**

gohovany
A species of arbor tree. **BFM** *XIV*

golasma
"... an organic crystal with a large number of peripheral fibers", translucent and "...the pallid blue color of Roquefort cheese." It was used to achieve the transfer of personalities between bodies. **CD** *V*

gol'eszitra
A Pnume policeman: "Listening Monitor" would be "a somewhat unwieldy translation of the contraction *gol'eszitra*, from a phrase meaning 'supervisory intellect with ears alert for raucous disturbance'." **Pn** *III**

golse
A "pantheon of demons" worshipped by the Shker cult. **BFM** *IV*

gomapard
"One of the few electric instruments used on Sirene. An oscillator produces an oboe-like tone which is modulated, choked, vibrated, raised and lowered in pitch by four keys." It was used on ceremonial occasions. **MM***

gonaive
A variety of mountain tree. **GPr** *II*

gorgolium
A perfect substance if you want to keep a sharp edge forever: "Those are gouges, with blades of an artificial substance called 'gorgolium', which never grows dull." **NL** *XX-2*

gorusjurhe
"The language of Shant discriminates between various types of sunsets. Hence: [*gorusjurhe* is] a flaring, flamboyant sunset encompassing the entire sky." See also *arusch'thain, feovhre, heizhen* and *shergorszhe*. **BFM** *V**

goumbah
"A pejorative term used by Darsh women in reference to men: a person of vulgar futile stupidity." **F** *V**

Gradencia

A beverage. "There'll be showers of flowers, and big iron jugs brimming with deep purple Gradencia." **NL** *VIII-3*

grass-pipe

A type of musical instrument made by fairies: "Fairies constructed viols, guitars and grass-pipes of fine quality, but their music at best was a plaintive undisciplined sweetness, like the sound of distant windchimes. At worst they made a clangor of unrelated stridencies, which they could not distinguish from their best." [Compound.] **L** *XIII*

gravinul

An anti-gravity material used in space travel: "... an airship left the roof, floated off on its shimmering plane of gravinul." [From "gravity" and "null".] **OM** *I*

gravitron

The discovery of the gravitron (by Chiram) led to the development of inertia-negative destriation fields for spaceship propulsion. [From "gravity" and "electron".] **UQ**

graybloom

A flower whose benign perfume was transformed into the deadly poison *tox meratis* (q.v.) when it was turned upside down in the dark for a month. [Compound.] **PL** *II*

greenock

A type of foliage. [? from "green" and "hillock".] **ShW** *XIV*

gregarization

Fraternizing for the sake of social advancement. [From "gregarious".] **DJ**

greph

A member of a bloodthirsty, militant race of mutant dragons from the planet Coralyne; they were also known as the "Basics", and were capable of space travel. **DM** *II*

griamobot
A species of "Savage river beasts. Horrible." However, the serpent-like creatures were actually vegetarians. The Magickers were concealed inside of craft made to look like griamobots. *BP VI*

grichkin
A variant individual of the Seishanee race. "…one of every two hundred Seishanee is a sport; as he grows, he becomes something other than the usual Seishanee, and is known as a grichkin." *NL XVI-1*

grinder-fish
A dangerous species of ocean fish, also referred to as "grinders". [Compound.] *MT XIV*

griswold
A species of predatory forest animal. *L XIX*

grotock
A wild creature, not described. *ShW III*

grsgk y thgssk trg
A phrase of uncertain translation in the language of the Water-folk; concerning the performance of *The Barber of Seville* by Dame Isabel's company, the Water-folk's representative stated that he "…found the duet about halfway through interesting because of the unusual but legitimate *grsgk y thgssk trg*." *SO VIII*

grue
A species of dangerous forest-dwelling creature; according to the casebook of the mad wizard Follinense (EO), the *grue* was a hybrid of "man, ocular bat, the unusual *hoon* [q.v.]." [Variant usage.] *EO III, Mo*

gruff
A baked brown dough, constituting the wholesome staple food of Arrabus, on Wyst; see also *bonter, deedle* and *wobbly.* [Variant usage.] *W I*

gryph
A species of griffin which guarded the portal to Murgen's castle. [From "gryphon", alternate spelling of "griffin".] **M** *V*

guizol
A common musical instrument. **BFM** *VI*

gungeon
An unspecified item which a *twastic* (q.v.) offered to Rhialto for sale by the gross. (He refused.) **Rh** *II*

gutch
Poor food: "The Domus [a fancy restaurant] serves insipid gutch." **F** *III*

gutreek
A smelly lout. [Compound.] **AOC**

guttrick
1. A knave. (GP) 2. Any visitor who grumbled over the lack of natural food, or *bonter* (q.v.) on Arrabus, Wyst. (W) **GP** *XII*, **W** *I*

gyjit
A species of night insect; it produced a creaking sound. [Onomatopoeia.] **MT** *XIV*

Gynodyne
Literally, "powerful woman"; Paphnis was "Goddess of Beauty and Gynodyne of the Century." [From the Greek *gyne*, "woman", and *dynamis*, "power".] **CS** *II-2*

Gzhindra
"Pnumekin [men associated with the Pnume over thousands of years] ejected from the underground world, usually for reason of 'boisterous behavior'; wanderers of the surface, agents of the Pnume." They were also referred to as "Ground-men". **Pn** *I**

H

hackle-bush
A common variety of shrub. [Compound.] *An IV*

hacknut
A variety of wood used for carving. [Compound.] *E V*

hackrod
An ordinary plant, commonly stewed and eaten with mealcake. [Compound; by association with "goldenrod".] *D V*

hadaul
"A Darsh game, combining elements of conspiracy, double-dealing, cunning, trickery and a general free-for-all melee."

Further: "Hadaul like all good games is characterized by complexity and the multiple levels upon which the game is played.

"The basic apparatus is simple: a field suitably delineated and a certain number of players. The field is most often painted upon the pavement of a plaza; occasionally it will be constructed of carpet. There are many variations, but here is a typical arrangement. A pedestal stands at the center of a maroon disk. The pedestal can be of any configuration, and customarily supports the prize money. The diameter of the disk ranges from four to eight feet. Three concentric rings, each ten feet in width, surround the disk. These are known as 'robles' and are painted (from in to out) yellow, green and blue. The area beyond the blue ring is known as 'limbo'.

"The rules are simple. The roblers take up positions around the yellow roble. All now are 'yellow roblers'. As the game starts they attempt to eject the other yellow roblers into the green roble. Once thrust or thrown into the green, a robler becomes 'green' and may not return to yellow. He will now attempt to eject other green roblers into the blue. A yellow robler may venture into the green and return into yellow as a sanctuary; similarly a green robler may enter blue and return to the green, unless he is ejected from blue by a blue robler.

"A game will sometimes end with one yellow robler, one green robler and one blue robler. Yellow may be disinclined to attack green or blue; green disinclined to attack blue. At this stage no further play is possible. The game halts and the three roblers share the prize in a 3-2-1 ratio, yellow receiving the '3/6th' or half share. Green, or blue, may wager new sums equal to the yellow prize, and by this means once again become yellow, a process which may continue until a single robler remains to claim the entire prize. Rules in this regard vary from hadaul to hadaul. At times a challenger may now propose a sum equal to the prize; the previous winner may or may not decline the challenge, according to local rules. Often the challenger may propose a sum double the prize, which challenge must be accepted, unless the winner has suffered broken bones, or other serious disability. These challenge matches are often fought with knives, staves, or, on occasion, whips. Not infrequently a friendly hadaul ends with a corpse being carried off on a litter. Referees monitor the play assisted by electronic devices which signal crossings of the roble boundaries.

"Conspiracy is an integral part of the game. Before the game starts the various roblers form alliances of offense or defense, which may or may not be honored. Tricks, crafty betrayal, duplicity are considered natural adjuncts to the game; it is surprising, therefore, to note how often the tricked robler becomes indignant, even though he himself might have been intending the same treachery.

"Hadaul is a game of constant flux, constant surprise; no one game is ever like another. Sometimes the contests are jovial and good-natured, with everyone enjoying the tricks; sometimes tempers are ignited by some flagrant act of falsity, and blood is wont to flow. The spectators wager among themselves, or, at major hadauls, against mutualization agencies. Each major shade [a Darsh oasis] stages several hadauls each year, on the occasion of their festivals, and these hadauls are considered among the prime tourist spectacles of Dar Sai."

For another elaborately detailed public sport, see *hussade*. **F** *V**, *IX*

haemaphyll
A biochemical present in many forms of alien vegetation. [From "haematin" and "chlorophyll".] **WB** I

hag-bush
A common variety of bush bearing edible berries. [Compound.] **An** I

haggot
A popular food, possibly fish. **W** XII

hag-tree
A variety of tree indigenous to Big Planet. [Compound.] **ShW** III

halash
A type of peppery stew, commonly garnished with parsley. [? by association with "goulash".] **GPr** V

halcoid
A member of "... a long-known class of materials which emerges from the retort as an extremely dense white material of waxy and somewhat fibrous texture. They show a most curious propensity. When a surge of electricity passes through them, they alter to a translucent crystalline solid, with an appreciable increment in size." Certain *halcoids* "altered" with such force and speed that they were, in effect, explosives. **BFM** VII

Halcoid-Prax
A variety of *halcoid* (q.v.) which "... additionally is harder and less susceptible to atmospheric friction." It was used to produce a type of cannon which was accurate up to a mile. **BFM** X

halcositic
A term used to describe the dendrons overlooking Coble. **ShW** VII

half-aud
See *aud*. **Ma** VIII

hallucinizer
A hallucinogen present in *Fraze* (q.v.). [From "hallucinate".] **SK** I

halpern

A kind of hat: "...a person wearing a black halpern fletched with a yellow plume." **BD XIV**

hand-conic

A hand weapon used by Druids. [Compound.] **ST XI**

hange

A light bulb on a three-foot pedestal carried by each captain in the sport known as *hussade* (q.v.). **Tr VII***

harbite

A popular but despicable Sarkoy sport consisting of the baiting and torture of a *harikap* (q.v.). **SK IV***

hariah

An odious variety of weed. **MT I**

harikap

"...a large bristle-furred semi-intelligent biped of the north forests" and indigenous to the Sarkoy steppes. In the sport known as harbite, "The wretched creature, brought to a state of tension by hunger, would be thrust into a circle of men armed with pitchforks and torches, stimulated to wild activity by being set on fire, thrust deftly with pitchforks back into the center of the circle as it sought to escape." **SK IV***, **PL II**

harquisade tree

An exquisite cultivated tree having glass foliage. **Rh II**

hawber

A variety of tree. A local superstition held that, "A cudgel cut from a nine-year old hawber and soaked nine nights in water which has washed no living hand: that's the best fend against witches." **W XII**

Hearth-O-Matic

"...a screen built into the wall, usually under a mantel. A turn of a switch projected the image of a fire upon the screen, anything from a crackling conflagration to a somber bed of coals, while infrared projections radiated a corresponding degree of heat." It was invented by Vincent Rodenave. See also *infra-radiator*. [From "hearth" and "automatic".] *TLF XI*

heceptor
A marsh-dwelling monster having clammy skin and gray, long-fingered hands with knobby knuckles. *L XIX*, *M VII*

heelcorn
A common variety of tree. [Compound.] *E VI*

heizhen
"The language of Shant discriminates between various types of sunsets. Hence: [*heizhen* is] a situation where the sky is heavily overcast except for a ribbon of clarity at the western horizon, through which the sun sets." See also *arusch'thain, feovhre, gorusjurhe* and *shergorszhe. BFM V**

hemmer
A type of foodstuff, not described. [Variant usage.] *E VII*

heptagong
A popular musical instrument played aboard the ship *Miraldra's Enchantment*, and presumably consisting of seven gong-like appliances. [From the Greek *hepta*, "seven", and "gong".] *ShW IX*

heptant
A neurotransmitter compound which "…appears only during the process of thought transfer." Its chelating agent, *anti-heptant*, "…acts like the eraser button of a recorder, canceling whatever circuits are active, but inactive toward those not in use." Basil Thinkoup used *anti-heptant* in a partially successful attempt to cure a manic-catatonic psychotic, or *catto* (q.v.). [From the Greek *hepta*, "seven".] *TLF VII*

herculoy
A very strong material used to make cable. [From "Hercules" and "alloy".] *HB*

herndyche
A liquid "dermal irritant" applied as part of an official punishment. *MT VI*

Herpetanthroid

A species of intelligent creature indigenous to New Hellas. [From the Latin *herpes*, "snake", and the Greek *anthropos*, "man".] **SP** *XIII*

hespid batrache

A creature which, when bred with man, had "…arms like baulks of timber, a heavy gray hide proof against spear, arrow, claw or fang." One such hybrid was dispatched by Kul, a *syaspic feroce* (q.v.). **GP** *XVI*

hesso-penthol

A gluey chemical used in the processing of *resilian* (q.v.). [? from "hessite", the mineral silver telluride, and "pentothal".] **HB**

hexafoam

A material commonly hardened with magnesium and used to provide structure for such items as car seats. [From the Greek *hex*, "six", and "foam".] **BD** *XVIII*

hexamorph

A variety of *sandestin* (q.v.); the term implies that it could assume six forms. [From the Greek *hex*, "six", and *morphe*, "form".] **L** *XV*

hilk

A food, probably a vegetable, sometimes served with bread and steamed eel. **D** *III*

hilp

A common herb, sometimes used in wizard's potions. **EO** *VII*

hinano

A variety of garden plant. **ArS** *VII*

histels

A percussive musical instrument which produced a rattling sound. **BFM** *VII*

hisz

The number six in the Dirdir language. **D** *X*

hity-tity
Hoity-toity. *W* V

hivan
The number seven in the Paonese language. *LP* X

hola
An interjection used as the equivalent of "hello" or "hollo". *DE* VI

hollip
A large purple vegetable having a musty flavor and used to brew ale.
E IV

Homo gaea
The human race in the Gaean Reach. *MT* Intro.

Homo mora
An ancient race of humans, divergent from *Homo gaea* (q.v.) and
living on planets around the star Mora. *MT* Intro.

honeybutton
A variety of fruit. [Compound.] *W* X

honeygrub
A variety of edible insect or its larva. "The next shop sold comestibles:
small bitter kumquats; cakes of compressed honeygrubs; cartons of
yeast; strings of myriapods, dragged squirming from the sea, drowned
in formaldehyde, then dried and cured in the smoke of smouldering
algae." [Compound.] *PoC* II-2

hoo
A dangerous night creature, extant during *mirk* (q.v.). *Ma* VII

hoochy-macooch
Sinuous or deceptive. During their voyage to Jexjeka, Howard
Thifer said to Magnus Ridolph, "John Southern told me you were a
detective, not an incense-swinging hoochy-macooch witch-doctor."
[By corruption of "hootchy-kootchy".] *TB*

hoon
A dangerous night-wandering creature. *EO* V, *CS* IV-2

hork

A foodstuff served with *pummigum* (q.v.) and tankards of must, victuals favored by the master criminal Lens Larque. *F III*

Horlogicon

A clock store. [From "horloge", meaning "a timekeeping device", and the pseudo-suffix "-icon", as in "stereopticon".] *BD II*

hormagaunt

One of "…the folk who soak up other folk's lives and then go off to live on Thamber. Aging is pursuivant to a condition in which the ichors of youth have been exhausted: so much is inherently obvious. The *hormagaunt* will desire to replenish himself with these invaluable elixirs from the most obvious source: the persons of those who are young.

"From the bodies of living children, the *hormagaunt* must procure certain glands and organs, prepare extracts, from which a waxy nodule might ultimately be derived. This nodule implanted in the hormagaunt's pineal gland forfends age." The process involved the loss of face and nose.

The criminal Kokor Hekkus proved to be a hormagaunt. *KM I*

horsewhistle

A common shrub which tended to grow in thickets. [Compound.] *E XI*

hs'ai

Dirdir: to call "*hs'ai hs'ai, hs'ai*" invokes an obligation of assistance, which Adam Reith incorrectly took to be a call for arbitration (*dr'ssa*). *D XX*

h'so

The Dirdir term for "marvelous dominance". *D IV*

huffaw

Bluster. "Certain smug boffins whose names I will not mention, though I can see their hangdog grins from where I stand, would boom and huffaw to their tenure committee as slavishly as ever." [Amalgam of "huff" and "guffaw".] *NL XI-2*

Hummer
The middle in status of three castes among the Blenks of Blenkinsop, a sort of nouveau riche; "[Hummers] comprising high-level financiers and mercantilists; professionals legal, medical and technical; and general intelligentsia. Their mansions, situated along the slopes of the highlands, were notably more pretentious than the simple and elegant Shimerati palaces." cf. *Shimerati*. [One who is very active; variant usage.] *Lu VII-1*

hurlibut
A wild creature of some kind: "Enemies and hurlibuts surround me, and stare with mad eyes. They flaunt their insolent haunches as they pass by on the run." [? from "hurlbat", a club-like weapon.] *BD XIV*

hurlo-thrumbo
1. A hullabaloo or foofaraw; a fuss. (KM) 2. "This device, intended for the training of swordsmen, that they might learn deftness and accuracy, dealt the clumsy challenger a mighty buffet if he failed to thrust into a small swinging target." This "perverse engine" served as a source of amusement for the young folk at Castle Sank. (L) 3. "An unspecified gambling game". (PoC) [from a play reference in the novel *Tom Jones*: "A more curious or a more insane production has seldom issued from human pen." (OED)] *KM VI, L XXII, PoC IV-2*

hurse
A moderately noxious plant bearing brown flowers. *CS IV-1*

hurusthra
"Roughly, musical panoramas and insights." *BFM V**

hushberry
A bush whose roots and berries were favored by *merlings* (q.v.) but poisonous to men. [Compound.] *Tr IV*

Husler
An "honorific appellative, applied to all persons. Eisel society lacks formal caste distinctions, status being essentially a function of wealth." *MT X**

hussade

A popular game played at Cluster Stadium. "The hussade field is a gridiron of 'runs' (also called 'ways') and 'laterals' above a tank of water four feet deep. The runs are nine feet apart, the laterals twelve feet. Trapezes permit the players to swing sideways from run to run, but not from lateral to lateral. The central moat is eight feet wide and can be passed at either end, at the center, or jumped if the player is sufficiently agile. The 'home' tanks at either end of the field flank the platform on which stands the sheirl.

"Players buff or body-block opposing players into the tanks, but may not use their hands to push, pull, hold, or tackle.

"The captain of each team carries the 'hange' — a bulb on a three-foot pedestal. When the light glows the captain may not be attacked, nor may he attack. When he moves six feet from the hange, or when he lifts the hange to shift his position, the light goes dead; he may then attack and be attacked. An extremely strong captain may almost ignore his hange; a captain less able stations himself on a key junction, which he is then able to protect by virtue of his impregnability within the area of the live hange.

"The sheirl stands on her platform at the end of the field between the home tanks. She wears a white gown with a gold ring at the front. The enemy players seek to lay hold of this gold ring; a single pull denudes the sheirl. The dignity of the sheirl may be ransomed by her captain for five hundred ozols, a thousand, two thousand, or higher, in accordance with a prearranged schedule."

"Hussade puts a premium not only on strength, but on skill, agility, fortitude, and careful strategy. Withal, hussade is not a violent game; personal injury, aside from incidental scrapes and bruises, is almost unknown." *Tr VII**, *Ma*, *W*

hust

An exhortation applied by a driver to his dragon, equivalent to "giddap". *DM V*

hyllas

A climbable, pod-bearing tree. *Rh II*

hymerkin
A musical instrument on Sirene: "...that clacking, slapping, clattering device of wood and stone used exclusively with the slaves." **MM**

Hynomeneural
See *Pattern of Hynomeneural Clarity.* **DE** *VI*

hyolone
A substance which, when dropped into the "thrust-box" of a spaceship's engine, caused it to "...leave a trickle of luminescence behind", thus allowing it to be followed at a safe distance. [? from "Hyolithes", a genus of mollusks.] **SSP** *II*

hyperas
"...a hyperaesthesic agent and a glottal inhibitor." Administered as official punishment by means of a *bladder-sting* (q.v.), it induced hypersensitivity of the skin and inflamed the brain. [By shortening of "hyperaesthetic".] **MT** *VI*

hyperglossom
A potable essence, served in tots on special occasions. [From the Greek *hyper*, "above", and a corruption of "blossom".] **Rh** *II*

Hyperordnets
A category of knowledge in the Museum of Man; it was subdivided into "Attractive and Detractive" sections. **DE** *VI*

hypnidine
A type of sedative-hypnotic drug. "The orderly administered a shot of D-beta hypnidine. The chief relaxed, his eyes open, vacant, his skinny chest heaving." [From "hypnotic" and possibly "anodyne".] **DSB**

Hypogrote
An adherent of a heretical sect. [? from "hypocrite".] **F** *XV*

hypolite
A red stone; it was used to fashion a model of the *Pectoral Skybreak Spatterlight* (q.v.). **CS** *VI-1*

hypospray

An instrument acting as a hypodermic syringe by high-speed percutaneous injection. [From the Greek *hypo*, "under", and "spray".] *MD, UQ*

hyrcan major

A clever and sometimes savage animal indigenous to Upper Phrygia, a continent on the planet Alphanor. [? from "Hyrcania", a province of the ancient Persian and Parthian empires, and "Ursa Major", the Great Bear constellation.] *SK IV, PL*

hyslop

A category of imaginary creatures, distinguished from fairies: "In the nomenclature of Faerie, giants, ogres and trolls are also considered halflings, but of a different sort. In a third class are merrihews, willawen and hyslop." See also *skak*. *L X**

I

iban
A variety of wood which was used to form polished posts for construction. *An* V

ibix
A hardy variety of tree, commonly found isolated and having a black trunk and mustard-colored foliage. *GPr* IV

ilkness
Genealogy; in his *Book of Dreams* notebook, Howard Alan Treesong asserted: "For ilkness I claim the line of Demabia Hathkens, specifically from his union with Princess Gisseth of Treesong Keep." [From "ilk" and the suffix "-ness".] *BD* XIV

Ilsday
A day of the week. *SvW* VII

imagicon
A device, placed about the head and neck, which allowed the projection of one's thoughts and images onto an auditorium screen for purposes of artistic competition. [From "image" and the pseudo-suffix "-icon", as in "stereopticon".] *BG*

impenetrex
A hard material used for windows in concrete buildings on the planet Skylark. [From "impenetrable" and ? "Plexiglas".] *SO* IX

impet
A common bird; it dove down upon its prey, which consisted largely of mud eels. *E* XI

imple
The number eight in the Paonese language. *LP* X

implet

See *impling.* **M** *VIII*

impling

A variety of small supernatural creature: "I cite also the Talisman of Saint Uldine, who worked to convert Phogastus, troll of Black Meira Tarn. Her efforts were extended; indeed, she bore Phogastus four implings, each with a round bloodstone in the place of a third eye." Also implet. [From "imp" and "-ling", diminutive suffix.] **M** *VI**

inchskip

See *Velstro inchskip.* **DJ**

Indescense

See *Pink Indescense.* **ArS** *I*

infra-radiator

An infrared room heater; in old-fashioned country inns it was "suspended obtrusively from the ceiling." [From "infrared" and "radiator".] **KM** *VIII*

ing

1. On Cadwal, the metal lead; when capitalized, the term also referred to Wednesday. For details, see *Ain* and *glimmet,* also *milden, ort, smollen, tzein* and *verd.* [Variant usage.] (ArS) 2. A costly wood used for carving. (E) 3. A natural material, commonly black, used to carve such items as antique desks. (MT) **ArS** *I,* ***E*** *V,* **MT** *VII*

inger

An animal whose eggs were eaten as a delicacy: "...while you dine on pomfret and inger eggs at the Old Pagane." [Variant usage: "a district of early Russia" (also spelled "Ingria".] **An** *X*

inoptative

Hazardous or uncontrollable, in relation to dreams; synonym *intractive.* [? by association with "inoperative"; and/or from "optative", a mood in some languages which expresses wish or desire.] **Rh** *I*

insidiator
A chained, man-like creature in the custody of Zanzel; after death, its ghost could bring bad luck. [From "insidious".] **Rh I**

insul
An insulating material; Magnus Ridolph protected himself from electrically heated wire by applying *insul* tape to his arms and legs. See also *glochrome*. [By shortening of "insulate".] **HLD**

intercongele
A variety of metaphysical interconnection or bond. [From the Latin *inter*, "between", and *congelare*, "to freeze".] **EO IV**

interflux
The stuff of the cosmos. [From the Latin *inter*, "between", and *fluere*, "to flow".] **Mo**

Interlocking Sequalion
A category of scale from the disintegrated corpus of the demon Sadlark; its value was twenty terces. See also *Clover-leaf Femurial*, *Malar Astrangal*, *marathaxus*, *Pectoral Skybreak Spatterlight* and *protonastic centrum*. **CS I-1**

intersplit
See *Jarnell Intersplit*. **SK I**

intractive
See *inoptative*. **Rh I**

intression
A kind of "psychic accommodation", performed silently and often in small groups. [? from "intress", shortened form of "interess", an obsolete term meaning "right or interest".] **LC I**

IOUN stones
Floating, fiery, variously shaped magical gems about the size of small plums. They were mined from nests of black dust at the edge of nothingness, and were considered by the *archveults* (q.v.) to be the *brain-eggs* of *fire-folk* living within stars. **Mo**

irchment

A fearful creature: "I have many fears. Mad dogs, lepers and leper bells, hellhorses, harpies, and witches; lightning-riders and the creatures who live at the bottom of wells; also: hop-legs, irchments and ghosts who wait by the lych-gate." [? from "irk".] **M** *III*

irix

An extinct tree whose sap was useful as a vermifuge. **CS** *V-2*

iron-web

Woven iron, used for such purposes as edging swords (BFM) or making door hinges and magnetic motor cores (An). [Compound.] **An** *III*, **BFM** *IX*

Irredemptible

A member of an incorrigible group on the Unspeakable Fourteenth spaceship landing on Maske; they "... refused to acknowledge either the Credence or the sublimity of Eus Thario; they were driven away from Thaery. (...) The descendants of the Fourteenth, mingled through some freakish process with *Homo mora* (q.v.), comprise the Waels of Wellas." Also *irredemptibility*. [From "irredeemable" and "redemption".] **MT** *Intro.*

irregulationary

Contrary to government regulations. [From "regulation".] **E** *IV*

irrevox

An extremely durable substance, useful in constructing knives. "... four knives with edges of the substance irrevox ... I want good carvings of animals! ... and take the cutting knives, with which you may carve many more such objects, since the edges never grow dull." [From "irrevocable".] **PoC** *XII-1*

irutiane

A variety of flower used in bouquets. **BFM** *VII*

iseflin

A material used in rugmaking, "a flat resilient matrix containing entrapped air bubbles. Designs of choice are printed upon this material; the resultant rug is inexpensive, durable, and decorative." [? by association with "isinglass", a very pure gelatin.] **MT XI**

iskish
"Darsh jargon for anyone other than a Darsh." **F VI***

Isoptogenesis
Uncertain; "Vodel's Doctrine of Isoptogenesis" was argued around a campfire one evening during Cugel's caravan journey to Kaspara Vitatus. [? from "isoptera", the order of insects consisting of the termites.] **CS IV-2**

isp
See *chill isp* and *aud*. **Ma III**

issir
The Dirdir word for sword. **D X**

isthiate
To modify or reduce in some way: "The first of these [regions of the universe] is compressed and isthiated." [? by amalgamation of "vitiate" and "asthenic".] **GM**

isthoune
An ineffable quality: "...exalted pride and confidence." **Tr XIV***

itling
A rascal: "Come, you raddle-topped little itling!" [From "it" and -ling, diminutive suffix.] **M III**

Ivensday
A day of the week. **SvW IV**

ixxen
"The white foxes of Maz. They're blind, but they run in packs of two or three hundred. They're dreadful creatures; they capture baby Gomaz and raise them to be ixxen, so sometimes you'll look out on the plain and see naked Gomaz running on all fours, and they're the eyes for the pack until the pack decides to tear them apart." They were found on the Steppe of Long Bones. [From "vixen", a female fox.] **DTA X**

J

Ja
One of the four secondary strings of the *khitan* (q.v.). **BFM** *IV*

jajuy
A species of arbor tree common to the mountains of Palasedra. **BFM** *XIV*

jangal
A type of foliage. **ShW** *XIV*

jaoic
A fruit grown locally on Sarkoy and served in crystallized form. **PL** *II*

jard
A species of plant, probably a weed. **Tr** *IX*

Jarnell Intersplit
The device on a rocketship which permitted travel through hyperspace. Kirth Gersen explained, "Space-foam is whorled into a spindle; the pointed ends crack and split the foam, which has no inertia; the ship inside the whorl is insulated from the effects of the universe; the slightest force propels it at an unthinkable rate. Light curls through the whorl, we have the illusion of seeing the passing universe." The intersplit emitted certain "mysterious effluviae" from which spacemen traditionally protected themselves by the application of blue-brown tone to their skins. It was also referred to as the Jarnell Overdrive. [From the Latin *inter*, "between", and "split".] **SK** *I*, **PL** *X*, **KM** *I*

jectrolet
A type of boat engine. [By reversal of "electrojet".] **MT** *XV*

jeek
A species of alien creature having a tail horn, "secondary stubs" and an "...organ above the dorsal horn ... [which] ejects body-tar, which

smells like nothing on Earth." *Jeeks* were mentioned as keeping shop in the Parade of the Alien Quarter on Light-year Road; they were partial to blue lights and liked to ingest salt-froth. See also *tinko* and *wampoon*. **AOC** *II*

jelosaria
A luxuriant variety of arbor plant. **ArS** *II*

jerdine
A black, stately tree commonly lining the shores of the Trullion waterways. **Tr** *I*

jetta
A variety of hedge. **E** *XXII*

jigger-plane
A flying machine consisting of "…little more than a seat suspended from four whirling air-foils." [Compound.] **AA**

jilberry
A variety of creeping seaside vegetation, which "squeaked when trod upon." **W** *XII*

jin
A ubiquitous species of tree with a tendency to rampant growth; they were cultivated in groves by the Waels, who regarded them as sacred. **MT** *XV*

jingle-bar
A type of percussive musical instrument. [Compound.] **An** *IV*

jinjiver
A reputedly healthful herb. "He has been taking jinjiver tea to help his ague, but it only seems to make his eyes water." [From *Zingiber officinale*, the latin name for ginger.] **NL** *XV-3*

jinket
In the Maunish dialect, a magazine. **BD** *XII*

jinko
A blue forest tree whose Uaian variety grew to enormous heights.
GPr VII

jinxman
A master of voodoo and spells for use in combat and political intrigue.
[Compound.] *MW I*

joho-wood
A type of wood, commonly black and used for carving masks. *ArS IV*

jorgiana
A beach plant, commonly pink. *FT XI*

jossamer
A hardy variety of tree. *GPr IV*

judas-dolly
A slotted device acting as a keel for a passenger balloon. [Compound;
by association with "Judas goat".] *As II, BFM II*

Jugger-tank
A variety of military tank. [From "juggernaut" and "tank".] *FHB*

junkberry
A common variety of bush. [Compound.] *GPr IV*

justiciant
A member of the judiciary; a judge. "This man was dignified and
handsome, like a retired justiciant." [From "justiciary".] *NL X-3*

K

Ka
One of the four secondary strings of the *khitan* (q.v.). **BFM** *IV*

kachemba
"A secret Uldra cult-place, dedicated to divination and sorcery, usually located in a cave." (The Uldras were a nomadic people on Koryphon.) **GPr** *I**

kachinka
A card game. "He thrives on five-star monte, stingaree, layabout, kachinka, and any other whimsies of fate from which he thinks he can wring a profit." [Suggestive of "pachinko", a Japanese pinball game.] **PoC** *III-1*

Kadant
A class of spaceship. **SvW** *XIII*

kahalaea
A variety of garden plant. **ArS** *VII*

kaiark
The highest rank among the Rhune hierarchy of aristocrats; the next two were *kang* and *eiodark*, respectively (q.v.). See also *lissolet*. **Ma** *IV*

kakajou
A type of fruit. **W** *X*

kakaru
A species of bird with a distinctive cry. [? onomatopoeia.] **MT** *VI*

kaleidochrome
A complex artistic technique for use of color. [From the Greek *kalos*, "beautiful", *eidos*, "form", and *chroma*, "color".] **TLF** *VII*

kalingo
A popular sport, not described. **KM** *VIII*

kalychrome

A color "…far up on the spectrum, a glorious, misty color"; it was visible only to Phalids, with their two hundred eyes. "…the Phalid word for the color was phonetically 'zzz-za-mmm', more or less." [From the Greek *kalos*, "beautiful", and *chroma*, "color".] **PF I**

Kanetsides Day

A major holiday on Pao, celebrated at mass meetings known as "drones". **LP XIV**

kang

1. A sprawling forest tree, sometimes inhabited by *grues* (q.v.). (Mo)
2. The second highest rank among the Rhune hierarchy of aristocrats. (The first and third were *kaiark* and *eiodark*.) See also *lissolet*. (Ma) **Mo, Ma IV**

kangol

A common foodstuff, sometimes mixed with clams, barley etc.; when served aboard the ship *Avventura*, passengers were required to pay a surcharge. **CS IV-1**

kaobab

A variety of forest tree. **EO III**

Kar Yan

"…subtle gray beasts slinking through the rocks, sometimes erect on two legs, sometimes dropping to all six." **SvW XII**

karkoon

"In the Alastrid myths karkoons are a tribe of quasi-demonic beings, characterized by hatred of mankind and insatiable lust." In the games of *hussade* (q.v.) at Uncibal, the defeated team's *sheirl* was given to the *karkoon* Claubus. **W V***

karoo

"Uldra festivities, including feasting, music, dancing, declaiming, athletic contests. An ordinary karoo occupies a night and a day; a Grand Karoo continues three days and nights, or longer. The karoos of the Retent tribes are wild and often macabre." The Uldras were a nomadic people on Koryphon. *GPr II**

karpoun
"A feral tiger-like beast of the Shamshin Volcanoes." *Tr XIV**

kasic
"A dark brown liquid, semi-viscous, with a bad smell" imported to Star Home from Cax, packed in carboys (narrow-necked bottles which typically hold corrosive liquids). It is an essential ingredient of *schmeer* (q.v.). " 'Curb your wonder!' Gontwitz told him. 'Thirty-two carboys of kasic is barely adequate. The rugmaker's worst fear is that his pot will go dry.'" *Lu IV-5*

katch
"The masculine Eisel headgear: a rimless hat of pleated cloth, ordinarily worn at a jaunty angle." See also *quat* and *dath*. *MT X**

kazatska
A type of dance. *CS IV-2*

keak
"A horrid hybrid of demon and deep-sea fanged eel." *CS II-3**

Kelt
The air-car owned by the District Thearch, a Druid; possibly a generic term. [By association with "Celtic".] *ST I*

kercha'an
"Effort conducing to superhuman feats of strength and will." *Tr X*

khet
An epithet, "...a metaphor linking Dasce to the obscenely fecund Sarkovy mink." *SK IX*

khitan
A musical instrument made from *blackbirk* (q.v.) and having a crooked neck, bronze hinges and "brilliancy buttons" (An). It had a "scratch-box" or "rattle-box" containing resonating fibers (which were played with the elbow), five prime strings and "four second strings

of unknown significance: Ja, Ka, Si, La." (BFM) [Variant usage: a medieval Chinese tribe; or from the Greek *kithara*, root of the word "guitar".] **An I, BFM II**

khoontz

An aged Darsh virago: "But who caught me but the vile old khoontz who terrorized the place, With her biffle belly, monstrous arse and gibble-gobble face." On moonlit nights, according to custom, they chased after the Darsh men, who in turn were pursuing *kitchets* (q.v.). [? from "cunt".] **F VI**

kial'etse

"In Shant no color could be used arbitrarily. A green gate bulb implied festivity, and in conjunction with purple or dark scarlet lusters gave hospitable welcome to all comers. Grayed golds told of mourning; violet indicated formality and receptiveness only to intimate intrusion; blue, or blue with violet, signified withdrawal and privacy. The word *kial'etse*, the mingling of violet and blue, might be used as an epithet, for example, *ls Xhiallinen kial'etse*: the snobbish and hyperaesthetic Xhiallinens." **BFM VI***

kianthus

A variety of grove tree. **Pn IX**

kiki-nuts

A delicacy which has "engaged epicurean appetites everywhere across the Reach." They grow on stalks rising from the swamp at the bottom of the Great Gorge at Felker's Landing, on the world Mariah. Their harvesting requires a special (and dangerous) technique: see *sprangs* and *sprang-hoppers*. [Compound; ? by association with "kiwi" (the fruit) and/or "kaki", a type of persimmon.] **PoC XI**

kil

A forest tree. **MT I**

kinderling

The children of the Kokod warriors. [From the German *kinder*, "children", and the diminutive suffix "-ling"; and by association with "kindling".] **KW**

kirkash
A resinous tree having a strong, sweet smell. **W** *IV*

kitchet
"After adolescence and until she grows her facial mustache, usually after six to eight years, [a Darsh girl] is a 'kitchet'. Thereafter she may incur any number of epithets, usually derogatory. The women use an equivalent set of terms in reference to the men." Another term for a young girl was *chelt*. [? by association with "kit" or "kitchen".] **F** *VI**

kite-copter
A flying machine beneath which a passenger car was suspended by cables. [From "kite" and "helicopter".] **KW**

kitkin
A small female child: "There need be no bedizenry of precious gems or yellow gold; such adjuncts would go unnoticed on this barely female slip of a kitkin." [From "kit", a small fur-bearing animal, and "-kin", diminutive suffix.] **M** *IX*

kiv
A musical instrument on Sirene: "five banks of resilient metal strips, fourteen to the bank, played by touching, twisting, twanging." It was used to accompany "casual polite intercourse". **MM***

klapper
An old-fashioned hat of black velvet, having "... a wide rolled brim, a coil of dark-green ruche and a small stiff brush of black bristles." [? from "clapper".] **BD** *II*

KLARO
An exclamation appearing on a sign before Murgen's castle; the sign read, in part: "WARNING! TRESPASSERS! WAYFARERS! ALL OTHERS! ADVANCE AT RISK! If you cannot read these words, cry out, 'KLARO!' and the sign will declare the message aloud." [From German *klar*, "clear" and colloquialism *klaro*, "you betcha".] **M** *V*

knoblolly
A heavy stick or cudgel. [Compound.] **DE** *V*

kodilla

A variety of wood used for carving. *E III*

kopf-nocker

A type of hand weapon. "Wayness looked wildly around the room. On the shelves were weapons: scimitars, kiris, yataghans, poniards, kopf-nockers, long-irons, spardoons, quangs and stilettos." [From the German *kopf*, "head", and English "knock".] *EOE VI*

koromatik

Chromatic, in the language of Shant; see also *aernid*. **BFM** *II*

koruna

A fragrance applied by Darsh men to augment their "fust", or odor. *F V*

krabenklotter

A species of beast wont to become bogged down in swamps, and ungrateful when rescued. [From "kraken", a Scandinavian sea monster, and "clot".] **ArS** *IV*

kragen

A sea monster; the greatest of them was King Kragen, whose "... body was tough black cartilage, a long cylinder riding a heavy rectangle, from the corners of which extended the vanes. The cylinder comprising King Kragen's main bulk opened forward in a maw fringed with four mandibles and eight palps, aft in an anus. Atop this cylinder, somewhat to the front, rose a turret from which the four eyes protruded: two peering forward, two aft." It devoured sponges in huge quantities and terrorized the island colonies of Blue World. [From "kraken", a fabulous Scandinavian sea monster.] **BW** *I*

kraike

The wife of a *kaiark* (q.v.); the term was applied as an honorific. **Ma** *IV*

kribbat

A carrion-eating animal. **Ma** *I*

krodatch
"A small square sound-box strung with resined gut. The musician scratches the strings with his fingernail, or strokes them with his fingertips, to produce a variety of quietly formal sounds. The krodatch is also used as an instrument of insult." **MM***

kruthsh'geir
"An untranslatable word, roughly: a man who has defied and defiled his emblem, and hence perverted his destiny." After death he was sent to the blue moon Braz, a place of torment. **CC II***

krystallek
A liqueur. [From "crystal".] **PL VI**

Kud
A class of spaceship. **SvW XIII**

kurdaitsy
"...a rather repulsive trained beast which squeals when its tail is pulled"; it was thus used as a sort of musical instrument, often accompanied by gongs and water flutes. **BD IV**

kxis'sh
An attribute of the Gomaz warriors: "...a lordly and contemptuous disregard for circumstances below one's dignity to notice." **DTA XI**

Kyalisday
A day of the week. **An VIII**

L

La
One of the four secondary strings of the *khitan* (q.v.). **BFM** *IV*

Laganetic
See *Thasdrubal's Laganetic Transfer.* **EO** *I*

laharq
"A creature of vicious habits, native to the tundras north of Saskervoy."
CS *II-3**

Lallankers
Outlier youths of the Ritters who cast aside certain restraints. They
are tolerated as sowers of wild oats. "Gontwitz spat on the ground.
'...Sometimes a youth with doting parents becomes an adolescent
convinced of his own sublime importance. He daydreams, shirks his
work and joins the girls at play, wearing a blue sash, and makes no
effort to learn the creed of the Ritters.'" [Portmanteau word, from
"lallygaggers" and "wankers".] **Lu** *V-1*

lalu
A wild animal heard at night on the Steppe of Long Bones. **DTA** *X*

Lamster
"...contraction of *Landmaster* — the polite appellative in current use."
UR

lancelade
A tall tree "...with a glossy dark red trunk and feathery black foliage."
CS *II-2*

landfish
A dinner item sometimes served devilled and put in pastry shells with
sauce. [Compound.] **NL** *III-3*

Landmoote

One of three agencies in *The Parloury* (q.v.), representing the middle and lower castes. [From "land" and the Old English *gemot*, "judicial assembly".] *MT Glossary*

langtang

A common variety of mountain tree. *GPr II*

lank-lizard

A variety of lizard which, when hybridized with bear, man and demon, produced an *erb* (q.v.). [Compound.] *EO I*

lanslarke

"A predacious winged creature of Dar Sai, third planet of Cora, Argo Navis 961." It was suggested as one of the possible origins of Lens Larque's name. "From UTCS [Universal Technical Consultative Service] I [Maxel Rackrose] extracted full particulars regarding the lanslarke. It is a four-winged creature with an arrow-shaped head and a stinging tail, reaching a length of ten feet exclusive of the tail. It flies over the Darsh deserts at dawn and twilight, preying upon ruminants and occasionally a lone man. The creature is cunning, swift, and ferocious, but is now rarely seen, though as a fetish of the Bugold Clan it is privileged to fly freely above their domains." *F III*

Larcener

A member of the caste of tower-builders on Blue World. The towers "stood sixty to ninety feet high at the center of the float, directly above the primary stalk of the sea-plant." [From "larceny".] *BW I*

latifers

Bushes, not described. [? by association with *conifers*.] *Rh II*

laud

A Badaic word meaning " 'well-appointed knight' in the Robin Hood tradition"; Paddy Blackthorne used it as a euphemism for "rascal". *SP V*

lavengar

A species of black tree; it was referred to by Druid Pruitt. *PL XI*

Lavrentine Redoubtable

A grandee in barbed, spiked armor and a helmet "crested with tongues of blue fire". *Rh II*

layabout

A card game. [Variant usage.] *PoC II-2*

lazy-tang

A type of tool used for wood carving. [Compound.] *E III*

lemurka

A type of musical instrument having a plaintive tone; it was played in the Carnevalle. *TLF I*

leobar

A creature whose habitat was crumbling masonry. *BG*

lep

A word of insult. "Don't you see the sign? It reads: 'Gaks, moops, leps and schmeltzers: Keep out!'" [From "leper".] *NL IX-4*

lessamy

A common type of food: "I was just about to cook up some hotchpotch Gladbetook-style, and a dish of lessamy." *BD XVII*

lethipod

A variety of grove tree. *Pn IX*

leucomorph

A dangerous, nocturnal, forest-dwelling creature; it was probably a hybrid, though according to the casebook of the mad wizard Follinense (EO), its origins were unknown. [From the Greek *leuko*, "white", and *morphe*, "form".] *EO III, CS I-2*

libram

An arcane or sorcerous book. [From the Latin *liber*, "book", and by association with "dram", "Libra" (sign of the Zodiac"), etc.] *DE I, EO, M VII, OM et al.*

Liddrsk
A musical mode of the Lekthwan race: "an underlying base or legato, with notes falling on it like rain." See also *Cmodor* and *Lyzg*. **GI** V

lillaw
A variety of tree protected at Bethune Preserve: "...that acre supporting the single and unique lillaw tree, whose provenance is a total mystery." **BD** XV

liltaphone
A musical instrument. [From "lilt" and the Greek *phone*, "tone" or "voice".] **BD** XII

limberleaf
A variety of black plant indigenous to the Great Salt Bog. [Compound.] **BFM** XIII

limequat
A cultivated fruit. [From "lime" and "kumquat".] **W** IV

lincture
An anatomic part of a ship's giant propulsive worm. [Variant usage: a syrup-like medicine.] **CS** II-1

linderling
A mythical creature, akin to ogres and dragons. [From the German *Lindwurm*, "dragon", and "-ling", diminutive suffix.] **KM** I

ling-lang
1. A type of toddy served in the bar of the Arkady Inn. (ArS) 2. A variety of tree having a thick, gnarled trunk and blue foliage. Also linglang. (BD) **ArS** IV, **BD** XI

linslurk
"A moss-like growth native to the swamps of Sharmant, Hyaspis, fifth planet of Fritz's Star, Ceti 1620." It was suggested as one of the possible origins of Lens Larque's name; see also *lanslarke*. **F** III

lippet

A small defenseless animal: "...the madmen who invaded the Carabas and slaughtered Dirdir as if they were lippets." **D X**

lirkfish

A species of fish cultivated in shallow ponds. [Compound; ? from the Scottish *lirk*, meaning "wrinkle".] **CS IV-2**

lissolet

A young female member of the Rhune aristocracy; the term was applied as an honorific. See also *eiodark, kaiark, kang* and *kraike*. [? from "lissome".] **Ma IV**

litholite

A variety of stone, a fused black form of which was commonly used as a writing surface. [From the Greek *lithos*, "stone".] **EOE III**

livret

A choice variety of purple-black seaweed often eaten as garnish with *hemmer* (q.v.). **E VII**

loitre

A kind of musical instrument. **BD XII**

Lorango

A gambling game on Fan, the Pleasure-Planet. It consisted of "...a large globe full of liquid and swimming balls of various colors." Winners were determined by the positions of the balls after the spinning globe came to rest. The colors were remarkable in themselves: vermilion, sapphire, flame, royal, topaz, zebra, opal, emerald, jet, white, olivine, indigo, silver, gold, ruby, fawn, diorite, harlequin, teal, amethyst and aqua. **SSh**

louthering

Literally, "defiance of the constellation-heroes", and, by extension, the IPCC. An activity of the Vongo gypsies of Camberwell. "At first they stood drunkenly reeling, peering up at the sky, pointing to the constellations they intended to disparage. Then, one after another, they threw clenched fists high, shouted taunts and challenges toward their opponents." [From "lout", and by association with Martin Luther — sometimes spelled *Louther* in German — who was an icon of defiance; portmanteau.] *NL I-2*

loutrano
A giant forest tree having a "straight black trunk" which supported a "disproportionately small parasol of dough-colored pulp." *BFM XIV*

ls
The article "the"; see *kial'etse*. *BFM VI**

lucanthus
A species of tree. "A waiter led them out upon an open terrace overlooking the river Chaim, and seated them at a table to the side, in the shade of a lucanthus tree." [From "acanthus", a variety of shrub.] *PoC I-7*

luciflux
A type of glowing material; a white bar of it marked the Parade in the Alien Quarter, where *jeeks*, *tinkos* and *wampoons* (q.v.) kept shop. [From the Latin *lux*, "light", and *fluere*, "to flow".] *AOC II*

lulade
A variety of flower having lavender blossoms; it was carried as a symbol by the *Grand Unctator of the Natural Rite*. See also *Unctator*. *MT III*

lume
A floating, glowing ball of plasm, used for illumination. [From the Latin *lumen*, "light".] *ArS*, *KM I*, *Rh II*, *TLF*

lumenifer
The illuminating device of a lighthouse, commonly having "twin shafts of red and white." [From the Latin *lumen*, "light", and the Latin *ferre*, "to bear".] *WFMR*

luminant
A street lamp. [From the Latin *lumen*, "light".] *SvW IX*

luminifer

A biological organ capable of luminescence; see *gaid*. [From the Latin *lumen*, "light", and *ferre*, "to bear".] **BD** *V*

lurlinthe

A garden plant, not described. **BFM** *V*

lurulu

An inexpressible state of mind which one may attain in seeking the satisfaction of his life's quest or heart's desire, embodying the idea that the journey itself, not its end, is the reward. " 'Lurulu' is a special word from the language of myth. It is as much of a mystery to me now as when I first yearned for something which seemed forever lost. But one day I shall glance over my shoulder and there it will be, wondering why I had not come sooner." *PoC Epilogue,* **Lu** *Intro*

lychbug

A stinging insect. [? from "lich", meaning "corpse".] **Ma** *I*

lyssum

A variety of vine. **W** *IV*

Lyzg

An especially complicated musical mode of the Lekthwan race; see also *Cmodor* and *Liddrsk*. **GI** *V*

M

Maasday
A day of the week. *F IV*

macro-gauss
A type of electrical generator used in vehicles made by the Yao people. [From the Greek *makros*, "long", and "gauss", a unit of electromagnetic induction.] *SvW IV*

macroid
Greatly enlarged; Cugel threatened to deploy the *Spell of the Macroid Toe* against Fianosther, "whereupon the signalized member swells to the proportions of a house." (EO) The term was also applied to outer space (WLA). [From the Greek *makros*, "long", and *oïdes*, "resembling".] *EO VII, WLA*

macrolith
A large stone; the *Shrouded Macrolith* was one of the "competing religions" subscribed to by the animate mountains in the realm of Irerly. [From the Greek *makros*, "long", and *lithos*, "stone".] *L XV*

macroscope
A device on board rocketships for producing enlarged images of the environment. [From the Greek *makros*, "long", and *skopein*, "to view".] *SK I, KM I*

macro-unit
A large unit. [From the Greek *makros*, "long", and "unit".] *DJ*

macro-viewer
A *macroscope* (q.v.). *SO XII*

maddercap
A plant of the Ushant jungle, sporting rigid, two-hundred-foot spines. "Each spine terminated in a ten-foot knob, from which spurted a corona of orange flames, regular as flower petals. The flames burned

perpetually, and by night, from an altitude, the [jungle] seemed a field of flameflowers." [Compound; from "madder", a plant in the bedstraw family.] **NL IX-1**

madlock
A large creature "…with heavy arms, staring green eyes and no neck"; two of them were sent by Iucounu to attack Cugel, but assaulted Lorgan after Cugel switched inn-rooms with him. **CS VI-2**

magmold
A variety of purple desert flora found on the planet Dar Sai. [? from "magenta" and "mold".] **F X**

Magna-fluke
A class of giant worm used to propel merchant ships; see also *Motilator*. [From the Latin *magnus*, "great", and "fluke".] **CS II-2**

magner
A malignant creature produced by black magic. **GM**

magniscope
See *proton magniscope*. **CD X**

magnoflux vortex
An energy source having commercial potential. [From the Latin *magnus*, "great", and *fluere*, "to flow".] **HB**

mais
A type of marine glue: "They cut the wood into strips and then weld them to the hull with *mais* — 'the stuff of life', which they keep in bottles of black glass. What is *mais*? No one knows but the Waels. If they curse a ship, the *mais* loosens in midocean and the ship becomes a tangle of sticks." **MT XVI**

makara
A stout forest tree, from which "…the staunchest hulls were fashioned." [Variant usage: a Hindu water monster.] **S**

Malar Astrangal
A type of scale from the elbow of the third arm of the disintegrated

corpus of the demon Sadlark; see also *Clover-leaf Femurial, Interlocking Sequalion, marathaxus, Pectoral Skybreak Spatterlight* and *protonastic centrum*. **CS** *I-1*

malditty
An offensive bit of doggerel: "The toper [a drinker] ... soils his clothes and commits malditties." [From the Latin *malus*, "bad", and "ditty", a song or trivial verse.] **BD** *XII*

malengro
A nonsense term in the ditty sung by Mikelaus the circus performer. **M** *VIII*

malepsy
A violent malaise; *Xarfaggio's Physical Malepsy* was one of the spells listed in "*Killiclaw's Primer of Practical Magic*". [Probably from "malevolent" and "epilepsy".] **Rh** *Foreword*

malleator
A spaceship drive part which is essential to the prevention of "bounces, bumps and jerks." "...mechanics installed a new-type nine-mode malleator which was guaranteed to keep the entire anathrodetic mesh in synchrony." [From the Latin *malleus*, meaning "hammer".] **PoC** *VI-1*

Malpractor
A member of the caste of tooth-pullers on Blue World; they wore "nondescript snuff-colored smocks." [From "malpractice".] **BW** *I*

Mamarone
See *neutraloid*. **LP** *II*

mana
"The emotion which compels heroes to reckless feats; a word essentially untranslatable." [Variant usage; the English "mana" is derived from the Polynesian meaning "impersonal supernatural force or power that may be concentrated in objects or persons, and that may be inherited, acquired, or conferred".] **DTA** *III*, **Tr** *XIV**

managa

The number eight in the Dirdir language. **D** *X*

Manciple

See *Chief Manciple*. **BW** *XIV*

mandoril

A wild animal on Cadwal, present principally in various hybrid forms; see also *banjee* and *yoot*. [? from "mandrill", a ferocious species of baboon.] **ArS** *I*

mangoneel

1. An edible species of scarlet eel. (CS) 2. A variety of forest tree. (GPr) **CS** *V-1*, **GPr** *VII*

manicloid

A substance used in making machinery. **SP** *I*

maniple

A prehensile extremity: "His flippers ended in long maniples." [Variant usage: an ecclesiastical vestment or subdivision of Roman soldiers; and by association with "manipulate", from the Latin *manus*, "hand".] **UM**

mank

A tailed, forest-dwelling animal, not further described. **Rh** *II*

man-river

A form of conveyor belt for the transportation of masses of people on Arrabus; also known as a *slideway*. [Compound.] **W** *I*

mantic

A double-winged creature in the retinue of Holy Symas. [Variant usage: the science of divination.] **F** *VII*

mantric

An expostulation or exegesis; a section of Howard Alan Treesong's notebook, *The Book of Dreams*, was headed *Mantrics*. [? from "*mantra*", a Vedic hymn.] **BD** *XIV*

marathaxus

An anatomic part of the *Malar Astrangal* (q.v.), a scale from the demon Sadlark's disintegrated body; its value was reduced if it had a greenish tinge. See also *Clover-leaf Femurial, Interlocking Sequalion, Malar Astrangal, Pectoral Skybreak Spatterlight* and *protonastic centrum*. **CS** *I-2*

marmarella

An edible oil, probably plant-derived, which could be used to cover up the hint of poison. "The girl lifted the lid to the box. 'Try one of these wafers! They are baked from sweet seeds and the oil of marmarella. No? You should at least taste! The flavor is pleasant.'" [? by association with "Nutella", a popular spread containing hazelnuts and oils.] **PoC** *VI*

marmelize

To transform all or part of a body into a white, marble-like material; in the land of Maunish this process was applied to the dead, creating statues (known as marmels) which populated their cemeteries. The legs of the villain Howard Alan Treesong were thus embalmed while he lived. [From "marmoreal", meaning "like marble or a marble statue", and "carmel".] **BD** *XII*

marmont

A large land animal: "…running in a frenzy like a bull marmont, braying at the top of his lungs." **Pn** *XI*

maroe

A fruit used to make jelly. **BFM** *V*

matanne

A type of luxury upholstery, commonly brown-violet. **SP** *VI*

Maugifer

A maker of spite. [From the obsolete "mauger", meaning "ill-will", and the Latin *ferre*, "to bear"; see Introduction.] **CS** *III*

maunce
A foodstuff: "...a kind of put-together, from herbs and river-fish." *BD XII*

mead-apple
A variety of cultivated fruit. The term "mead" may be a reference to the archaic word for "meadow", or to the alcoholic beverage derived from honey. [Compound.] *DE V*

mealie-bush
A common cultivated plant. [Compound.] *W IV*

Mechanismus
In the Museum of Man, a complex device of bobbins and rotors which was used to unravel the monster Blikdak. [From "mechanism".] *DE V*

megaphot
An industrial-grade camera. [From the Greek *megas*, "large", and *phos*, "light".] *KM VIII*

meioral
A potent parenteral sedative. [? from the Greek *meiōsis*, "lessen".] *TLF VII*

melantid-worm
A species of segmented, mud-dwelling worm in Bethune Preserve. *BD XVII*

mematis
A popular plant commonly having a dense, dark green growth and cultivated indoors. *BD I*

memril
"...gracile creatures apparently all legs and arms of brown chitin, with small triangular heads raised twenty feet above the ground; it was said that the magician Pikarkas, himself reportedly half-insect, had contrived the memrils from ever more prodigious versions of the executioner beetle." Memrils were used in battle by the Bohul battle-gangs. *Rh II*

mena
A variety of gray-green tree. *Tr I*

Mendolence
See *Violet Mendolence.* *CS I-1*

meng
"A small lizardlike creature." *PL II*

mephalim
A substance whose ichor, along with cacodyl and cadaverine, could be produced by a magical vessel given to Madouc by her fairy mother, Twisk. [Probably from "mephitis", meaning "a stench".] *M IX*

Mephitoline
A vile concoction created by Magnus Ridolph for commercial purposes. [From "mephitis", meaning "stench".] *SpS*

mepothanax
A plant from which powerful poisons were derived, e.g. *extin* (q.v.). *LP III*

mercade
A shopping center or bazaar, e.g. the South Ebron *Mercade.* [From "mercantile" and "arcade".] *SvW VIII*

mereng
A "savagely ferocious predator" indigenous to Star Home, which "lives hidden in narrow tunnels under the grass." "Merengs are long, supple, six-legged creatures which may attain a length of twelve feet, dreaded by the Ritters but occasionally hunted for meat and hides." *Lu IV-5*

meriander
A fragrance applied by Darsh men to augment their "fust", or odor. [? from "coriander".] *F V*

merlank
A species of lizard; the continent of Merlank was so named because it "...clasps the equator like a lizard clinging to a blue glass orb." *Tr I*

merling

A species of "… amphibious half-intelligent indigenes of Trullion, living in tunnels burrowed into the riverbanks. Merlings and men lived on the edge of a most delicate truce; each hated and hunted the other, but under mutually tolerable conditions. The merlings prowled the land at night for carrion, small animals, and children. If they molested boats or entered a habitation, men retaliated by dropping explosives into the water. Should a man fall into the water or attempt to swim, he had intruded into the domain of the merlings and risked being dragged under. Similarly, a merling discovered on land was shown no mercy." *Tr I**

mermelant

A large, intelligent animal used for drayage. "Ordinarily amiable, they are fond of beer, and when drunk rear high on their splayed rear legs to show their ribbed white bellies. At this juncture any slight provocation sends them into paroxysms of rage, and they exercise their great strength for destruction." See also *belch-wort* and *nuxium*. *CS III-2**

mernache

A species of tree, not described. *CS I-2*

mernaunce

An aromatic chemical in the workshop of Iucounu the Laughing Magician. *EO VII*

Merner

"Usual polite appellative of the Jingkens' worlds", comparable to "Mister". *FT XI**

merridown

See *merrydown*. *L XXIV*

merriehew

"A supernatural creature of delicate beauty, something like a fairy, with gauzy hair and webs between its fingers." Variant spelling of *merrihew* (q.v.). *NL VI-2*

merrihew
A variety of benign creature produced by white magic, and distinguished from fairies and various other halflings. "In a third class are merrihews, willawen and hyslop, and also, by some reckonings, quists and darklings. (...) Merrihews ...may manifest human semblance, but the occasion is one of caprice and always fugitive." (L) See also *skak*. **GM, L X*, M VII**

merrydown
A lively dance tune, with "unexpected halts and double beats" (An); see also *tantivet*. [Compound.] **An XI, GP XVI, L XXVII**

mervan
A poison which "...migrates harmlessly to the skin, and becomes a lethal principle only upon exposure to direct sunlight." **PL II**

metachronics
Flim-flam science purporting to encompass techniques of repairing or reversing aging. From an article in *Innovative Salubrity*: "Kodaira is known as the 'World of Laughing Joy' and the 'Palace of Resurgent Youth'. The source of this wonderful ambience is the unique fountain known as Exxil Waters, where a scientist called Dr. Maximus (not his real name) first studied the remarkable power of the water and eventually evolved the science of metachronics." [From the Greek *meta*, "beyond" and *kronos*, "time".] **PoC I-2**

metallite
A metallic material used in Kyash rugmaking. [From "metal" and "-ite", suffix meaning a salt or ester.] **MT XI**

metaphotic
Having the light-altering property of the glass used on Kyash to protect the citizens from the rays of their sun, Bhutra; Vance uses the term "photo-selective" synonymously. [From the Greek *meta-*, "above", and *phos*, "light".] **MT X**

metathasm
An ancient science or secret lore known to Rogol Domedonfors;

other such disciplines included *superphysic numeration* and *corolopsis.* [In part from the Greek *meta-*, "above".] **DE V**

metathiobromine-4-glycocitrose
An artificial flavoring used in soda pop. [Corruption of ISV.] **UR**

methycin
A solvent used for certain poisons. **PL II**

mian
A species of fly which was crushed to obtain a valuable musk, which was then "…brought in by the bulb-men of McVann's Star a half ounce at a time." **PBD**

micromac
A personal appliance of unspecified usage. [In part from the Greek *mikros*, "small".] **KT**

micro-unit
A small unit. [From the Greek *mikros*, "small", and "unit".] **DJ**

microvies
Small materials, possibly viable; an edition of *Characteristic Stuffs: Dusts and Microvies of the Latter Aeons* was consulted by Rhialto and Ildefonse. [From the Greek *mikros*, "small", and ? the Latin *vita*, "life".] **Rh II**

milden
On Cadwal, the metal silver; when capitalized, the term also referred to Saturday. For details, see *Ain* and *glimmet*, also *ing, ort, smollen, tzein* and *verd*. [Variant usage.] **ArS I**

millicent
A grain used to make a cake which was sometimes served with flower syrup. **W VII**

mina
The number four in the Paonese language. **LP X**

mind-weft
The weavings of the mind: "We go in the mental frame of adventure,

aggressiveness, zeal. Thus does fear vanish and the ghosts become creatures of mind-weft; thus does our elan burst the under-earth terror." [Compound.] *DE VI*

mini-film
Microfilm, used for archival storage. [From the Latin *minimus*, "smallest", and "film".] *DJ*

minkins
A nonsense term in the ditty sung by Mikelaus the circus performer. *M VIII*

mirk
A period of darkness and unreality on Marune. "About once a month, the land grows dark, and the Rhunes become restless. Some lock themselves into their homes; others array themselves in odd costumes and go forth into the night where they perform the most astonishing deeds. The baron whose rectitude is unquestioned robs and beats one of his tenants. A staid matron commits daring acts of unmentionable depravity. During mirk, the Majars lock themselves in their huts, and by the light of oil lamps chant imprecations against Galula the Goblin who mauls and eviscerates anyone unlucky enough to be abroad after dark. During mirk, *sebalism* [q.v.] is rampant. Indeed, sexual activity occurs only as a night-deed, only in the guise of rape." See also *aud*. [Variant usage: alternate spelling of "murk".] *Ma IV*

mishkin
A variety of pet animal. *OM V*

miswink
An error at "hoodwinking", the method of communication by signal machine on Blue World. [From the Old English *missan*, "to miss", and "wink".] *BW II*

mitre-bush
A stately, dark blue plant commonly found in clumps. [Compound.] *An VIII, CS I-1*

mitrox

A high explosive; it was used in construction and in tiny projectiles: "... a little metal box no larger than a match-case. From a tiny hole in its side a sliver of a dart would plunge six inches into a human body, and the little thread of mitrox would explode." (ChC) **ChC** *VII*, **T** *II*

mixistaging

A data-sorting process in the *Actuarian* (q.v.). [By contraction of "mixing" and "staging".] **TLF** *XIII*

mnemiphot

An information storage device with video screen and keyboard input. [From the Greek *mneme*, "memory", and *phos*, "light".] **KW, SP** *VIII*, **SSt**

mogrifier

A kind of transforming device used by magicians. [By shortening of "transmogrify".] **L** *IV*

moidras

Probably a type of metal. "From the west comes Shing, built of jet and silver. From the east comes Shang, built of copper and green moidras." **NL** *X-4*

moir

A common tree having a dank odor and sometimes planted along boulevards. **MT** *III*

molk

A common grain having white stalks, grown for cereal. **GPr** *X*

monic

Single, unified: "The Grand Unctator of the Natural Rite will conduct the eulogy and guide his monic spire toward the Lambent Nescience." See also *Unctator*. [From the Greek *monos*, "alone, single".] **MT** *III*

monitor fomories

Insects found in swarms on the surface of the oceans of Dimmick, covered with a mat of algae. Their "disciplined tactics" are said to be amusing. [By corruption of "formic", "of or relating to ants".] *PoC II-1*

monitor trapenoid

A monstrous oceanic creature found near the beaches of Songerl Bay, on the world Mariah. It lies in wait offshore, its black eye-tube emerging six feet above the surface, and seizes its prey with three or four tentacles to bring it to its jaws. [By corruption of "trapezoid".] *PoC X-1*

monkey-pole

"The Pedestal overlooking the Field of Voices." It consisted of a circular platform mounted on a pylon and covered by a glass parasol, and served as a podium for important speeches by the "Whispers". [Compound.] *W VI**

Monomantic Syntoraxis

An arcane discipline taught at the seminary of the Zubenites on Pogan's Point; its first principles were known as *Syntoractic Elementaries*. "Syntoraxis is essentially a progression of axioms, each deriving from the so-called Fundamental Verity." [From the Greek *monos*, "alone, single", and the English "romantic"; and in part from the Greek *syn*, "with", and the English "parallaxis".] *ArS VII*

monomarch

A sole sovereign; the term was applied to the *Connatic* (q.v.), ruler of the Alastor Cluster. [From the Greek *monos*, "alone, single", and *archos*, "ruler".] *W I*

Monstrament

The textual wisdom in the crypt at Fader's Waft; it was engraved in the blue *Perciplex* (q.v.) and projected onto a slab of dolomite. [From the Latin *monstrare*, "to show or instruct".] *Rh II*

monstrator

A guide during religious rituals. [From the Latin *monstrare*, "to show or instruct", and by association with "monitor".] *An III*

monstratory
A large room for display of artifacts. [From the Latin *monstrare*, "to show".] *EOE V*

moon-mirkin
A variety of whimsical creature having a whimpering cry. *LC III*

moop
Among the "strivers" of Gallingale, the most pathetic of *nimps* (q.v.). See also *gak*, *lep* and *schmeltzer*. "If you come upon a very timid nimp who wets the bed and wouldn't say 'peep' to a pussycat you have found a moop." [Combination of "miserable" and "droop".] *NL III-1*

mordet
1. "A fairy invocation, usually of bad luck; a curse". (GP) 2. "A unit of acrimony and malice, as expressed in the terms of a curse". (L) *GP IX*, L XXI**

mordyke
A type of piece in the chess-like game played by Vus and Vuwas, the two *gryphs* (griffins) which guarded the portal to Murgen's castle; other such pieces included the *bezander*, the *darkdog* and the *reignet*. *M V*

morphote
"...a malicious, perverse and unpredictable race, esteemed only for their weird beauty." The *morphotes* were one of the two quasi-intelligent races indigenous to Koryphon, the other being the *erjins* (q.v.).

"Morphote viewing is a sport on many levels. The morphotes stimulate upon themselves all manner of growths — spines, webs, wens, fans, prongs — to make themselves objects of fantastic splendor. Morphote viewers have contrived an elaborate nomenclature to define the elements of their sport." Examples: "...a twelve-spine devil-chaser with triple fans and a purple lattice", and "a red-ringed bottle-head". *GPr Prologue, GPr I**

Motilator
A class of giant worm used to propel merchant ships; distinguished from the *Magna-fluke*. [From the Latin *motus*, "moved".] **CS** *II-2*

mo-wood
A variety of wood, from which Lord Kandive the Golden carved a barge. **DE** *IV*

moy
A widespread plant, commonly purple. **An** *V*

mud-scut
A derogatory epithet; it was applied by Apollon Zamp to a *bulwig* (q.v.). [Compound.] **ShW** *I*

mulgoon
A variety of tall tree. **CS** *VI-2*

munit
A basic unit of currency. [Contraction of "monetary unit".] **HB, KW,** *SSt et al.*

murdock
A highly prized grain, milled for flour. **BD** *XII*

murre
Among the mountain peaks of Marune: "...the Two Hags Kamr and Dimw, rancorous above Danquil, enchanted and sleeping under a blanket of *murre* trees ..." **Ma** *VIII*

murst
"The meaning of this word, like others in *The Book of Dreams* [the childhood notebook of the criminal Howard Alan Treesong], can only be conjectured. (Must: urgency? With *verst*: in Old Russia, a league? Farfetched, but who knows?)" The pertinent text reads: "Gallop forward along your mad and reckless murst, oh Loris, on and ever on!"

Vance's footnote is convincing evidence of his intuitive etymological thinking; see Introduction. **BD** *XVI**

murvaille
A material commonly used to make tablecloths. [? from "murva", a variety of silky Asian hemp.] **M** *VIII*

musker
A kind of delicacy used as a sauce. [? from "musk".] **W** *VII*

muskit
"... a new breed of rough and ready young cats ... (in analogy with 'cowboys')." [? from "musketeer" and "kitten".] **CI**

mutachrome
A kind of optical filter used in night-glasses. [From the Latin *mutare*, "to change", and the Greek *chroma*, "color".] **KM** *VIII*

mycosetin
A medical antidote to Lyma's Virus, an organism indigenous to the planet Alphard. [From the Greek *mykes*, "fungus".] **MD**

mylax
A variety of tree having black bark and broad pink leaves. **CS** *III-2*

myradyne
A form of high explosive. [In part from the Greek *dynamis*, "power".] **TLJ**

myrhadion
A variety of tree with long purple blossoms. **CS** *I-1*

myrophode
A species of plant whose filaments were the principal source of food for "slimes"; see also *shdavi*. **MT** *X*

N

naae

"A set of aesthetic formulae peculiar to the Space Ages: that critique concerned with the awe, beauty and grandeur associated with spaceships. Such terms are largely untranslatable into antecedent languages." *W XVIII**

Nacnoc

A strong brew of Romarth. "On the following day another Loklor band appeared and collected another toll of the strong brew known as 'Nacnoc'." [? by association with "eggnog".] *NL XIII-7*

naisuka

A Beaujolais word meaning "…what makes a person decide to do things for no reason whatever"; also, "The reason that is no reason at all." *BP II*

narciz

"…a sharp, faintly salty beverage derived from seaweed, consumed in quantities by the Iszics of the Pheadh." *HI VI*

narcogen

Generally, a soporific drug. [From the Greek *narkoun*, "to benumb", and *genus*, "class" or "kind".] *MT VI*

narcotiana

The hallucinations peculiar to the narcotized state. [From the Greek *narkoun*, "to benumb", and the Latin *-ianus*, "a collection".] *CD IV*

naroko

A variety of wood: "They sang and danced by firelight to the tinkle of small lutes fabricated from dry red naroko wood." *Th VI*

narwoun

A type of "coiled full-throated instrument", played to the accompaniment of drums and horns or oboes. *Tr XIX*

natrid

A species of noxious creature having a sharp sting and brass horns. *L XIII*

needlegong

A musical instrument. [Compound.] *NL III-2*

nefring

A noxious fish of Songerl Bay on Mariah. "There are also nefring with needle-noses ... Songerl Bay is not a favored venue for aquatic sports." *PoC X-2*

nene

A truth drug. [Variant usage: a species of goose.] *ArS II*

Neophasm

Uncertain; one of the scientific subjects available in the microfilm viewer at the Kamborogian Arrowhead resort. [From the Greek *neos*, "new", and "*phasm*", a meteor or apparition.] *SP XIII*

nephar

A variety of tree with sprawling, black-green foliage: "I first saw light at Gaggar's Shade beneath the nephar tree." *F VI*

neutraloid

A member of the Mamarone: "...enormous creatures tattooed dead-black ... [wearing] magnificent turbans of cerise and green, tight pantaloons of the same colors, chest emblems of white silk and silver." They were eunuchs, and served as bodyguards. [From the Latin *neuter*, "of neuter gender", and the Greek *oïdes*, "resembling".] *LP II*

nging

A type of *pold* (q.v.), whose effect was "...to minimize the importance of serious business. It allows one to live without tension or care." *EOE VIII*

nibbet

"Vitalizing tea". It had "...flavors to which [Gersen] could put no names. One of the ingredients seared first the tongue, then the entire oral cavity." *BD XII*

nif
The number five in the Dirdir language. **D** *X*

night-whisk
A flying animal with small, glittering red eyes, which looked "…like a big bundle of black fluff. It's mostly air, a mouth, a gut and black plumes. It vibrates fibrils which create lift, and the creature flies." The creature perched in cardamom trees and ate insects; its plumes were illegally taken by poachers. [Compound.] **ArS** *V*

nimp
"One who refuses to participate in the striving for status and thus commands no respect, regardless of any other accomplishments." A term of disparagement on Gallingale; cf. *schmeltzer*. "As you know, your father and I belong to no clubs. We are 'Non-orgs', or 'nimps', and we have no social status." [Probable contraction of "not important", and by association with "wimp".] **NL** *II-1*

Nip-doodle
A variety of beer; it was favored by the drunken roustabout Bengfer. [Compound.] **BD** *XII*

nitsnip
A type of small hand tool. [Compound.] **M** *VIII*

nocumene
A type of flammable liquid. "Strangely, all the guards who had aided the scientist were housed in the same barracks, and this barracks was fumigated one night with nocumene." [By extension of "cumene", synonym for "isopropylbenzene".] **SEB**

Nolde
"The official responsible for the inhibition of caprice and abnormality", a post roughly equivalent to mayor. In the town of Gundar, the Nolde was Huruska. **CS** *V-1*

nona
The number five in the Paonese language. **LP** *X*

noncup

A colloquial term for *noncuperative* (q.v.). **E III***

noncuperative

"A nonrecipient of welfare benefits, reputedly all Chaoticists, anarchists, thieves, swindlers, whoremongers." [? from "non-cooperative", and/or "nuncupative"; see *nuncupatory*.] **E III***

Non-Sob

A variety of *Stimmo* (q.v.) which "minimized emotional response", and was used as an "anti-grief pill". [Compound.] **TLF VIII**

noop

A nonsense term in the ditty sung by Mikelaus the circus performer. **M VIII**

nopal

A malignant, phantomlike, parasitic creature whose presence distinguished the Chitumih from the Tauptu. It had "great bulbous eyes" and "a proud bank of bristles ... sprouting from a wad of dark fuzz the size and shape of a football", and clung to its prey's "neck and scalp by means of a gelatinous flap." Fibrils penetrated the victim's brain to influence his emotions and suck nourishment. The origin of the nopals was Nopalgarth — Earth. See also *chitumih* and *tauptu*. **BE I**

nopal-stuff

The substance of dead *nopals* (q.v.); it was impervious to the creatures, and was therefore used to make transparent sacks to imprison and transport them. *Nopal-stuff* was "brittle ... like dry old egg-shell" and "almost infinitely extensible". When live *nopals* were crushed within such a sack, they "...disintegrated into powder, merged with the fabric of the bag." Also referred to as *nopal-cloth* and *nopal-matter*. **BE VI**

nulastic

A resilient material used to make boots. [From "new" and "elastic".] **SSt**

Nunciant
A formal speaker in the *Parloury* (q.v.). [From the Latin *nuntiare*, "to report".] **MT** *III*

nuncupatory
Impertinent or irrelevant. Typical Vancean use is "The question is *nuncupatory*." [Probably from "nuncupative", an obsolete term meaning "oral", "not written" (especially of a will).] **CI, GP, L, Rh** *et al.*

nupper
A utensil used by the inhabitants of Cray, on the world Paghorn, to crack the shells of boiled bogworms. [? by association with "scupper".] **NL** *XIII-2*

nuptiarii
The perfumed consorts, of uncertain gender, favored by the Calbyssinians. [From "nuptial".] **GI** *XIV*

nuwai
The number nine in the Dirdir language. **D** *X*

nuxium
A plant from which, together with *belch-wort*, Faucelme prepared a noxious, beer-like tea for a group of importunate *mermelants* (q.v.). **CS** *III-2*

nyel
Literally, "horse-smell", a common pejorative "…applied by the Ska to all other men than themselves." The term "…made reference to the difference in body odor between Ska and other races, the Ska seeming to smell, not unpleasantly, of camphor, turpentine, a trace of musk." Another such derogatory term was "two-leg". **L** *XXI**

nyene
A poison given off by *trapperfish* (q.v.); see also *glemma*. **ArS** *VII*

nymode
An entity known for its speed, but not defined; the fairy Osfer said, "I

move with the speed of flashing nymodes when urgency is the call!"
M VIII

nympharium

A brothel to which the stoneworkers commissioned by the sorcerer
Pharesm were given privileges as part of their benefits. [From
"nymph" and the Latin *arius*, "a connected thing or place".] *EO IV*

O

---

oak-wort
A parasitic plant found on oak trees. [Compound.] *DE VI*

oast
A moronic giant used by certain villagers as a horse. "In a litter of filth and matted straw stood a number of hulking men eight or nine feet tall. They were naked, with shocks of dirty yellow hair and watery blue eyes. They had waxy faces and expressions of crass stupidity. As Guyal watched, one of them ambled to a trough and noisily began gulping gray mash."

A villager added that they "...carry us easier and appear to be less vicious [than horses]; in addition no flesh is more delicious than oast properly braised and kettled." [Variant usage: "kiln"; and by association with "hostler", a handler of horses, and "roast".] *DE VI*

Oblatic
An adherent of a heretical sect. [From "oblate", meaning "to offer".] *F XV*

obstrepery
Unruliness; boisterousness. "LOCAL ORDINANCES STRICTLY ENFORCED. OBSTREPERY FORBIDDEN." [From "obstreperous".] *PoC III-2*

occurgle
A nonsense verb used in a bit of doggerel concerning "Tim R. Mortiss" (the latter a play on the Latin words *timor mortis*, "fear of death"). It was written by the mad poet Navarth. *PL V*

ocholo
A probably derogatory term used by the Brumbos to refer to a Paonese. *LP XVII*

odorifer

A small well containing scent, activated during a *sherdas* (q.v.). [From "odor" and the Latin *ferre*, "to bear".] **Ma** *XI*

oel

See *swamp-oel*. **ShW** *III*

oe-pod

A plant product used by the Saponids: "They are the fruit of a great vine, and grown in scimitar-shape. When sufficiently large, we cut and clean them, slit the inner edge, grapple end to end with strong line and constrict till the pod opens as is desirable. Then when cured, dried, varnished, carved, burnished, and lacquered; fitted with deck, thwarts and gussets — then have we our boats." **DE** *VI*

ogave

A fruity ingredient of *pummigum* (q.v.), a victual favored by the fiend Lens Larque. **F** *III**

Oikumene

The civilized universe; beyond the Pale at its perimeter countless criminals took refuge. [From the Greek *oikoumene*, "inhabited".] **SK** *II et al.*

Old Gaboon

An ale served at the Owlswyck Inn, at Port Tanjee on Taubry. It is "strong, bitter and a trifle fowsty — still, all in all, palatable." Hilmar Krim unwisely took four portions, to his misfortune. **Lu** *Intro*

oliolus

A species of plant; one of the showboats plying the Lower Vissel River was named the *Perfumed Oliolus*. **ShW** *XIV*

olophar

A variety of thick-boled tree. **CS** *V-2*

ombril

A species of tall shade tree. [? from the Latin *umbra*, "shade".] **Tr** *IX*

omnigraph

A universal communications device, which also incorporated an automatic recording mechanism. [From the Latin *omnis*, "all", and the Greek *graphein*, "to write".] **Th** *V*

onniclat

A species of dangerous wild animal having a long neck. **Th** *VIII*

Oomp

"… (contraction of Oomphaw's Police Sergeantry): members of an elite militia, responsible only to the Oomphaw [chief]. They were men of extraordinary physique, with heads shaved bald, ears cropped to points and lips tattooed black. They wore crisp tan tunics, white knee-length kirtles, and ankle boots of a tough black metalloid substance exuded by a sea snail. A band of this same glossy black substance encircled their foreheads; to this band were attached spikes symbolic of rank. Most intriguing of all was the emblem, or ideogram, embroidered on the back of each tunic, in black and red: a symbol of unknown meaning."

Also: "They were handsome men of early middle age, golden-skinned, golden-haired, wearing neat uniforms of white, yellow and blue." (Th). **ArS** *IV**, **EOE** *I*, **Th** *VI**

opo

A punch made from pure fruits, natural honey and sweet *sessamy* (q.v.), and enjoyed by the people inhabiting an unclassified dream explored by Vermoulian. **Rh** *I*

optator

A button which each member of the Amaranth Society could press at his seat, thus illuminating a color-coded light on a master board to indicate his vote on a given issue. [From "optative", a mood in some languages which expresses wish or desire.] **TLF** *XVIII*

opticon

A device which reverses the usual visual process by displaying the output of the brain's visual center. See also *optidyne*. [From "optic", "relating to the eye or sight".] **EP** *I*

optidyne

A small, transparent hemisphere which, when placed over the eye, functioned as a powerful microscope or telescope. "The enormous range of [its] power is controlled by the ocular muscles and the eyelids." [From the Greek *opsis*, "sight", and *dynamis*, "power".] ***LP II***

orgote

A ganglionic structure resembling a jellyfish, on the body of Miss Aries 44R951, an extraterrestrial participant in the Miss Universe contest; it "should give off no perceptible odor" in order to be attractive. Related terms were *agrix*, *clavon*, *orgote*, *therulta* and *veruli* (q.v.). ***MMU IV***

orpoon

A variety of tree in Maunish. ***BD XI***

ort

On Cadwal, the metal iron; when capitalized, the term also referred to Monday. For details, see *Ain* and *glimmet*, also *ing*, *milden*, *smollen*, *tzein* and *verd*. [Variant usage.] ***ArS I***

ossip

1. A gnarled, silver-gray tree; its large, silver-green berries yielded a wax which induced an anti-gravity effect when applied to one's boots. (CS) 2. A dangerous creature with a large maw. (L) ***CS III-1, L XXI***

ouinga

A variety of aquatic tree having purple wood and an aromatic scent. ***Pn V***

Outker

"The general term for tourists, visitors, recent immigrants: essentially all persons other than Uldras or Wind-runners." [From "out".] ***GPr Prologue****

ozol

The basic unit of currency in the Alastor Cluster: "A monetary unit roughly equivalent to the Gaean SVU [Standard Value Unit]: the value of an adult's unskilled labor under standard conditions for the duration of an hour." ***Tr III, Ma, W III****

P

pacer
"A draft beast evolved from bullocks brought to Durdane by the first settlers." The wagon it pulled was known as a *pacer-trap*. [Variant usage.] *An I, As II**

padisks
"Number nine in series ten — or eleven — of the artificial elements." It was used in the construction of *verktt*, or "radiation valves" (q.v.). *GI XVI*

padroons
The ruling caste on the world Blenkinsop. They "do as they please", and "are not always reasonable"; a strong caste indeed. [From the Italian *padrone*, "ruler" or "master" and by association with "poltroon", a coward.] *PoC IX-1*

palliatory
An institution for the incarceration and treatment of psychotics. [From "palliate".] *TLF I*

pallow
A color in the realm of green magic. [? by amalgamation of "pall" or "pale" and "yellow".] *GM*

palmatic
A type of ochre and gray forest-plant. [From "palmate", meaning "hand-shaped".] *Rh II*

palodendron
A form of sparse vegetation on Smade's Planet. [? from the Latin *palus*, "pole", and the Greek *dendron*, "tree".] *SK I*

Panarch
The absolute tyrant of the planet Pao: "Deified Breath of the Paonese, Tyrant-Absolute of Eight Continents, Ocean-Master, Suzerain of the

System and Acknowledged Leader of the Universe", among other titles. [From the Greek *pan*, "all", and *archos*, "ruler".] **LP** *II*

Pancomium
See *Universal Pancomium.* **ShW** *VII*

pandalect
Generally, a powerful figure, e.g. the *Pandalect Cosmei.* [? by association with the English "pandect", meaning "a complete legal code".] **CS** *II-2*

Pan-Djan Binadary
"A secret organization …apparently dedicated to the expulsion of the Thariots from Maske. The Binadary mystified responsible officials, since neither Djan nor Saidanese were notably adept at intrigue." Its members often performed aggressive acts during the eclipse of the sun Mora. **MT** *Intro. et al.*

pandy-suit
A suit, commonly gray, worn by "rogues of the moor". [Compound; probably from "Pandy", a mutineer in India.] **DE** *III*

paney
A species of black tree referred to by Druid Pruitt. **PL** *XI*

pangolay
A bread-stuff baked from pollen. **BW** *XI*

panibal
A foodstuff, not defined. **CC** *VIII*

pannax
A film used in medical applications. "…we isolated Ogg's Plaque from its input of nervous impulses, sheathing it in pannax film and totally surrounding it with an insulating capsule." **NL** *IV-8*

Panortheism
A cult, one of many "…motivated by abstractions four or five or six times removed from reality." [In part from the Greek *pan*, "all", and *theos*, "god".] **GPr** *IV*

Pansogmatic
All-encompassing; *Pansogmatic Gnosis* was a religion subscribed to by the citizens of Gozed. Some favored it over *Tutelanics* (q.v.) because of its greater simplicity: "You merely recite the litany and then you are done for the day." [In part from the Greek *pan*, "all", and "automatic".] *SvW III*

pantavist
An optical enlarging device used by magicians. [From the Greek *pan*, "all", and "vision".] *Rh II*

Pantechnic Metaphysic
A metaphysical discipline well known to Rianlle. [From the Greek *pan*, "all", and *technikos*, "art".] *Ma XIII*

Panticle
A religious doctrine, as in the Panticles to be declaimed by the cadres of Marmaduke. [? from the Greek *pan*, "all", and "canticle", a hymn or poem.] *F XV*

Pantologue
A master linguist (?); suggested by a street named the Way of the Ten Pantologues. [In part from the Greek *pan*, "all", and *logos*, "word".] *EOE II*

parabamin-67
A medicament "for use in [and adjustment to] oxygen-rich atmospheres." *OM III*

parasphere
A parallel realm referred to by the mad poet Navarth in connection with the psychic world: "…every human thought disturbs the psychic parasphere." [From the Greek *para*, "beside", and "sphere".] *PL VII*

paray
"…that easy skirtlike garment worn by man and woman alike," probably resembling a lavalava. [From "pareu", a Polynesian loincloth.] *Tr I*

Parloury

A state council: "The Parloury at Wysrod consists of three agencies, with their various bureaus: the *Landmoote* [q.v.], representing the middle and lower castes; the Convention of Ilks; and the Five Servants. The grand structure on Travan Square is also known as 'The Parloury'." [From "parlour".] *MT III*, *MT Glossary*

parment

A pale gray tree with strings of dangling, spherical black nuts. *CS III-2*

pa-siao-tui

A variety of tree whose saplings were used as masts for catamarans. *S*

Pattern of Hynomeneural Clarity

A state of mental normality induced by the Chair of Clarity, in the Museum of Man. *DE VI*

patziglop

A form of poison; for selling it to Viole Falushe outside the decreed price schedule, Kakarsis Asm was sentenced to death by "cooperation", i.e. by public ingestion of a selected poison. *PL II*

paunce-wort

A variety of lush plant. *CS I-1*

pechavies

Sluggish, yellow-furred, sheep-sized animals husbanded on Big Planet. [? from "peccary".] *ShW XIII*, *BP IV*

Pectoral Skybreak Spatterlight

The crowning scale from the disintegrated corpus of the overworld demon, Sadlark. It had a red node at its center, and was pilfered by Cugel. See also *Clover-leaf Femurial*, *Interlocking Sequalion*, *Malar Astrangal*, *marathaxus* and *protonastic centrum*. [Compound.] *CS I-1*

pedestrip

A public walkway. [From "pedestrian" and "strip".] *CD VI*

pelgrane

A large, predatory, high-flying creature with white fangs, clawed hands and a head of black horn; "…gargoyle creatures, with wings creaking like rusty hinges …a hard leathern body, great hatchet beak, leering eyes in a wizened face." (DE) See also *flantic*. **CS** *III-2*, **DE** *II*, **Rh** *II*

pengelly

On Fluter, a local crowlike bird. There is a village "of considerable antiquity by that name on the Suametta River, with a population of about four hundred, occupied principally with fishing and agriculture. Pengelly figures to a small extent in historical lore and at one time was the lair of the bandit Rasselbane." **Lu** *III-4*

pentabrach

A small, edible, five-limbed sea-creature, possibly a starfish. [From the Greek *pente*, "five", and the Latin *brachium*, "arm".] **Tr** *XI*

pepperfish

A species of edible fish. [Compound.] **BW** *IV*

perceb

"A small mollusk growing upon sub-surface rocks along the shores of the Moaning Ocean. The percebs must be gathered, husked, cleaned, fried in nut oil with aiole, whereupon they become a famous local delicacy." [From the Spanish *percebes*, "goose barnacles".] **W** *XII**

Perciplex

"…a blue prism four inches tall, inwardly engraved with the text of the Monstrament [q.v.] Through the window the Perciplex projected an image of the Monstrament in legible characters upon a vertical dolomite slab, and so charged with magic was the Perciplex that should an earthquake or other shock cause it to topple, it must right itself immediately, so that it should never present a faulty image, or one which might be misconstrued, to the viewer." [From "percipient" and "complex".] **Rh** *V*

perdura

A dark, hard, glossy wood used in carving. [From the Latin *per*, "thoroughly", and *durus*, "hard".] **E** *IX*

peripatezic

A corruption of "peripatetic", as in *Framtree's Peripatezic Entercationers*. See also *Entercationer*. **E I**

permobeam projector

A piece of laboratory equipment. [From "permanent" and "beam".] **SSt**

perriault

Not described; a hawk-like bird? **CC III**

Perrumpter

A leader of a religious sect. "I am Deter Kalash, from Loisonville on the world Komard. My status, as you can readily detect, is good; in fact, I am Perrumpter of the Clantic Sect, and I now serve as Wayfinder for a contingent of ten pilgrims." [From the Latin *per*, "through", and *rumpere*, "to break". See also *Perrupter*. The spelling with an m suggests a caricature of the figure as having a large behind.] **Lu Intro**

Perrupter

A Saidanese warrior. "The usually mild Djan, when isolated from his fellows, is apt to become a rogue. When solitary Djan are recruited as perrupters, they are required to wear masks to prevent them from establishing normal social relationships with their fellows, to the detriment of their fighting qualities." They wore brown tunics and black breeches. [From the Latin *per*, "through", and rumpere, "to break".] **MT Intro., MT XIII***

perturgle

A nonsense verb used in a bit of doggerel concerning "Tim R. Mortiss" (the latter a play on the Latin words *timor mortis*, "fear of death"). It was written by the mad poet Navarth. **PL V**

pervolve

To involute. [From the Latin *per*, "through", and *volvere*, "to roll".] **EO IV**

pervulsion
A violent spell or one of its manifestations. [By amalgamation of "perversion" and "convulsion".] *EO VII*, *Rh II*

petradine
A biochemical component of vegetation on some alien planets: "No chlorophyll, haemaphyll, blusk, or petradine absorption ... in short — no native vegetation." *WB I*

pfalax
A heavy wood used to construct furniture. *ShW I, II*

phaltorhyncus
A variety of forest tree on the planet Pao. *LP XIII*

phalurge
A variety of tree. *DE VI*

photochrometz
A material used for the panes in spaceyachts. [From the Greek *phos*, "light", and *chroma*, "color".] *MT XI*

photoscape panel
A pictorial wall decoration used in houses. [By amalgamation of "photograph" and "landscape".] *MT XI*

phyle
(Singular and plural) The five levels of achievement by which one's lifespan was determined, according to the Fair-Play Act: Base, or Brood; Wedge; Third (or, rarely, Arrant); Verge; and Amaranth, i.e. immortal. See also *glark*. [From "phylum".] *TLF I*

pilkardia
A unique and beautiful species of tall tree: "Chilke called attention to a towering tree with masses of small rectangular leaves shimmering in waves of dark red, pale red and vermilion. 'That is a pilkardia, but it is usually called an "oh-my-god tree".'" This term reflected the consequences of being struck by "stink-balls" of fiber and gum thrown down on visitors by the tree-waifs. *Th IV*

pinct
A piece of equipment used by a *worminger* (q.v.). **CS II-1**

Pingis Rejuvenator
The fourth variant of *Pooncho Punch* (q.v.), " '…occasionally administered to the dead or unconscious.' 'Indeed!' marvelled Wingo. 'To what effect?' " **Lu I-3**

Pink Indescense
A sweet, heavy wine formulated by the Wook oenologists. [? by contraction and alteration of "incandescence".] **ArS I**

pinker
A type of sharp hand-weapon. "Now then, are any of you carrying power guns, flashaways or pinkers? It is imperative that we keep such gear from the local thugs, which is to say, most of the population." [From to "pink", meaning "to stab", and more ominously, "to punch something with decorative holes".] **PoC V-1**

pinkum
A species of very tall tree cultivated on ranches on Rosalia. "Pinkums are black and yellow, with pink strings dangling from the branches. The tree-waifs use these strings to make rope." See also *chulka*. **Th II**

pinky-panky-poo
Hanky-panky: "…while you played blindman's buff and pinky-panky-poo with your eight girls." **ArS V**

plambosh
The quality of pride, as expressed in the Darsh male: "…a swaggering willful flamboyance, a reckless disregard for consequences, a perversity which automatically conduces to contempt for authority. If, by one means or another, such as public humiliation, this pride is fractured or destroyed, the man is 'broken' and thereafter becomes almost eunuchoid.

"In women, the quality is more difficult to define, and takes the form of studied inscrutability." [? by association with "panache" or "swashbuckle".] **F VII**

plancheen
A glossy construction material sometimes substituted for steel. [From "planch", meaning "a flat metal plate".] **CD** *IV*

planetta
A gambler's card game played on Fan, the Pleasure-Planet. [From "planet".] **SSh**

plastrol
A synthetic material; it was used to make the Ten Books, a treasured encyclopedia. [? from "plastic".] **MTB**

Pleasaunce
An opulent lounging chamber on Abercrombie Station. [variant usage.] **AbS** *III*

plench-box
See *froghorn*. [? by association with "clench".] **NL** *III-2*

pleurmalion
A tube-shaped device used by Rhialto to divine the location of the *Perciplex* (a prism engraved with textual wisdom; q.v.), even at great distances in space and time. See also *farvoyer* and *pantavist*. [From the Latin *pleura*, meaning "side" or "rib", and ? "Pygmalion", the mythic artist who fell in love with his sculpture of a woman and persuaded Aphrodite to bring it to life. The relationship of *pleurmalion* to the *Perciplex* is thus analogous to that of the biblical rib to a woman, bringing it into view and thus to life. A similar metaphor is realized in *Thasdrubal's Laganetic Transfer* (q.v.). See Introduction.] **Rh** *II*

plinchet
A variety of salad vegetable. **E** *V*

plion
A flexible synthetic material used to make clothing. [From "pliable".] **ChC** *VI*

pliophane
A material used to make clothing suitable for space travel. [From "pliable" and "diaphanous", meaning "transparent".] **ST** *I*

plumanthia

An arbor plant. [? from the English "plum" or "plume" and the Greek *anthos*, "flower".] **GP, Rh** *I*

pn'hanh

A doctrine used by the highest Dirdir castes: "corrosive or metal-bursting sagacity." See also *zs'hanh*. **D** *IV*

pogget

"Shredded seaweed, wound around a twig and fried in hot oil." **W** *V**

poinct

To puncture: "…a man's vitality is like air in a bladder. Poinct this bubble and away, away, away, flees life, like the color of fading dream." **DE** *V*

poincture

A tiny entity; the Murthe was compressed to a *poincture* by the three magicians Teus Treviolus, Schliman Shabat and Phunurus the Orfo. [By amalgamation of "point" and "puncture".] **Rh** *I*

pointane

A variety of tree, "each a perfect tear-drop" in shape. **F** *VIII*

pold

On the planet Nion, a compound of pollen and water: "While the climate was generally mild, the topography was diverse and the habitable areas separated by deserts, steep-sided plateaus, tracts of weird wonderful forests and 'water-fields'. These latter were suspensions of pollen blown from forests and 'flower-fields' into areas originally lakes and seas, where the sedimented pollen became the substance known as 'pold'." Further, "In order to understand the intricacies of life on Nion, one must understand pold. There are hundreds of types of pold, but basically they are either 'dry', derived from loess-like beds of pollen and spores transported by the wind, drifted and ultimately compacted; or the 'wet', from deposits laid down in the ancient lakes and seas. The sub-varieties of pold derive from age, curing and blending, the action of morphotic agents, and thousands of secret processes. Pold is ubiquitous. The

soil consists of pold. Beer is brewed from pold. Natural raw pold
is often nutritious, but not always; some deposits are poisonous,
narcotic, hallucinogenic, or vile-tasting. The Gangrils of the Lankster
Cleeks are experts; they have built a complex society upon their
manipulation of pold. Other peoples are not such connoisseurs, and
eat pold like bread, or pudding, or as a substitute for meat. The flavor
of pold depends, obviously, upon many factors. Often it is bland, or
somewhat nutty, or even sour, like new cheese.

"By reason of pold, everywhere available, hunger is unknown."
EOE VIII

Polymantic

A member of a cult opposed to the Monomantics; see also
Monomantic Syntoraxis. [From the Greek *polys*, "many", and
"romantic".] *ArS VIII*

polyptera

A variety of plant growing in clumps. [From "Polypteridae", a family
of fishes.] *W VII*

pomardo

A popular table beverage. *E VIII*

pooder

A kind of food: "The sublime tuber", eaten with a "crunch, crunch,
crunch!" A central prop of the ever-popular Po-po the Pooder Boy's
act at the Trevanian on Blenkinsop. *Lu VII-5*

poomsibah

On Star Home, a derisive term for a bacchanal. "…they are rumbling
their wumps [q.v.] across the steppe to Maiden Water, or some
other notorious resort, and will convert the kasic [q.v.] into a grand
poomsibah of sybaritical follies." *Lu V-4*

Pooncho Punch

The specialty of the Pingis Tavern on Fluter. The recipe is a "guarded
family secret". There are four varieties; the most recommended is
Number Three: "It is bracing and flavorful, yet never sits heavy on the
tongue." [Echoic.] *Lu I-3*

pooter

An old solivagant: "Now that I'm a pooter bold, I wander where I please." **F VI**

pop-bark

A species of plant. [Compound.] **PL II**

Portinone

An unspecified structure in the realm of Green Magic. [? from "portico".] **GM**

post-pot

"The accumulation of challenge money; the victor's prize" for the game of *hadaul* (q.v.). [Compound.] **F IX***

potentium

The central, perpetual power source in the Museum of Man; it contained "prismatic fervor" which Kerlin the Curator hoped to spray on the demon Blikdak to destroy him. [From "potent".] **DE VI**

poulder

A dire supernatural being. "[*Shrikes* (q.v.)] consort with ghosts and know what human men should never know. Don't so much as look at them! They will send poulders to sit on your neck of nights." [By association with the German *Poltergeist*, a "noisy ghost".] **PoC VII-2**

pourrian

A kind of "fine Darsh provender" served at Tintle's Shade; its taste, however, was vile. **F III***

praesens

A Paonese "vitality-word", not further elucidated. [Latin, "present in the same place".] **LP X**

Presbyte

A Druid official. [From "presbyter", an official in the early Christian church.] **ST III**

Preterite Recordium

A sibilant, horn-like instrument of convoluted bronze tubes, acquired by Rhialto from among the effects of the *archveult* (q.v.) Xexamedes. [From the Latin *recordari*, "to call to mind".] **Mo**

prickle-sac
A form of weapon containing anodyne (tranquilizer). [Compound.] **KM** *VIII*

prickle-withe
A variety of twig used to make brooms which were held to be effective in repelling witches. [Compound.] **W** *XII*

printhene
A species of creature indigenous to the Bethune Preserve: "Sinuous black printhenes skulked through the meadows on splayed legs. These were voracious, cunning and capable of prodigious feats of savagery; still they avoided the vile-smelling *balt-apes* [q.v.]." **BD** *XVIII*

printogram
A large machine in the *Actuarian* (q.v.) into which blank forms were fed. [From "print" and the Greek *gramma*, "record".] **TLF** *XIII*

procourse
A prescribed sequence of instruction, usually religious, as "Argument One of the Chilite Procourse". [From the Latin *pro*, "for", and *currere*, "to run".] **An** *III*

proctosculation
Obsequious flattery. "How did 'Careless Clois' achieve this office? By assiduous proctosculation, so I am told." [From the Greek *proktos*, "anus" or "rectum", and "osculation", meaning "kissing".] **NL** *XI-2*

projac
A type of handgun which projected a dazzling "stalk of blue-white energy." An indicator displayed the amount of charge remaining; its power pack was replaceable. **BD** *VIII*, **F** *IX*, **KM** *I*, **SK** *IX*

proscedel
A precious powder sifted from the Dust of Time and comprising part of Uthaw's treasure. **CS** *V-2*

proton magniscope

A device for extreme magnification at distance, the opposite of an electron microscope. [From the Latin *magnus*, "long", and the Greek *skopein*, "to view".] **CD** *X*

protonastic centrum

The anatomic term denoting the demon Sadlark's central scale, the *Pectoral Skybreak Spatterlight* (q.v.). See also *Clover-leaf Femurial, Interlocking Sequalion, Malar Astrangal* and *marathaxus*. **CS** *VI-2*

pro-ubietal

Correctly or forwardly placed; the term was applied by the sorcerer Pharesm to the metaphysical chute created by his elaborate rock-carving. See also *cryptorrhoid* and *suprapullulation*. [From "ubeity", meaning "position".] **EO** *IV*

prut

A type of soft peasant hat favored by the residents of the hamlet Poldoolie. **BD** *VIII*

prutanshyr

A macabre ritual of gelding and public execution by suspension from hooks in a glass cauldron of boiling oil, all to the accompaniment of sad, sweet music. **Tr** *I*

psilla

A variety of tree having shaggy bark and papery, russet leaves; its black wood was used to make doors. **D** *II*, **Pn** *VIII*, **SvW** *IV*

psychodele

A mentalist. [From the Greek *psyche*, "soul", and *delein*, "to make manifest".] **MZ** *II*

Pubescentarium

A hostel for adolescents. [From "pubescent" and the Latin *arius*, "a connected thing or place".] **DE** *V*

puffworm

A species of worm popularly sold by vendors who blew bugles to attract customers. [Compound.] **W** *IX*

pulsor
A propulsive device for a small boat. [From "pulse".] *Tr I*

pummigum
"A pudding of yellow meal, meat, tamarinds, ogave, scivit and like fruits, served in a thousand variants at restaurants catering to spacemen across the human universe." It was favored by the criminal Lens Larque. [? from "pemmican", meaning "venison" or "emergency rations".] *F III**

punchern-gun
A weapon carried by the feluccas of the Long Ocean. [From "punch".] *MT Glossary*

pungko
A species of thin black tree. [? by association with "gingko".] *CS III-1*

pungle
Nose or other part of the anatomy. "AND A TWEAK IN THE PUNGLE FOR SCHMELTZERS" (q.v.). *NL III-1*

puzzle-bush
A littoral shrub. [Compound.] *W XII*

pyreumator
A large weapon used by the Brumbos. [? from the Greek *pyr*, "fire", and "decimator".] *LP XVII*

pyrong
A new and potent poison prepared by Guildmaster Petrus. *PL II*

pyroxilite
An underground mineral occurring in large crystals of "russet-brown, black-brown [and] greenish-black." [From "pyroxenite", a form of igneous rock, and/or "pyroxylin", a cellulose nitrate compound.] *Pn II*

pysantilla
A dangerous creature inhabiting the chasms on Tschai. [? a play on the word "piss-ant".] *D II*

Q

quain
A flowering domestic tree. *FT I*

quainterie
Quaintness; the term "self-conscious *quainterie*" was applied as an epithet by citizens of Cuthbert to the architecture of New Wexford. *PL III*

quake-tree
A tree native to Fluter. "Quake-trees, nectarcups hanging on corkscrew tendrils, bobbed and bounced to spill perfume into the air." [Compound.] *Lu I-3*

quampic
A gray shadow manipulated by the sandestin Osherl. *Rh II*

Quaners
"A caste of engineers, architects and builders, active everywhere across the Dalkenberg." *ShW III**

quang
A type of hand weapon. "Wayness looked wildly around the room. On the shelves were weapons: scimitars, kiris, yataghans, poniards, kopf-nockers, long-irons, spardoons, quangs and stilettos." *EOE VI*

quarti-quartino
A liquid measure: a fourth of a *quartino*. "Magnus Ridolph sat on the glass jetty at Providencia, fingering a *quarti-quartino* of Blue Ruin." [From the Italian *quartino*, "a small wine-measure, usually a pint".] *KW*

quat
"A flat four-cornered hat, sometimes no more than a square of heavy fabric, occasionally weighted at the corners with small globes of

pyrite, chalcedony, cinnabar, or silver." See also *dath* and *katch*. **MT VI***

quist

A category of supernatural creature distinguished from fairies and certain other halflings: "In a third class are merrihews, willawen and hyslop, and also, by some reckonings, quists and darklings." See also *skak*. **L X***

quorl

"A type of mollusk living in beach sand." **Tr XV***

R

rachepol

"A person driven away from his native shade [a Darsh desert oasis]; an outcast; a homeless wanderer, more often than not a criminal." A literal translation was "crop-ear", because the punishment included the ceremonial cutting off of one ear. *F III, F VII**

rackbelly

A poisonous plant. [Compound.] *D II*

rackleg

A dangerous species of jungle creature on Shattorak. [Compound.] *EOE II*

racq

A distilled beverage consumed by the Trevanyi; it "...influences the nerves and makes them none the kindlier." [From "arrack", any of various liquors found in the Middle-East, distilled from a variety of fermented organic materials.] *Tr XIX*

radne

A nonsense term in the ditty sung by Mikelaus the circus performer. *M VIII*

rado-cooker

A domestic device probably resembling a microwave oven. [? from "radon" or "radio".] *HB*

raho fibers

A material used by the Sah and Aianu to wind rope. *As IX*

rainberry creamcakes

A fancy pastry. [Compound.] *Lu IX-5*

ramcopter

A helicopter powered by ram-jet. [From "ram" and "helicopter".] *T II*

ramifolia

A garden plant which stood "…high on ten crooked legs." [From the Latin *ramus*, "branch", and *folium*, "leaf".] *ArS VII*

raptap

A species of insect infesting the beaches of the Torpeltine Islands. [Compound.] *FT IX*

raptogen

A type of tranquilizer, administered in the form of an exhalation. [From "rapt" and the Greek *genes*, "born".] *EO VII*

rascolade

A sort of bull-run for unransomed hostages. The captive was kept in a cage or hutch. "After a year or two, if ransom isn't paid, the captive is brought out to run down a course. After him come warriors on erjins [q.v.], armed with lances. If he reaches the other end of the course he's set free." [? from "rascal" and the French *roulade*, "rolling down".] *GPr III*

rashudo

Among the Roum: reputation, self-respect, honor. "'Rashudo' included flair, grace, impassive bravery, rituals of courtesy, exact to the flick of the little finger, and much else." [By association with Japanese words in which the suffix *-do* means "the way of", as in bushido, "the way of the warrior", the code of the samurai.] *NL XIII-7*

rattle-bush

A common variety of plant: "…a sad little garden of rattle-bush, pilgrim vine, rusty fungus." [Compound.] *ChC XIX*

rat-whisk

A punitive instrument similar to a cat-o'-nine-tails. [Compound.] *MT XIV*

raudlebog

One of "…the semi-intelligent beings of Etamin Four, who were brought to Earth, trained first as gardeners, then construction laborers, then sent home in disgrace because of certain repulsive habits they refused to forgo." *LC II**

rawn
A color in the realm of green magic. *GM*

Recordium
See *Preterite Recordium*. *Mo*

reeber
A black tuber having a rancid odor, often boiled and "…tingled with pap and bug-spice" for the table, or pickled; it frequently caused bloating and dyspepsia, but was nonetheless regarded as a staple. *E XVII*

Refluxive
A member of a tendentious cult: the "Society of Yearning Refluxives" was formed by a group of Dirdirmen who had been expelled from the academies at Eliasir and Anismna "for the crime of promulgating fantasy." They offered twice-weekly classes in "thought-control and projective telepathy." [From "reflux".] *SvW II*

refrax
A hard material used to make shields. [? from "refract".] *LP II*

Refunctionary
On Scropus, in the town Duhail, a penal institution housed in an ancient palace (Fanchen Lalu) which had belonged to Imbald, Sultan of Space. Its methods were original, and its superintendent was quite skilled in hypnosis techniques, as the crew of the *Glicca* eventually discovered. "At the Refunctionary we have learned to avoid static solutions to evanescent situations, which come and go like the flicker of fireflies. Each type of mischief-maker has a generic pattern of behavior, which can to some extent be classified. We never deal with our animal-torturers as we do our widow-swindlers; each must be processed in subtly different ways, to match his or her predilections. We must act tactfully; some of our murderers are damnably proud folk, and we do not want to inflict new lesions upon their self-image." [From "function".] *PoC IV-2*

reignet
A type of piece in the chess-like game played by Vus and Vuwas, the two *gryphs* (griffins) which guarded the portal to Murgen's castle. Other such pieces included the *bezander*, the *darkdog* and the *mordyke*. [From "reign".] **M** *V*

resilian
An elastic, tensile substance derived from the *ticholama* bush (q.v.) and having many industrial applications. [From the Latin *resilire*, "to rebound".] **HB**

Retrotropic
A spell of return. [From the Latin *retro*, "backward", and the Greek *tropos*, "turning".] **Rh** *I*

rhodopod
A common domestic tree. [From the Greek *rhodon*, "rose", and *pod*, "foot".] **MT** *III*

rhumbo
A gambling card-game played on Fan, the Pleasure-Planet; see also *Lorango* and *planetta*. **SSh**

rhume
A species of noisome herb. **ShW** *III*

riddleberry
A variety of low, green bush whose dark red berries were pressed by fairies to make wine. [Compound.] **L** *XIII*

rigoband
A clown or buffoon: "Silly rigobands at a carnival." **BD** *XII*

rigoroid
A material in which psychotic patients were swaddled to produce a mild therapeutic massage; it was used in a *palliatory* (q.v.). [From "rigor" and the Greek *oïdes*, "resembling".] **TLF** *VI*

Ritter Way
The guiding philosophy of the nomads of Star Home. "I am a Ritter of

Star Home! I am self-guided, self-determined, autonomous! On Star Home there are neither rules nor statutes." *Lu IV-5*

robler

"A participant at *hadaul* [q.v.]." *F X**

robles

"The concentric rings of a hadaul [q.v.] field, painted yellow, green and blue." *F IX**, *F X**

rock orchid

An unusual plant having glass flowers. [Compound.] *ArS V*

rock-rack

A species of edible fish: "I recommend the baked rock-rack and greenfish." [Compound.] *Th I*

Rondler

An honorific title earned by one who has circumambulated the world Kyril on pilgrimage (which requires about five years). [? by association with "rambler", "rondo", a musical form characterized by repetition, and/or the Yiddish *hondler*, meaning "bargainer".] *PoC IV-2*

roqual

A shrub commonly grown as a hedge. *DE II*

rostgobler

A dangerous, white, vaguely-shaped creature, also known as a "hyperborean sloth". *CS I-1*

rotomatic

A small, automatic device, not specified. [? from "rotor" and "automatic".] *OM III*

roverball

A team sport practiced on the world Gallingale. Since it requires "several strong agile forwards ready for a mix-up" and an "ace roving plunger", we may assume the game is similar to American football or rugby. [Compound.] *NL III-1*

Rt.

"Abbreviation for Recipient, the usual formal or honorific title of address." *E III**

rubant

A creature in an imaginary realm discussed by two "efferents" controlled by the magician Shimrod: "The gray-pines are on regular duty, and there is never a tweak from the rubants." *M VII*

rufflewort

A gigantic species of plant commonly decorating urban roadsides. [Compound.] *MT* X

rug-fish

A fish whose skin was used to make sandal leather. [Compound.] *BW IV*

Ruha

The sixth and most secret of a Yip's six names, two of which, including the Ruha, were self-applied. In the Caglioro, a cavernous gambling hall, "When an unlucky or unskillful gambler loses all he owns, what then does he use for his desperate wager? He puts up a fragment of his Ruha: in effect, himself. If he wins, he is once more whole. If he loses (and being unskillful or unlucky, this is often the case) he parts with a one-fortieth portion of himself, such being the recognized fractions into which a Ruha may be divided.

"This deficiency is noted by fixing a white cord to the hair at the back of the head. Often he continues to lose, and pieces of him may be scattered all over Yipton, and ever more white strands dangle down his back. If and when he loses all forty parts of his Ruha, he has lost all of himself and is no longer allowed to gamble. Instead he is called *No-name* and made to stand at the side of the Caglioro, staring blankly over the scene. His Ruha is gone; he is no longer a person. His first four names are meaningless, while his wonderful fifth name [designating 'a quality to which the person aspired, such as "the Lucky" or "the Harmonious" '] has become a horrid joke.

"Out on the floor of the Caglioro, another process starts — the negotiations between those who owned parts of the Ruha, in order that the entire property may be brought under a single ownership. The bargaining is sometimes hard, sometimes easy; sometimes the parts are used as gambling stakes. But in the end the Ruha is brought under the ownership of a single individual, who thereby augments his status. The 'No-name' is now a slave, though he owes neither service nor duty to his master; he obeys no orders and runs no errands. It is worse; he is no longer a whole man; his ruha has been taken into the soul of his master. He is nothing: before he is dead he has become a ghost.

"There is a single mode of escape. The man's father and mother, or his grandfather and grandmother, may give up their ruhas to the creditor, so that the first ruha is returned to its original owner. He is once more a whole man, free to gamble as he chooses out on the floor of the Caglioro." *Th Glossary*

rumblesnout

A species of bug-sucking animal. [Compound.] *Tr VIII*

Rumfuddle

An eccentric party whose participants were "cognates", or surrogates from an alternate universe, of famous or notorious historical personages. [From "rum" and "befuddle".] *R*

rumplinga

A pejorative term applied to a woman. [? from "rumple".] *FT XIII*

S

sacerdote
One of a race of handsome, naked, subterranean autochthons with
golden hair. See also *tand*. [From the Latin *sacerdos*, "priest".] *DM II*

sachuli
A pearl-colored wood used for interior carpentry. *GPr V*

sad-apple
An enormous fruit tree having yellow-green foliage and an acrid scent.
[Compound.] *E XI*

saddleband
A band of cloth used to restrain a sleeper in his bunk while in the
weightless environs of Abercrombie Station. [Compound.] *AbS IV*

sad-horn
A musical instrument of coiled bronze. [Compound.] *Ma VI*

sagmaw
A creature with a stentorian voice. [Compound.] *ShW XIV*

Sainh
The Iszic equivalent of "Mister" or "Sir", but appended after the name
of the person addressed, as the Japanese *-san*. *HI I*

sako
A variety of fine wood, commonly gray-green and used for paneling
interior walls. *E IV*

salmatic
A species of plant having "...drooping branches and blue-green
leaves." *ArS VII*

sal-negative
A medicament for treatment of heat rash. [Compound.] *SP VIII*

salpiceta

A species of cultivated plant; its nubbins were edible. *ArS IV*

salpoon

A type of black timber. *Tr XVIII*

sampang

A rich material, probably wood, used for interior paneling. *BD II*

sand-creeper

A common littoral creature taken as food. [Compound.] *GPr III*

sandestin

A type of demon commonly indentured to a magician: "a class of halfling which wizards employ to work their purposes. Many magical spells are effected through the force of a sandestin." One such was Sarsem, "the Adjudicator", who was trained in interpretation of the *Monstrament* (q.v.); another was Osherl, an irascible, red-eyed creature in the service of Ildefonse (Rh).

"Sandestins, most powerful of all, are in a class by themselves"; they were distinguished from fairies and the class of halflings which included giants, ogres and trolls. The creatures could take on many appearances, e.g. "...the form of a fresh-faced boy", iron scorpions, or "...that sort known as a hexamorph." Three sandestin scales were used by Shimrod, with only partial success, for protection in the realm of Irerly (L). See also *chug, falloy* and *skak*. *GM, GP*, L X*, M III, Rh*

sand-tripe

A variety of desert flora found on the planet Dar Sai. [Compound.] *F X*

saniflex

A white material used as upholstery for the beds of the clinical laboratory in a *palliatory* (q.v.). [From the Latin *sanitas*, "health", and "flexible".] *TLF VII*

sanivacity

Healthful vigor. [From the Latin *sanitas*, "health", and "vivacity".] *BD XI*

sanoe
A variety of wood used in shipbuilding. **ShW** *XIV*

sanque
"A complicated game of assault and defense, played on a board three feet square, with pieces representing fortresses, estaphracts [q.v.] and lancers." It was commonly played in public inns. **W** *XI**

sansuun
"The evening breeze which follows the sun around the planet [Dar Sai]." **F** *IX**

sarai
"Untranslatable: a limitless expanse, horizon to horizon, of land or water, lacking all impediments or obstacle to travel and projecting an irresistible urgency to be on the way, to travel toward a known or unknown destination." [? by shortening of "caravanserai", an inn for desert caravans.] **GPr** *VII**

sarcenel
A red, jewellike object found in the sensorium (brain) of a *Flamboyard* (q.v.), a bizarre and sometimes ferocious creature indigenous to the Torpeltine Islands; the node could be taken violently, particularly by members of the Arsh race, for use as barter. **FT** *IX*

sark
A variety of wood used for carving. [Variant usage: a shirt.] **E** *VII*

sashei
"…that wild and gallant élan [in a *sheirl*] which inspires a [*hussade*] team to transcend its theoretical limitations." See also *sheirl* and *hussade*. [? by association with "sashay".] **Tr** *X*

Saskadoodle
A cocktail described as "a pale green liquid, mildly effervescent, with a subtle bite which tingled pleasantly on the palate." One of Vermyra Garwig's specialties. **PoC** *VII-1*

scalmetto

A species of tree. [? by corruption of "palmetto".] *SK II*

scanscope

"A binocular photo-multiplying device, with a variable magnification ratio up to 1000 x 1: one of the articles Reith had salvaged from his survival kit." [By shortening of "scanning telescope".] *D I**, *Pn I**, *SvW I*

scape

A form of swift, silent military airship, often armored. [Variant usage; and by association with "escape".] *MT XIII*

scattlebogger

An incompetent amateur musician: "...there are other local [orchestral] groups: scattleboggers, bang-and-bump groups and the like." *BD XII*

scaur

A variety of tree. *Ma VI*

sceleone

"...that fragile metal forged from water-reflected beams of moonlight." The fairy-king, Throbius, had a crown made of sceleone. *GP IX*

schkt

The syllable whose pronunciation activated the spell known as *Sissle-way* (q.v.). *M IV*

schmeer

A substance used by the Ritter rugmakers: "Schmeer is the adhesive which binds our rugs. It is indispensable." A "short pot" of *schmeer* is a source of anxiety. "The recipe is standard. Into a forty-gallon vat she pours twenty gallons of green grass gum, adds ten gallons of barnacle slurry, ten pounds of mereng [q.v.] bladder-wax for unctuousness, three gallons of boiled red kelp, a jug of emalque extract [q.v.], a gallon of fire oil for bite, and two gills of kasic [q.v.]. The vat is brought to a boil, simmered for two hours, strained and allowed to rest. After a week the schmeer is ready." [Probably from the Yiddish *schmear*, "a spread such as cream cheese on a bagel".] *Lu V-1*

schmeltzer
"One who attempts to ingratiate himself, or mingle, with individuals of a social class superior to his own." A term used by the "strivers" of Gallingale. [By association with the Yiddish *schmaltz*, meaning "chicken fat or lard", and the Yiddish *schmoozer*, meaning "one who chats casually, sometimes to gain an advantage." (Similarly the word "unctuous", from the Latin *unctum*, "ointment", means both "ingratiating" and "oily".) Portmanteau.] *NL II-1*

scimitar trees
A tree of Terce. "At the back a row of scimitar trees cut across the enormous globe of the orange sun; black shadows were in violent contrast to the wan orange sunlight." [Compound.] *PoC V-1*

scivit
A fruity ingredient of *pummigum* (q.v.), a victual favored by the master criminal Lens Larque. *F III**

scoon
A species of edible fish. *Th VIII*

scorposaur
A species of dinosaur at the Bethune Preserve. [? from "scorpion" and the Greek *sauros*, "lizard".] *BD XVII*

screedle
A popular musical instrument. *ShW III, IV*

screedle flute
A musical instrument; see *froghorn*. [Compound; ? by association with "screed", meaning "a long monotonous speech or writing".] *NL III-2*

scroff
A bum or looter. [From "scrofulous", meaning "having a diseased appearance".] *AOC III*

scruff
A variety of nondescript plant: "The landscapes of Yaphet [the eighth of 11 planets attending Gilbert's Green Star] lacked interest; the native flora consisted mainly of marsh-pod, algae and a drab bamboo-like shrub known as 'scruff'." [Variant usage.] *Th IV*

scudhorn
An indigenous plant of Camberwell. "Along the ridges stood rows of orange-russet scudhorn, glowing like flame in the low sunlight." [Compound.] *NL I-4*

scumble
A play tactic in *double-moko* (q.v.). [By association with "scramble" and the rugby term "scrum", meaning "to mass players around the ball".] *PoC IV-4*

scurch
"Untranslatable into contemporary terms; generally: 'susurration along the nerves', 'psychic abrasion', 'half-unnoticed or sublimated uneasiness in a mind already wary'. 'Scurch' is the stuff of hunches and unreasoning fear." [? by amalgamation of "urge", "ouch" and/or "scourge".] *GP VI**

scurrilize
To disparage. [From "scurrilous".] *W XII*

scutinary
Protective; the *Celestial Handbook* referred to the *Scutinary Vitalists*, an organization at Bethune Preserve. [From the Latin *scutum*, "shield".] *BD XV*

sea-calch
A seafood, sometimes candied for eating. *E VII*

sea-lympid
A marine creature having a proboscis which was used to inject a complex nutrient liquid into tree-pods. *HI III*

sebalism
"...the special Rhune concept for sexuality, which the Rhunes find disgusting." *Ma IV*

sebax
A variety of plant or tree. "...layers of broad sebax leaves for the thatch." *NL VI-2*

sei
The number two in the Dirdir language. *D X*

seiach
An annual festival: "...a vast wash of sound swelling and subsiding like wind, or surf, with occasional tides, vague and indistinct, of clear little waif-bells. More general was the music played by wandering troupes: jigs and wind-ups; set-pieces and sonatas; shararas, sarabands, ballads, caprices, quick-steps." *An IV*

semir
A vine found in the hanging gardens of Ampridatvir. *DE V*

semola
A common foodstuff; it was served with flat beans aboard the *Avventura*. [Probably by shortening of "semolina".] *CS IV-1*

semprissima
A species of tree. *Tr I*

sensenitza
A social class on Marmone. "My mother is very beautiful. On Marmone she belongs to a social class known as the 'Sensenitza', the 'People of Grace'. She is Naonthe, 'Princess of the Dawn', which is quite important, and she can't be bothered with us poor provincials at Thanet." [From "sensitive" and/or "sentient".] *NL VI-2*

sentinel syrax
A black plant. *ShW XIII*

sentinello
A species of tree. *Tr IX*

Sequalion
See *Interlocking Sequalion*. **CS I-1**

sessamy
A sweet seed or herb comprising one of the ingredients of *opo* (q.v.). [? from "sesame".] **Rh I**

sexivation
"To emphasize sexual differences … for a girl to primp or show her figure to best advantage." It was considered a serious offense. [By combination of "sex", "deviation" and ? "salivation".] **W III**

shachane
A species of flower "… from which the Djan derived their purple dye." **MT XV**

shag-head
A derogatory term applied to off-worlders by the denizens of Sogdian, who shaved their scalps "as clean as an egg." [Compound.] **PL X**

shag-tree
A species of urban shade tree. [Compound.] **MT X**

shagwort
A sprawling decorative plant. [Compound.] **MT XI**

shairo
A massive black tree. **Rh II**

shamb
A dangerous, wild, six-legged creature with a moaning call. [? by shortening of "shamble".] **CS V-1**

sharara
A dance-like musical form; see *seiach*. **An IV**

shardash
A species of tree suitable for a hanging, according to Bodwyn Wook. **ArS VI**

sharloc
A "lumpish bristle-backed creature" on Shattorak. "According to the [almanac] index, the sharloc was notorious for 'an odorous exudation secreted by bristles along the dorsal integument. The odor is both repulsive and vile.'" When ruptured, its heavy gut "drained a yellow ooze." *EOE II*

shatterbone
A common but dangerous species of fish. [Compound.] *FT IX*

shauk chutt
A powerful oath in the Blale idiom. *W XII**

shdavi
"A tower supporting a residential globe high in the air, the construction resembling (and perhaps patterned upon) the stem and sporepod of the indigenous *myrophode* [q.v.]." *MT X**

shebardigan
A dance. "He moves with dramatic pride, like a cavalier of old, dancing the shebardigan." [? by association with "shenanigan", meaning "a prank".] *Lu II-3*

she-buffalo
A tiresome old virago; used in reference to Dame Clytie. [Compound; analogous to "she-devil".] *Th VIII*

sheirl
"An untranslatable term from the special vocabulary of *hussade* [q.v.] — a glorious nymph, radiant with ecstatic vitality, who impels the players of her team to impossible feats of strength and agility. The sheirl is a virgin who must be protected from the shame of defeat." Her white gown was gathered by a gold ring, which the members of the opposing team strove to yank and thus denude her. *Tr I**, *VII*

sherdas
A ceremony of inhalation: "Those attending a sherdas are seated around a table. From properly disposed orifices a succession of aromatic odors and perfumes is released. To praise the fumes too

highly, or to inhale too deeply is considered low behavior and leaves
the guilty person open to suspicions of gourmandizing." See also
odorifer. **Ma** *VI**

shergorszhe

"The language of Shant discriminates between various types of
sunsets. Hence [*shergorszhe* is] as above [i.e., "a flaring, flamboyant
sunset encompassing the entire sky"]; additionally with cumulus
clouds in the east, illuminated and looking toward the west." See also
arusch'thain, feovhre, gorusjurhe, and *heizhen*. **BFM** *V**

sherliken

A species of scaly beast. **Ma** *IV*

shiftill

A ne'er-do-well. [From "shiftless" and "ill".] **W** *VII*

shillick

A wild animal, suitable for roasting. **ShW** *XIII*

Shimerati

The highest caste of three among the Blenks of Blenkinsop. Relatively
few in number, they live "along the ridges of the southern highlands in
palaces behind exotic gardens." [Portmanteau word, from "shimmer"
and "glitterati", meaning "glamorous people".] **Lu** *VII-1*

Shivering Trillows

Trees (?) under which *Uthaw's zamanders* (q.v.) were buried. [By
association with "willows"?]. **CS** *V-2*

shrack-tree

A tree commonly found in groves and forests. **CS** *III-1*, **Ma** *VI*

shrai

The number two in the Paonese language. **LP** *X*

shree

A dangerous wild creature, not described; possibly a bird. [? by
shortening of "shreek", an alternate spelling of "shrike".] **CS** *V-2*

shrick
"Untranslatable"; a pejorative epithet. **W** *VII**

shrig
"Larva of a bog animal, notable for its sinuous dancing gait upon a pair of caudal feet. The shrig stands four to five feet high and emits a yellow phosphorescence. At night the shrig dance by the hundreds across the bog to create an eerie and fascinating effect." The word was sometimes used "…in a deprecatory sense to typify a dilettantish impractical fellow, out of touch with reality." **F** *IX**

shrike
A type of sorcerer. "I see only a pair of polite old men who are sitting quietly." …"They are shrikes of the deepest dye! They consort with ghosts and know what human men should never know." [Variant usage.] **PoC** *VII-2*

shrinken-bird
A species of bird common to mud flats. **E** *IV*

Shristday
A day of the week, possibly equivalent to Sunday. [? by alteration of "Christ's day".] **BFM** *X*

shulk
An ugly creature, commonly fat and yellow. **Pn** *I*

shunk
"Monstrous creatures indigenous to the Pombal swamps, notably cantankerous and unpredictably vicious. They refuse to thrive on Zumer [an island continent], though the Zur are considered the most adept riders. At the Arrabin stadia spectacles involving shunk are, along with the variety of hussade, the most popular of entertainments." These violent, competitive spectacles were referred to as *shunkery*. See also *hussade*. **W** *I**

shybalt
A species of moth-like, supernatural creature which could assume the

form of a man, and killed by exhaling a gust of poison from its mouth. *M V*

Si

One of the four secondary strings of the *khitan* (q.v.). **BFM** *IV*

sil

A unit of money (singular and plural). (This word appears in the version of the story edited by Underwood-Miller and retitled "Crusade to Maxus", in *The Augmented Agent*, 1986; the original version, "Overlords of Maxus", used the term *milray* instead). **OM** *I*

silicanthus

A species of plant commonly found in patches along the shore: "miniature five-pronged radiants of a stuff like frosted glass, stained apparently at random in any of a hundred colors." [? by combination of "silicon" and "agapanthus".] **W** *XII*

silvanissa

A tendril-bearing cultivated plant. [Probably from "silva", meaning "forest trees".] **Rh** *II*

Silver Thionists

A cult. [From the ISV *thion-*, "sulfur".] **TLF** *XVII*

silverstrack

A tonsorial fabric. "Dean Hutsenreiter burst into the room: a thin man, wearing a natty suit of pearl-gray silverstrack." [Compound.] **NL** *VI-3*

silverwood

A rare wood used to make drinking cups and shoulder-clips. [Compound.] **BFM** *I*

silvish

A nonsense term in the ditty sung by Mikelaus the circus performer. *M VIII*

sime
An ape-like creature; Nissifer was a hybrid of *sime* and *bazil* (q.v.). [From "simian".] **CS** *IV-2*

similax
A common variety of dark green bush. **BFM** *IV*

simiode
A species of beast; the one kept as a pet by Gilgad was stolen, chained and beaten by Hache-Moncour. [From "simian".] **Rh** *II*

sindic
A dangerous wild creature, not described. **CS** *V-1*

sipi-leaf
A common leaf, used as thatch. **S**

Sissle-way
A magical spell which induced its victim to perform involuntary jumping and dancing motions; according to Shimrod the magician, "There is a lesser effect known as the 'sissle-way', which also comes in three gradations: the 'Subsurrus', the 'Sissle-way Ordinary', and the 'Chatter-fang'." The spell was initiated by pronouncing the "activator" *schkt*; uttering the syllable twice invoked the *Chatter-fang*. [From "sissle", variant spelling of "sizzle".] **M** *IV*

sissy-panty
A prissy coward: "I'd like to catch that cod-faced sissy-panty." [Compound.] **ChC** *XIX*

sjambak
A bandit or flouter of authority; he was punished by public caging and the attachment of a carburetor-like device to his chest to supercharge his blood with oxygen. [From "sjambok", a type of South African whip (hence to "flout").] **Sj**

skak
"The least in the hierarchy of fairies. First in rank are fairies, then falloys, goblins, imps, finally skaks. In the nomenclature of Faerie, giants, ogres and trolls are also considered halflings, but of a different

sort. In a third class are merrihews, willawen and hyslop, and also, by some reckonings, quists and darklings. Sandestins, most powerful of all, are in a class by themselves." A small, yellow *skak* was confined in a bottle in Casmir's secret chamber. See also *falloy* and *sandestin*. **L** X*

skane
A common tree having edible bark. **W** *IV*

skaneel
A kind of wood carved into such items as armchairs. **MT** *XIV*

skaranyi
"A miniature bag-pipe, the sac squeezed between thumb and palm; the four fingers controlled the stops along four tubes." It was played in accompaniment to speech in selected situations. **MM***

skarat
A large, quick black insect which exhaled a foul odor or *chife* (q.v.); it was nonetheless used as a nutritious ingredient in many staple foods. **D** *IV*

skarmatics
A branch of *eidolology* (q.v.). **F** *XV*

skatfinch
An undesirable person; one who engages in petty crime. "WINKLERS AND SKATFINCHES BE WARNED! ALL ATTEMPTS AT INSEMINATION MUST BE LICENSED!" *PoC* III-2

skatler
A kind of horned creature. **Rh** *II*

skauf
A chewy, often pickled snack, popular among longshoremen. **E** *VII*

Skax
A gambler's card game, played at the Inn of Blue Lamps. **CS** *I-2*

skene
A type of edged weapon. "Do whatever you like; only make sure that

I carry neither skene, nor daggeret, nor flaying knife." [Variant usage.] *PoC* VI

skiddit
A wild animal, not described. *ArS* V

skirkling
" '…to send skirkling' denotes a frantic pell-mell flight in all directions accompanied by a vibration or twinkling or a jerking motion." Hence also to *skirkle*. *LC* II*

skitter
A three-wheeled vehicle of Fluter, an "ad hoc construction, with struts, frames and braces installed where the builder thought they would do the most good." It appeals to "…persons of feckless disposition who rode high behind the two after-wheels, with the third wheel on a boom thrust forward like an instrument of attack." They are abundantly decorated with "…vanities raised aloft on struts clamped to the forward boom: a peacock's fan, a winged cherub blowing a clarion, a grotesque head with features articulated to contort in hideous grimaces as the vehicle moved along." [Variant usage.] *Lu* I-3

sklam
A material used in the making of Kyash rugs. *MT* XI

sklemik
"Untranslatable: a fairy word signifying (1) passionate receptivity or involvement with each instant of life; (2) a kind of euphoria induced by close attention to unpredictable changes in the perceived surroundings as one instant metamorphoses into the next; a dedicated awareness to NOW; a sensitivity to the various elements of NOW. The concept of sklemik is relatively simple and quite bereft of mysticism or symbol." *M* VIII*

skull-buster
A potent beverage favored by the *erjins*. [Compound.] *GPr* III

sky-flitter
A kind of flying conveyance. [Compound.] *E XVIII*

sky-lice
The pejorative term applied by the *byzantaurs* (q.v.) to the members of Dame Isabel's space-traveling opera troupe. [Compound.] *SO VI*

sky-shark
"A crude one-man aircraft, little more than a flying plank fitted with a gun or some other weapon, used by Uldra nobles for attacks upon enemy tribes or duels among themselves." [Compound.] *GPr I**

slane
"The mild and placid Djan, if kept in solitude, is apt to erupt in berserk fury upon trivial provocation. If thereafter he escapes to the wilderness he becomes a cunning and sadistic beast — a 'slane' — committing atrocity after atrocity until he is destroyed." The Djan were Saidanese, a human species known as *Homo mora* (q.v.). [? from "slay".] *MT I**

slang
"A hairless rodent, long and slender, capable of producing a variety of odors at will." [Variant usage.] *W VI**

slange
A form of iron *culbrass* (q.v.) worn by the Ymphs on their waistcoats. *MT III*

slankweed
A species of noisome herb. *ShW III*

slarsh
"Fojo term for a preadolescent girl. Slarsh-tit is a vulgar colloquialism for 'trifling amount', or 'to an almost negligible degree'." *BD VIII**

slarsh-tit
See *slarsh*. *BD VIII**

slaverfish
A species of ocean fish. [Compound.] *MT XVIII*

slayvink
A species of arboreal animal, not described. **Th** *II*

slfks
In the language of the Water-folk, the sound(s) made by a conductor's baton, or *air-swish* (q.v.). **SO** *VIII*

slideway
See *man-river*. [Compound.] **W** *I*

slipway
A moving pedestrian pathway. [Compound.] **T** *III*

slobo
A Sirenese musical instrument. **MM**

sloebank
A plum field (?). [Compound.] **ChC** *II*

slova
A nonsense term in the ditty sung by Mikelaus the circus performer. **M** *VIII*

slue
A type of food, as in Woudiver's order of "*gargan-flesh* [q.v.] and slue." **Pn** *I**

sluteberry
A variety of berry, often eaten as a mash. **CS** *I-2*

slutes
"...a flat waste of black stone, flowing with water from the sea. When the tide is out, there are pools and puddles and the water-waifs skip like black mad things. When the tide turns, sheets of water come swirling and foaming, as far as you can see. When storms blow in off the ocean, waves move across the slutes, breaking and reforming to break again. [They are] sometimes blank and wet, sometimes wild and terrible. Sometimes on a calm sunny morning even weirdly beautiful." Also: "...a peneplain of black rock, stark, bare, flat as a table except for shallow basins where water reflected the sky." **Th** *V*

smaidair

A "deed-debtor", i.e. "…a person who has gained *mana* at the expense of another person, thus establishing a psychic disequilibrum. The imbalance is often mutually recognized and a voluntary reparation made. In other cases the balance is forcibly restored, and is barely distinguishable from 'revenge', though the distinction is very real." See also *mana*. **MT** *V**

smaragd tree

A variety of tree. "…shaded under a pair of monumental smaragd trees." [From the Greek *smaragdos*, "emerald".] **NL** *VI-2*

smaudre

The entrancing color of a gem from the realm of Irerly; it was irresistible to fairies. **L** *XXV*

smokewood

A common domestic tree. [Compound.] **FT** *I*

smollen

On Cadwal, the metal gold; when capitalized, the term also referred to Sunday. For details, see *Ain* and *glimmet*, also *ing, milden, ort, tzein* and *verd*. [Variant usage.] **ArS** *I*

smollock

A kind of fish. **W** *XII*

smur

A species of fearsome, "sinuous half-reptilian beast" inhabiting the Boundary Wood. **D** *V*

snapple

A variety of hand-weapon which fired darts. [From "snap".] **ShW** *I, V*

snaveler

An entertainer, particularly a "whip-dancer" or similar buffoon; also snavelry. **F** *VI*

snerge

A thief; to "put the snerge on" something was to pilfer it. **W** *III*

snoozle
To insinuate. "Apparently he hopes to snoozle his way into the Sempiternals by means of the exclusive development." [? by association with "bamboozle", "schmooze" and/or "sneak".] *NL IX-3*

snuff-flower
A common species of plant having black flowers which produced whitish-yellow ash when burned. [Compound.] *BW XII*

soa-gum
A variety of tree, commonly black and used to carve guitars. *S*

solvicine
A detergent for personal washing. [From the Latin *solvere*, "to dissolve".] *T VI*

solypa
A nonsense term in the ditty sung by Mikelaus the circus performer. *M VIII*

sombarilla
A species of grove-tree. *Tr XIX*

sometsyndic
Properly patterned; Kerlin the Curator insisted on the "correct sometsyndic arrangement" of the manual controls on his Chair of Knowledge. *DE VI*

somnol spray
A volatile liquid "...to be used on drunks and roughnecks." [By shortening of "somnolence".] *SpS*

sonfrane
A specialized translucent material which was used to fashion the hood placed over Wratch's head so as to restrict his visual input. *PF I*

sonophone
An automatic music-reproducing device; dirt or thumbprints on the composer's input draft produced unwanted hissing and buzzing.

[From the Latin *sonus*, "sound", and the Greek *phone*, "tone" or "voice".] **TLF XII**

sorarsio
A nonsense term in the ditty sung by Mikelaus the circus performer. **M VIII**

soum
"The thick, tough, dun lichen which carpets most of the Palga [flatland]." **GPr VIII***

soursnap
A common variety of beer, kept in flasks. [Compound.] **E VI**

soursop
A garnish commonly served with poached *sand-creepers* (q.v.). [Compound.] **GPr III**

sour-wabble
A kind of pudding. [Compound and variant usage: "wabble" is a botfly larva.] **CS I-2**

spag
A state of rut; see also *spageen*. **Tr IV***

spageen
An individual in a state of rut — a derogatory term. **Tr IV***

spang
A vicious purple-and-silver fish: "…ten feet of prongs, barbs, hooks and fangs." [Variant usage.] **GPr I**

spardoon
A type of hand weapon. "Wayness looked wildly around the room. On the shelves were weapons: scimitars, kiris, yataghans, poniards, kopf-nockers, long-irons, spardoons, quangs and stilettos." **EOE VI**

sparkle-stone
An often blue and white stone used in floor designs. [Compound.] **DJ**

spase-bush
A plant whose buds were ground up probably for use as a spice, and accepted as barter. *DE IV*

spatterack
A type of gnarled tree. [? by amalgamation of "spatter" and "tamarack", a variety of larch tree.] *ShW III*

Spatterlight
See *Pectoral Skybreak Spatterlight*. *CS I-1*

spernum
A popular foodstuff, commonly served fried. *GPr III*

sphanctonite
A jewel from a dead star. *ArS I*

spharganum
A common herb having a pleasant odor. [? from "sphagnum", a type of moss.] *DM I*

sphid
A naturally occurring food: "[The Yips] built huts of palm thatch and lived in blessed indolence, nourished by wild fruit, pods, tubers, molluscs, sphids and coconuts ..." *Th VI*

sphigale
A crustacean eaten as a delicacy. "The typical sphigale measured eight inches in length, with a pair of powerful pincer-claws and a whip-tail sting." *CS I-2*

sphincter-clasp
"An awkward rendering of the more succinct *Anfangel dongobel*." The device was used by Koyman, embalmer to the town Saskervoy. [Compound.] *CS I-2**

spiderclam
A variety of edible clam, commonly black. Its presence in the Yip diet was believed to induce sterility in the union of Yip with non-Yip persons. *Th IV*

spider-leg

A forest plant. [Compound.] *W VII*

spinth

A variety of oak tree. [? from the Greek *spinther*, "spark".] *EO V*

spiral-bug

An insect which emitted a droning sound. [Compound.] *An III*

spockow

"A debased caste of dog-breeders" of Dimmick, as opposed to the ones who "keep dogs in their homes, and dress them in fancy suits." *Lu Intro*

sporade

A variety of tree indigenous to Rosalia. [? from "sporadin", a genus of protozoa.] *Th IV*

spraling

Small, delicate *bidechtils* (q.v.) caught and prepared as appetizers by the women of Lausicaa to lure men into their huts. *CS II-2*

sprang-hoppers

Workers in charge of harvesting the nut pods which produce *kiki-nuts* (q.v.). To that effect, they use the *sprangs* (q.v.). It is a dangerous job. Some of them have become legendary "through feats of agility, remarkable leaps; also for gallantry in connection with the dramatic duels which had occurred out along the *sprangs*, the loser toppling into the soft blue-green core of the ferns, to be swarmed over by foot-long insects." [Compound; from "spring".] *PoC XI*

sprangs

A mesh of fragile walkways suspended from trusses extending over the Gorge at Felker's Landing, on Mariah, to provide access to the *kiki-nuts* (q.v.). Due to poisonous insects inhabiting the fronds, the nut pods can only be harvested from above. [From "spring".] *PoC XI*

spratling

A baby dragon. [From "sprat", a word which refers either to "a small or insignificant person" or to "any of numerous small fishes".] *DM III*

springback
A long, lank white beast having a voluted six-foot horn and no eyes, and traveling in herds. [Variant usage; and from "springbok", a species of African gazelle.] *ArS V*

sprinjufloss
A material sprayed on air-car frameworks as upholstery. *CD VIII*

sprugge
A variety of littoral bush. *FT IX*

spumet
An undesirable variety of plant. *D II*

spurgeon
A creature known for its fearlessness. [? by association with "sturgeon".] *BW XVI*

Squalings
Uncertain; Murgen said to Tamurello, "I will cite first, the Wastes of Falax; second, the Flesh Cape of Miscus; third, the Totness Squalings. Reflect; then go your way, and be grateful for my restraint." *L XXXI*

squallix
An edible wild plant. *CS V-1*

squalm
See *ensqualm*. *Rh II*

squalmaceous
See *ensqualm*. *Rh II*

squalmation
See *ensqualm*. *Rh II*

squeech
A noxious insect of Dimmick. "…the clouds of gnats, winged grubs, squeeches, and the like are unendurable in the absence of special precautions." [By association with "leech".] *PoC II-1*

squibboon

A hand weapon. [From "squib", meaning "a small pyrotechnic device".] *FT XIII*

squonk

A species of hairless white rat on the world Terce. Also a derogatory term used by the local inhabitants to designate pale-skinned off-worlders with highly desirable pelts. "Ugly milk-fed tourists! Go back to your wallow! In two more seconds I would have had the squonk's hide, and now I have lost my knife!" [Possibly derived from the noise produced by the animal; onomatopoeic.] *PoC V-3*

stangle

"The stuff of dead fairies, with implications of horror, calamity and putrefaction; a term to excite fear and disquiet among halflings, who prefer to think of themselves as immortal, though this is not altogether the case." *GP IX**

starbush

A riparian plant growing in black balls and having a predilection for sandstone. [Compound.] *SvW IX*

starlander

An off-worlder. [Compound.] *AOC I*

starment

One of "...a million sub-planetary oddments of iron, slag and ice" floating among the stars. [By amalgamation of "star" and "fragment" and/or "oddment".] *Tr Preface*

starmenter

One of the "...pirates and marauders, whose occasional places of refuge are the so-called 'starments'." [From "starment" (q.v.) and possibly also "foment".] *Tr Preface**

stelt

1. "A precious material quarried from volcanic necks upon certain types of dead stars; a composite of metal and natural glass, displaying infinite variations of pattern and color." (Tr) 2. "A precious slag mined

from the surfaces of burnt-out stars." (F) It was used to make jewelry, flooring and other items. See also *sphanctonite*. [? from "star" and "melt".] *F IV*, Tr VII*, W X*

stessonite
A form of high explosive. *SSt*

sthross
"…indicating a manner flawed by an almost imperceptible slackness and lack of punctilio." *LC II*

sthurre
A basic concept of *Monomantic Syntoraxis* (q.v.) taught by the Zubenites at their seminary on Pogan's Point. "Fundamental Verity is a node of intellectual force: a substance known as *sthurre*." To apprehend it required the study of various "Precepts, Laterals and Fluxions", "Useful Terminators", "Facts and Primordials" and "Tesseractic Conjunctions". See also *Thresis* and *Anathresis*. *ArS VIII*

stick-tight
A device or creature deployed for surveillance: "…these come in at least five varieties, suitable to various applications: The servo-optical — a spy cell supported on rotary wings, remotely guided by an operator. The automatic — a similar cell to follow a radioactive or monochromatic tag fixed to, or smeared upon a man or vehicle. The Culp spy master — a semi-intelligent flying creature trained to follow any subject of interest; clever, cooperative, reliable, but relatively large and noticeable. The Manx spy bird — a smaller, less obtrusive creature, trained to perform similarly; less docile and intelligent, more aggressive. The Manx spy bird modification — similar to the above, equipped with control devices." [Compound.] *KM VII, SK V*

stimic
A musical instrument on Sirene: "Three flute-like tubes equipped with plungers. Thumb and fore-finger squeeze a bag to force air across the mouth-pieces; the second, third and fourth little fingers manipulate the slide. The stimic is an instrument well-adapted to the

sentiments of cool withdrawal, or even disapproval." It was played in accompaniment to speech. **MM***

Stimmo

Slang for a pill which "...worked upon the brain to build synthetic moods. Orange Stimmos brought cheer and gaiety; red, amativeness; green, concentration and heightened imagination; yellow, courage and resolution; purple, wit and social ease. Dark blue Stimmos (the 'Weepers') predisposed to sentimentality and intensity of emotion; light blue Stimmos firmed the muscular reflexes and were useful to precision workers, operators of calculating machines, musical instruments and the like. Black Stimmos ('Dreamers') encouraged weird visual fantasies; white Stimmos ('Non-Sobs') minimized emotional response. It was possible to take combinations of up to three pills with a vast number of compound effects. A dosage of more than three Stimmos or too frequent use diminished the effect." Stimmos could be purchased at concessions in Carnevalle. [From "stimulate".] **TLF I, TLF X***

stimp

A variety of noxious fauna. "It's a breeding ground for stimps and leeches: sheer sodden wasteland." **NL XII-1**

stiple

The monetary unit on Kyril. [? by association with "staple" and "stipend".] **ST I**

stiver

"Colloquialism for the Connatic's head tax", paid yearly. See also *Connatic.* **W XII***

stletto

See *Xtl.* **FT II**

stone-foam

A material formerly used for construction of buildings. [Compound.] *ChC* V

strakh

"Prestige, face, *mana*, repute, glory: the Sirenese word is *strakh*. Every man has his characteristic *strakh*. There is no medium of exchange on Sirene; the single and sole currency is *strakh* ..." Edwer Thissell acquired enormous *strakh* by going without the culturally required mask in order to capture the notorious criminal Haxo Angmark. **MM**

strankenpus

A word of insult. "So, cut your stick and hop off on the double, like the good little strankenpus you are." [? by association of "strangle", "wank" ("a detestable person"), and "puss", meaning "face".] **NL IX-4**

strapan

"... a circular sound-box eight inches in diameter. Forty-six wires radiated from a central hub to the circumference where they connected to either a bell or a tinkle-bar. When plucked, the bells rang, the bars chimed; when strummed, the instrument gave off a twanging, jingling sound. When played with competence, the pleasantly acid dissonances produced an expressive effect; in an unskilled hand, the results were less felicitous, and might even approach random noise." It was used when dealing with social inferiors, or to insult someone. **MM**

streedle

A repetitive street-melody. **L XXVII**

strenuata

Nerve cells: "You can change your fingerprints [by surgical capping] but you can't change your brain strenuata." [From the Latin *strenuus*, "active".] **SP XVII**

striatics

A branch of physics. [From "striation", an ionized band in a vacuum tube.] **UQ**

stringbook

A diary of social debts. "A wonderful magic stuff is comporture, and your stringbooks make it all so easy. You record favors you have done for others against the favors you have received: the so-called 'Outs' and 'Ins'. Their ratio is your social buoyancy, and you must keep a careful balance sheet." [Compound.] **NL III-1**

string-twister
Entertainers at Girandole on Fiametta. "If the 'string-twisters' are boring, we can always leave." [Compound.] **PoC VII-2**

strochane
"A mythical being with supernormal powers, whose commands no mortal men can disobey." **MT III***

sturge
Raw food-slurry, the basis for *gruff, deedle* and *wobbly* (q.v.). Its sources included urban wastes and slops, as well as the macerated cadavers from the Pavilions of Rest in Disjerferact, where Arrabin citizens could find death in various colorful forms. **W I, V**

stylax
A species of worm on the planet Sabria; *dekabrachs* (q.v.) ingested it as food. [? from the Latin *stilus*, "stalk".] **GG**

suanola
An instrument based upon the ancient concertina, with a pump supplying the air flow and toggled keys controlling both upper and lower registers. "The Faths considered the suanola a trivial, or even vulgar, instrument." **NL VIII-1**

subaqueate
To execute by drowning; the victim's feet were "thrust into ballasted tubes" and he was thrown from a cliff into the sea. [From the Latin *sub-*, "under", and *aqua*, "water".] **LP II**

sublume
An orchard-grown fruit, often used to make cider (described as palatable but potent) and brandy. **FT IX**

submulgery
Misinterpretation of the *Monstrament* (q.v.) — a serious misdemeanor. [? by amalgamation of "subterfuge", "mugwumpery" and/or "skulduggery".] **Rh II**

sub-musk
A glandular derivative having a strong odor; it was sold in the bazaar at Smargash. [From the Latin *sub-*, "under", and "musk".] **D** *I*

subsede
To underlie: "...we have four different regions, two of which floresce from the basic skeleton of the universe, and so subsede the others." [Opposite of "supersede".] **GM**

subuculate
To truckle or be sycophantic; "He had watched his fellows jockeying; he knew all the tricks and techniques: the beavering, the *gregarization* [q.v.], the smutting, knuckling, and subuculation." [From "subucula", an ecclesiastical undergarment.] **DJ**

suheil
A special material having deadly powers against the *shybalt* (q.v.); when formed into a circlet, it could act as a noose. **M** *V*

sulpicella
A species of black tree, used at Port Maheul to decorate the picturesque central square known for its archaic standards of solidity. **Tr** *XVIII*

sunuschein
"Reckless, feckless gaiety, tinged with fatalism and tragic despair." **An** *I**

superphysic numeration
An ancient science or secret lore known to Rogol Domedonfors; others included *corolopsis* and *metathasm*. [From the Latin *super*, "above", and *physica*, "natural science".] **DE** *V*

suprapullulation
A hyper-germination or meta-growth; the term was applied by the sorcerer Pharesm to the convolutions of time and space induced by the elaborate rock-carving he created in an effort to induce the appearance of the creature "TOTALITY". (When TOTALITY at last

appeared, Cugel roasted and ate it.) [From the Latin *super*, "above", and "pullulate", meaning "to bud".] *EO IV*

sustenator

A living device cultivated by the Lekthwans aboard their air barges to extract carbon dioxide and water vapour from the air and produce oxygen and basic food-stuff. It was "a black case hanging on a tube, like a berry on a stalk." [From the Latin *sustinere*, "to sustain".] *GI XVII*

swabow

A popular table wine, served in pots. *E XVI*

swag-bottom

A jocular, derogatory term for an old Darsh woman, or *khoontz* (q.v.). [Compound.] *F X*

swamp-gnarl

A variety of dense dark wood from Mirsten which is turned into an appealing black tankard by an exacting process. Since "the tree cannot be cut in place, it must be pulled up entire by a floating derrick. The piece is trimmed, cut into baulks, and seasoned for five years. Then it is sliced into billets, and turned in a special lathe — to become unfinished vessels, known as 'blanks'. The 'blanks' are boiled in a special oil for three days, then are shaped, carved, and finished by hand. Now they are tankards, no two alike; they cannot be broken, and last forever." [Compound.] *Lu IX-2*

swamp-oel

A swamp-dwelling "Oel: a creature indigenous to Big Planet and found in many varieties. Typically the creature stands seven feet tall on two short legs, with a narrow four-horned head of twisted cartilage. Its black dorsal carapace hangs low to the ground; to its ventral surface are folded a dozen clawed arms. From a distance an oel might be mistaken for a gigantic beetle running on its hind legs." It could be trained to dance the mazurka. *ShW III*, VI*

swamp-shrimp

Poisonous creatures from Fenn, morsels of which could be used to control another person. "On Fenn, when a man wants to put another man in his power for a day or a week, he seeks these creatures, or shrimp like them, from the swamps. Their red sacs contain a toxic principle." [Compound.] *SU*

swange
A hand-tool used for cutting kelp, stone or other material. [From "swage", a type of tool used by metalworkers.] *EO IV, CS I-2*

swash-trap
A device for activating a citizen's "torc", an explosive collar worn around the neck by command of the *Anome* (q.v.). *An VI*

swill
A crude, mildly intoxicating, home-brewed beverage made from leftover *gruff* (q.v.). [Variant usage.] *W I*

swillage
Cheap liquor: "It is not good to inebriate nor to souse, using swillage, near or far beers, or distillations." [From "swill".] *BD XII*

swotsman
"Institute argot: a person who energetically strives to climb the ranks rapidly." See also *Dexad*. [From the British "swot", meaning "to study hard and constantly", and "man".] *BD IX**

syaspic feroce
A creature from the Dyad Mountains of Tanjecterly; one of them was owned by Murgen. "It stood a few inches over six feet tall and displayed a rudely man-like form, with a heavy head resting on massive shoulders, long arms with taloned hands and prongs growing from the knuckles. A black pelt covered its scalp, a strip down its back and about the pelvic region. Its features were heavy and crude, with a low forehead, a short nose and ropy mouth; tawny-gold eyes looked through slits between ridges of cartilage." It was strong, agile, loyal and fearless, but also "… savage and … prone to unpredictable frivolities which propel its kind on expeditions of ten thousand miles that they may dine on a particular fruit." [Partly by modification of "ferocious".] *GP XIV*

synchrocephaleison

The term given to a phenomenon among the Doppelgangers (also called "symbiotes"): each one required the presence of the others to exist. Didactor Clou prepared a treatise on the subject. [From the Greek *syn-*, "with", *chronos*, "time", *kephal*, "head", and *eleison*, "have mercy".] *TLF VI*

syncresis

Syncretism; a synthesis. [By amalgamation of "syncretic" and "synthesis".] *SvW III*

syndic

A unique species of tree "...whose seeds sprouted legs and poisonous pincers. After walking to a satisfactory location, each seed roved within a ten-foot circle, poisoning all competing vegetation, then dug a hole and buried itself." [Variant usage: "a government official having different powers in different countries".] *An V*

synthan

An artificial material used instead of glass to make cups and other containers, especially for use by prisoners. [From "synthetic".] *ArS IX*

Syntoraxis

See *Monomantic Syntoraxis*. *ArS VII*

syrang

A flower from whose blooms a valuable essence was extracted and then "...brought in by the bulb-men of McVann's Star a half ounce at a time." *PBD*

T

talisman tree
A tree native to Fluter, one of which overhung the Labor Exchange; not further described. *Lu* I-3

tamsour
An ineffable characteristic of the denizens of Dimplewater on Ushant. "It is an idea which baffles off-worlders, tourists and sociologists alike. Still, I can describe 'tamsour' and some of its effects. It seems to mean the totality of one's life, condensed into a single drop of essence, a single profound symbol, a single moment of total enlightenment. But these are words and tamsour can't be put into words." *NL* X-5

tamurett
A musical instrument. "Dorsen brought a fellow musician to the box, a somber young tamurett player, who tried to explain the music to Dame Ida." [? by association with "tambourine".] *NL* IX-6

tanchinaro
"A black and silver fish of the Far South Ocean." *Tr* X*

tand
A fetish which was the physical representation of the soul of a *sacerdote* (a free-living, subterranean autochthon with golden hair; q.v.): "...an intricate construction of gold rods and silver wire, woven and bent seemingly at random. The fortuitousness of the design, however, was only apparent. Each curve symbolized an aspect of Final Sentience; the shadow cast upon the wall represented the Rationale, ever-shifting, always the same.

"The object was sacred to the sacerdotes, and served as a source of revelation. There was never an end to the study of the *tand*: new intuitions were continually derived from some heretofore overlooked relationship of angle and curve. The nomenclature was elaborate: each part, juncture, sweep and twist had its name; each aspect of the relationships between the various parts was likewise categorized. Such was the cult of the *tand*: abstruse, exacting, without compromise. At his puberty rites the young sacerdote might study the original *tand* for as long as he chose; each must construct a duplicate *tand*, relying upon memory alone. Then occurred the most significant event of his lifetime: the viewing of his *tand* by a synod of elders. In awesome stillness, for hours at a time they would ponder his creation, weigh the infinitesimal variations of proportion, radius, sweep and angle. So they would infer the initiate's quality, judge his personal attributes, determine his understanding of Final Sentience, the Rational and the Basis.

"Occasionally the testimony of the *tand* revealed a character so tainted as to be reckoned intolerable; the vile *tand* would be cast into a furnace, the molten metal consigned to a latrine, the unlucky initiate expelled to the face of the planet, to live on his own terms." **DM II**

tangalang

A species of (purple) flower, among others which Frulk the Magician attempted to transform into a beautiful maiden. **ShW III**

tanglet

A glowing green artifact, several inches in diameter. "At first they were hairclasps, worn by the warriors of a far world. When a warrior killed an enemy he took the clasp and wore it on the scalp rope of his hair. In this way tanglets became trophies. The tanglets of a hero are even more; they are talismans. There are hundreds of distinctions and qualities and special terms, which make the subject rather fascinating, when you acquire some of the lore. Only a finite number are authentic tanglets, despite the efforts of counterfeiters, and each one is annotated and named and attributed. All are valuable, but the great ones are literally priceless. A hero's rope of six tanglets is so full of mana it almost sparks. I must take extraordinary care; a single touch sours the sheen and curdles the mana." [? from "tangle".] **EOE VII**

tangletone

A musical instrument. [Compound.] **NL III-2**

tanjee
A species of littoral tree. *ArS III*

tankle
A musical instrument; it was played in the house of Yaa-Yimpe. *Rh II*

tantalein
A kind of musical instrument. *BD XII*

tantivet
A dance. "Visbhume ... played a rousing selection of ear-tickling tunes: tantivets and merrydowns, fine bucking jigs and cracking quicksteps, rollicks, lilts and fare-thee-wells." See also *merrydown*. [Probably from "tantivy", a headlong dash or gallop.] *GP XVI*

tarable
A classical musical instrument; two were generally included in the Valdemar Kutte Grand Salon Orchestra. *BD XII*

tartlip juice
An ingredient of a popular punch, "... a greenish yellow mixture which Hetzel found pleasantly astringent." [Compound.] *FT IX*

tasp
A green, weasel-sized scorpion-thing; a horde of tasps were conjured up by Iucounu as a threat to Cugel. *CS VI-2*

tatap
The Dirdir word for "father". *D X*

Tatterblass
A type of ale; it was served at the Inn of Blue Lamps. *CS I-2*

tattersack
A species of vegetation commonly found on soggy wasteland. [Compound.] *W VII*

tattletag
A type of electronic spy device. [Compound]. *EOE VII*

tauptu

In the Xaxan tongue, "purged", i.e. rid of the parasitic *nopal* (q.v.); see also *chitumih*. **BE** *I*

taxiplat

A landing pad for air taxis. [Compound.] **CD** *VIII*

tayberry

A variety of tree. [Compound.] **SvW** *IX*

tchabade

"A hurting complex emotion, encompassing all the following: drained of mana; emasculated; forced to submit, as if to perverted sexual acts; demoralized; rendered negligible; defeated and left behind; stripped of all comporture. In short, a vicious, debilitating emotion." **NL** *IX-2*

Teach tac Teach

Mountain range paralleling the Atlantic coast of Hybras. "Literally: 'peak on peak' in one of the precursor tongues." **L** *IX**

Technicant

One of the three new languages (the others being *Valiant* and *Cogitant*) deliberately introduced into Paonese culture by Palafox for purposes of social engineering. "In this instance, the grammar will be extravagantly complicated but altogether consistent and logical. The vocables would be discrete but joined and fitted by elaborate rules of accordance. When a group of people, impregnated with these stimuli, are presented with supplies and facilities, industrial development is inevitable." [By contraction of "technical" and "cant".] **LP** *XII*

technist

A technician. **BFM** *VII*

telanxis

A flower whose blooms produced a desirable oil. **DE** *II*

teleologue

A teleologist, i.e. one who studied metaphysical purposes; Cugel claimed to have once "...served as an incense-blender at the Temple of Teleologues." [From "teleology".] **EO** *V*

teletactility
The ability to feel with one's mind: "…touch without use of the nerve-endings. Is not clairvoyance seeing without use of the eyes?" This skill was useful in manipulating *nopal-stuff* (q.v.). [From the Greek *tele*, "far", and the Latin *tactus*, "touched".] **BE** V

televection
An electronic surveillance and registration system used to record information concerning the whereabouts of citizens. [From the Greek *tele*, "far", and the Latin *vehere*, "to carry".] **TLF** IX

televector file
The electronic recording made of one's alpha waves upon registration into "Brood", the first of five stages, or phyle, culminating in immortality. [From *televection* (q.v.).] **TLF** IV

telex crystal
A valuable mineral found on Moritaba and used for interstellar communication. **KT**

Tempofluxion Dogma
The belief that "…as the river of time flows past and through us, our brains are disturbed — jostled, if you will — by irregularities, eddies, in the flow of the moment …if it were possible to control the turbulence in the river, it would be possible to manipulate creative ability in human minds." [From the Latin *tempus*, "time", and *fluere*, "to flow".] **BP** XII

terce
A standard coin. [Variant usage; and/or by shortening of "tierce", a unit of liquid capacity.] **DE** V

thabbat
"The Darsh hood, usually of white or blue cloth." **F** V*

thakal skth hg
See *brga skth gz*. **SO** VIII

thamber
A species of oak tree. **CS** I-2

thame

A powdered aphrodisiac collected in little pots by natives and traded for salt. **PBD**

Thariot

A member of a group which became known for their devious and secretive nature; see *Glint*. **MT Intro.**

Thasdrubal's Laganetic Transfer

The spell by means of which Iucounu banished Cugel on a protracted errand to retrieve the cusps of the overworld. The Laganetic Cycle contained at least eighteen phases, as detailed on a scroll obtained by Cugel. [From "lagan", meaning "goods thrown into the sea with a buoy attached" (a reference to Firx, the parasite installed by Iucounu in Cugel's liver to keep his mind on his task).] **EO I**

thawn

A cave-dwelling creature, commonly bearded but not otherwise described. **EO III**

thelu gy shlrama

A phrase of uncertain meaning in the language of the Water-folk; their representative used the phrase in criticizing the performance of *The Barber of Seville* by Dame Isabel's space-traveling opera company. See also *bgrassik* and *brga skth gz*. **SO VIII**

therulta

An anatomic structure on the body of Miss Aries 44R951, an extraterrestrial participant in the Miss Universe contest; related terms were *agrix*, *clavon*, *orgote* and *veruli* (q.v.). **MMU IV**

thimble-pod

A common bush. [Compound.] **W V**

thio-manual

A pellet-firing hand weapon used by the Hunge (a warrior tribe on Koryphon); a common model was the Two Star. [From the ISV *thion*, "sulfur", and the Latin *manus*, "hand".] **GPr IV**

Thionist

See *Silver Thionists*. **TLF** *XVII*

thracide

"A sour, intense carmine." **BFM** *VII**

threlkoid

A dangerous swamp-dwelling creature. **CS** *V-2*

Thresis

One of the "Natural Doctrines" taught at the Monomantic seminary of the Zubenites; others were *Anathresis* and *Syntoraxis* (q.v.). *ArS VIII*

Thribolt gun

"The Thribolt gun shoots a Jarnell-powered projectile toward its target. A quest-needle protrudes a hundred and sixty feet ahead of the projectile, at the so-called preliminary roil section of the intersplit, and is in tenuous contact with undisturbed space. Upon encountering matter, the quest-needle disengages the intersplit and triggers its charge: either adhesive paper disks or high explosives. In effect the Thribolt gun is an instantaneous weapon over vast distances, its effectiveness limited only by the accuracy of the aiming and launching techniques, since once in flight the projectile cannot change direction." The text elaborates further on the development of automatic sensors for guidance. See also *Jarnell Intersplit*. [? from "thrice", i.e. "three", and "bolt".] **PL** *III**

thrombodaxus

A species of creature at Bethune Preserve, probably resembling a dinosaur. **BD** *XVII*

throy

"The [third] cardinal number in the language of Ancient Etruria." *ArS I**

thrum-tree

A species of gigantic tree. Also referred to simply as a *thrum*. See also *bilibob* and *chulastic*. [Compound.] **Th** *IV*

thryfwyd
A kind of sea-monster. **CS II-3**

thump-box
A popular musical instrument. [Compound.] **ShW III**

thuripid
A species of dangerous wild animal. **ArS V**

Thurist
One of the Coramese *Thurists*, to whom Shimilko delivered the seventeen virgins. They wore "gowns of embroidered silks" and "splendid double-crowned headgear", and had "...pale transparent skins, thin high-bridged noses, slender limbs and pensive gray eyes." [Probably from "thurify", meaning "to burn or offer incense".] **CS V-1**

Thwarterman
An important resident political position at Vasconcelles. [From "thwart" and "man".] **BD IX**

thyle-dust
A kind of noxious powder. **DE II**

ticholama
A bush having "...a cluster of inch-long purple tubes, twisting and curling away from a central node. They were glossy, flexible, and interspersed with long pink fibers." The plant was cultivated for its content of *resilian* (q.v.). **HB**

tikki-tikki
A type of *pold* (q.v.), often formulated as a pastille with a "sharp but subtle" flavor which some found soothing. **EOE V**

time-light
"An untranslatable and even incomprehensible concept. In this context, the term implies a track across the chronic continuum, perceptible to an appropriate sensory apparatus." [Compound.] **Rh I***

timp
An infestation or disease to which a ship's giant propulsive worms were susceptible. **CS** *II-1*

tink-a-tink-tinkle
The sound of a small bell. [Onomatopoeia.] **L** *I*

tinkleweed
A variety of desert flora indigenous to the planet Dar Sai. [Compound.] **F** *X*

tinko
A species of alien creature; tinkos were mentioned as having shops in the Parade of the Alien Quarter on Light-year Road, and insisted on having yellow lights for decoration. See also *jeek* and *wampoon*. **AOC** *II*

tinselweed
A plant whose fluff was used to stuff mattresses. [Compound.] **ShW** *VI*

tipple
A popular musical instrument. [Variant usage.] **An** *VI*

tipsic
A stimulating beverage on Nilo-May. "Ah, my poor throat — dry as rusk! Woman, have we no tipsic to drink? Is not life to be lived as a glorious adventure, with tipsic to be shared among friends?" [From "tipsy".] **NL** *XV-3*

tirrilay
A light song or ditty. [From the onomatopoetic "tirralirra", meaning "a bird's song".] **BD** *XII*

tirrinch
A rare hardwood; it was used in the construction of Doctor Lalanke's manse. **CS** *IV-2*

tish-tush

Fuss or fanfare: "At Kyash everyone pursues the style he fancies most, without stricture or tish-tush." *MT X*

Titilanthus

A beverage. "Along with the Gradencia we'll serve iced Titilanthus in authentic milk-glass urns." [From "titillate".] *NL VIII-3*

titticomb

A kind of delicacy sometimes baked in a pie with diced morels and garlic. *W VII*

tittle-bird

A brisk bird. [Compound; and by association with "tittlebat".] *CS III-2*

titvit

A nocturnal animal, probably a rodent or bird. *EO IV*

tix

The number ten in the Dirdir language. *D X*

tockberry

A species of berry, commonly rose pink. [Compound; ? from "tock", an African species of hornbill.] *ArS IV*

toctac

A two-legged wolf, given to setting up elaborate ambushes. *ArS III**

toice

A sentiment encountered by Shimrod in the realm of Irerly; it "... chafed against his flesh." *L XV*

toldeck

The standard unit of currency on Maske, approximately equal to one Gaean Standard Value Unit (SVU). *MT II*

tom-ticker

An alien creature, not described. [Compound.] *SSt*

tonquil
A restless creature. *CS II-3*

ton-ton eskoy
A legal principle which invalidated the indentures of Pook, Flook and Snook as a result of their being removed from their home province. "He spoke in a strange, emphatic language: 'Ton-ton eskoy!' 'Exactly,' said Maloof." [? by association with "tontine", a form of investment plan, and "escrow".] *Lu VI*

toomish
A nonsense term in the ditty sung by Mikelaus the circus performer. *M VIII*

toricle
An alien creature from Cordova, not described. *SSt*

torquil
A large, gnarled plant which grew in dense clumps. *D VI*

tox meratis
A deadly poison derived from the *graybloom* (q.v.). [From "toxin".] *PL II*

trambonium
A musical instrument encountered at Owlswyck Inn at Port Tanjee on Taubry. "They mounted to the bandstand at the far end of the room and brought out their instruments: a flageolet, a concertina, a baritone lute and a trambonium." [Portmanteau of "trombone" and "euphonium", a large brass musical instrument.] *PoC III-2*

trangle
A common scarlet flower, planted in decorative banks. *MT III*

transgraph
An interstellar telegraph. [From the Latin *trans*, "across", and the Greek *graphein*, "to write".] *SSt*

translux

A transparent material used for windows. [From the Latin *trans*, "across", and *lux*, "light".] *LP XIX*

transpar

A material used to fabricate body armor: "…ingenious segmented suits, which became streamlined shells when the wearer's arms hung by his sides." [By shortening of "transparent" and/or from "feldspar".] *LP XVII*

transpolation

A form of magical manipulation. [From the Latin *trans*, "across", and *polire*, "to polish".] *GM*

transview

An electronic visual communications device. [From the Latin *trans*, "across", and "view".] *HB*

trapperfish

A species of fish; for defense it gave off *nyene*, a poison. See also *glemma*. [Compound.] *ArS VII*

trater

A nonsense term in the ditty sung by Mikelaus the circus performer. *M VIII*

tremblant

1. A gray-green and silver plant. (ShW) 2. A device used by an apothecary, probably a scale. (W) *ShW XIII, W XII*

tremble-rod

Part of a spaceship stabilization system. "The tremble-rods are out of phase with the new unit." [Compound.] *PoC VII-1*

Trillow

See *Shivering Trillows*. *CS V-2*

trimbles

"Small huts built upon the backs of *wumps*" (q.v.). "The high-pitched roofs were artfully concave, with quaint upturned eaves." [By association with "thimble".] *Lu V-2**

tringolet
A popular musical instrument. *An VI, BFM VI*

triskoid dynamics
A set of theorems generated by the mathematician Palo Laenzle (907-1070). [From the Greek *triskeles*, a figure of three branches radiating from a center, and *oïdes*, "resembling".] *F III*

trisme
A Rhune term meaning "... an institution analogous to marriage. 'Trismet' designates the people involved." Further: "These persons might be a man and his trismetic female partner; or a man, the female partner, one or more of her children (of which the man may or may not be the sire). 'Family' approximates the meaning of 'trismet' but carries a package of inaccurate and inapplicable connotations. Paternity is often an uncertain determination; rank and status, therefore, are derived from the mother." *Ma III, Ma IV**

tritesimals
A complex mathematical discipline. [From the Latin *tria*, "three", and "infinitesmal".] *TLF VII*

tri-type
"... a three-dimensional simulacrum ... [of a person] six inches high." *Feeler-planes* (q.v.) were used to conduct data from the subject to a machine; the resulting hologram was used by the authorities on Iszm as an advanced method of fingerprinting. [From the Latin *tria*, "three", and the Greek *typos*, "image".] *HI I*

triventidum
A potent poison. *DM VI*

tsau'gsh
The Dirdir term for an organized hunt: "Prideful endeavor, unique enterprise, lunge toward glory. An essentially untranslatable concept." *D IV, Pn I**

tsernifer

"The term *tsernifer*, here translated as 'Force', refers to that pervasion of psychological power surrounding the person of a *kaiark* [q.v.]. The word is more accurately rendered as *irresistible compulsion, elemental wisdom, depersonalized force*. The appellative 'Force' is an insipid dilution." **Ma VI***

tubegrass

A common species of grass having tubular blades. [Compound.] **DE IV**

tube-wort

A scant vegetation indigenous to Ixax. [Compound.] **BE I**

tudelpipe

A musical instrument. [? by association with "dudelsack", a bagpipe.] **NL III-2**

tulsifer

A species of reed growing in thickets. **CS IV-1**

tumble-bugs

Red and yellow insects swarming the mats of algae on the surface of the oceans of Dimmick. Their antics "are said to be amusing". [Compound.] **PoC II-1**

tumblewit

A lack-witted rustic; a hick or rube. "The Klutes of Numoy claim: 'We may have come down from the Bleary Hills, but we are not tumblewits.'" [Portmanteau of "tumbleweed" and "lack-wit".] **Lu VI**

tumper

A person of no great force; a bumbler. "…they hooted and jeered. 'Hoy there, old tumper! Why do you trot so briskly?'" [From "tump", meaning "a small round hill or mound".] **Lu VII-5**

tuppet

A type of stoneware wine jug. **L XXIX**

Tutelanics

A religion involving much memorizing and a Convocation of Souls "…where the priests were so [i.e. too] familiar." [From "tutelage".] *SvW III*

twastic

A bizarre creature commonly encountered in pairs: "…twenty-legged creatures eight feet long and four feet high, with large round heads studded with stalks, knobs and tufts, fulfilling functions not immediately apparent. Their caudal segments rose and curled forward in an elegant spiral, and each boasted an iron gong dangling from the tip. Smaller bells and vibrilators hung in gala style from the elbows of each leg. The first wore a robe of dark green velvet; the second a similar robe of cherry-rose plush." The *twastic* had a sibilant voice which it produced by the rapid clicking of its mandibles. *Rh II*

tweedle-pipe

A musical instrument, probably similar to a penny whistle. [Compound.] *F VI*

twicket

A type of sartorial contrivance: "Madouc was not happy with the gown. 'There are too many pleats and twickets.'" [From "twick", meaning "to twitch" (archaic).] *M IV*

twirp

A variety of vegetable, commonly served boiled or heavily spiced in jars. *BD VIII*

twitchery

A type of lively dance: "…he danced several gavottes, a hornpipe and a twitchery." [From "twitch".] *BD XVI*

twitterling

A stupid or careless individual. [Compound of "twitter" and the diminutive suffix "-ling".] *L XXIV*

twittle

A trivial thing: "Faith, and I smash so much as a twittle, he'll shove me head up my own bum." [? from "tittle".] **BD** *VIII*

twittler

An individual of lower caste. **Rh** *II*

twitus

"An excellent selective poison, fatal only if ingested twice within a week"; it would be used by a *venefice* (q.v.). **PL** *II*

tympanet

A type of small musical drum. [From "tympan", meaning "drum".] **PL** *VI*

tympanillo

A type of musical drum. [From "tympan", meaning "drum", and the Spanish diminutive suffix *-illo*.] **F** *XV*

tyreen

A musical instrument; it was played in the house of Yaa-Yimpe. **Rh** *II*

tzein

On Cadwal, the metal zinc; when capitalized, the term also referred to Tuesday. For details, see *Ain* and *glimmet*, also *ing, milden, ort, smollen* and *verd*. [Variant usage.] **ArS** *I*

U

ulgar
A poison derived from the *meng* (q.v.); when ingested, "...the symptoms are spasms, biting off of the tongue and a frothing madness." The same substance could also be sold and used as *furux* (q.v.), with different harmful effects. ***PL*** *II*

ulrad
A high frequency used for radio transmission. [From "ultra" and "radio".] ***KT, SSh***

umpdoodle
A frivolous creature: "You would be as wrong as an umpdoodle's trivet." ***L*** *X*

Unctator
A master of religious ceremonies. The *Grand Unctator of the Natural Rite* wore a white and black mitre; "In one hand he carried a crystal orb to represent the cosmos, in the other a lavender blossom signalizing the fragility of life." [From "unctuous" and "spectator".] ***MT*** *III*

under-god
A lesser divinity or non-deity: "...all are now arrived: a chosen group of nymphs and under-gods, poets and philosophers." [Compound.] ***PL*** *VIII*

unigen
"The unigen was an intelligent organism, though its characteristics included neither form nor structure. Its components were mobile nodes of a luminous substance which was neither matter nor yet energy. There were millions of nodes and each was connected with every other node by tendrils similar to the line of force in macroid space.

"The unigen might be compared to a great brain, the nodes

corresponding to the gray cells, the lines of force to the nerve tissue. It might appear as a bright sphere, or it might disperse its nodes at light speed to all corners of the universe.

"Like every other aspect of reality, the unigen was a victim of entropy; to survive, it processed energy down the scale of availability, acquiring the energy from radioactive matter. The unigen's business of living included a constant search for energy."

The entity was capable of hope, "an emotion compounded of desire and imagination." See also *macroid*. [From the Latin *unus*, "one", and *genus*, "class" or "kind".] **WLA**

Universal Pancomium
"…a floating museum owned by Throdorus Gassoon"; existence of the generic word *pancomium*, a thing worthy of all praise, is implied. [? by combination of the Greek *pan*, "all", and "encomium", meaning "high praise".] **ShW VII**

unmel
Uncertain: "Galexis, the nervous essence, corresponds to female women as the candy of unmel to tannery sludge." [? from the Latin *mel*, "honey".] **An II**

ursial loper
A tailed animal, not described; the name suggests similarity to a bear and the style of its gait. [From the Latin *ursus*, "bear".] **Rh II**

urush
"Derogatory Trevanyish cant for a Trill [a citizen of Trullion]." **Tr IV***

uslak
In Blale (the native tongue of Wyst), " '…devil's dross'; the adjective *uslakain* means unholy, unclean, profane, repulsive." **W XI***

V

Vaast ray
A powerful weapon. *FT XIII*

vam
The Dirdir word for "mother". *D X*

vamola
A variety of tree. *ArS V*

vandalia
A variety of bush, commonly orange and found growing in copses and clumps. *GPr IV*

vanzitrol
A high explosive. *PBD*

vardespant
"The word *vardespant* lacks contemporary equivalence. It includes the notions of obstinacy, perverse wrong-headedness, a jeering attitude toward somber rectitude." *BD XII**

variboom
A popular musical instrument played aboard the ship *Miraldra's Enchantment*, and presumably producing a deep, percussive sound. [? from "variable" and "boom".] *ShW IX*

varience
A kind of musical instrument. *BD XII*

varmous
"Dirty, infamous, scurrilous; an adjective often applied to the Trills." [From "varmint".] *Tr XVII**

vat-berry
A common cultivated bush. [Compound.] *W IV*

vaul-stone

A variety of deep blue stone. **DE** *V*

Vedanticizer

A follower of a particular religious cult. [From "Vedanta".] **TLF** *XVII*

Velstro inchskip

A heavy, irregularly contoured hand-tool. [Compound.] **DJ**

venefice

A Sarkoy artisan skilled in the use of poisons. "By practice and tradition the Sarkoy were accomplished poisoners. A Master Venefice reportedly could kill a man merely by walking past him." [From the Latin *venenum*, "poison", and *facere*, "to make".] **PL, SK** *II*, **SK** *IV**

ventrole

A volcanic vent; the *Fumighast Ventrole* was a vast chasm on the planet Shaul. [From "vent" and "fumarole", meaning "a volcanic hole".] **SP** *XVIII*

verbane

A fine wood used for interior paneling and moldings. **GPr** *V*

verd

On Cadwal, the metal copper; when capitalized, the term also referred to Friday. For details, see *Ain* and *glimmet*, also *ing, milden, ort, smollen,* and *tzein*. [Variant usage.] **ArS** *I*

verge

A species of imported tree, often purple-green. [Variant usage.] **ArS** *I*

verktt

"Radiation valves"; they were made from *padisks* (q.v.), an artificial element. **GI** *XVI*

versi-dimensional

Having reversed dimensions. " 'This one —' he indicated Picture No. 4 '— is identical to ours, except that it's seen from a versi-dimensional angle. Everything appears inside out.'" [From the Latin *versus* and "dimension".] **SEB**

veruli
A fibrous structure on the body of Miss Aries 44R951, an extraterrestrial participant in the Miss Universe contest; related terms were *agrix, clavon, gadel, orgote* and *therulta* (q.v.). **MMU** *IV*

vespril
A species of bird whose colorful feathers were used as decorative plumes. *L XXVII*

Viasvar
See *Visfer*. **DTA** *II**, **GPr** *II**

vibre
A classical musical instrument, usually included in the Valdemar Kutte Grand Salon Orchestra. [? from "vibrate".] **BD** *XII*

vibrilator
One of the devices hanging "...in gala style from the elbows of each leg" of a *twastic* (q.v.). **Rh** *II*

vida
The number three in the Paonese language. **LP** *X*

vincus
The narrow body-part connecting Nissifer's abdomen and thorax; see also *bazil*. [By contraction of "vinculum", meaning "a uniting band or bundle of fibers".] **CS** *IV-2*

violeer
An audacious person, prone to illegal acts. [From "violate" or "violent" and "buccaneer".] **W** *VII*

Violet Mendolence
A type of beverage, probably wine, served in a flask. **CS** *I-1*

virebol
A species of tree. [? from "virile" and "bole".] **SK** *II*

virtu
The undefinable charisma or personality-status cherished by the Kruthe "Emblem Men" (CC). "Physiognomically he was one of the

archangels, radiant with *virtu*." (OM) [Variant usage.] **CC II, OM VI** *et al.*

Visfer

"...originally Viasvar, an Ordinary of the ancient Legion of Truth; now a low-grade honorific used to address a person lacking aristocratic distinction." (DTA)

"The two most common appellatives of the Gaean Reach are Dm., for Domine [q.v.], which may properly be applied to all persons of distinguished or exalted station, and Vv., a contraction of Visfer ..., then a landed gentleman, finally the common polite appellative." (GPr) **DTA II*, GPr II***

visiphone

A communications device having both audio and video capabilities. [From the Latin *visus*, "seen", and the Greek *phone*, "tone" or "voice".] **KM I, SO II, SSP II, T II**

visp

A predatory creature; it "...stood nine feet tall and looked across the night through luminous pink eyes, and traced the scent of flesh by means of two flexible proboscises growing from each side of [its] scalp-crest." When wandering it emitted a melancholy call. **CS III-2**

vistgeist

"A term from the jargon of Teaching: essentially, the idealized version of one's self. Teaching defines the vistgeist rather narrowly and exhorts the individual to a lifelong attempt to match the beatitude of the vistgeist. Howard [the criminal Howard Alan Treesong], for vistgeist, formulated an entity totally emancipated from the strictures of Teaching." [? from the German *wissen*, "to know", and *geist*, "spirit".] **BD XIV***

Vital Exprescience

The Druids' great Tree: "A vast breathing sappy mass, a trunk five miles in diameter, twelve miles from the great kneed roots to the ultimate bud." **ST II**

Vitalistics

Vital statistics. [Amalgamation.] *TLF VII*

vitran

"A process of visual representation unique to Garwiy. The artist and his apprentice use minute rods of colored glass a quarter of an inch long, one twentieth of an inch in diameter. The rods are cemented lengthwise against a back-plate of frosted glass. The finished work, illuminated from behind, becomes a landscape, portrait, or pattern, vital beyond all other representational processes, combining radiance, chromatic range, flexibility, refinement, detail, and scope. Inordinate effort and time is required to produce even a small work, with approximately sixty thousand individual rods comprising each square foot of finished surface." [From the Latin *vitrum*, "glass".] *BFM II**

vitrean

Glass used in a showcase. [By alteration of "vitrine".] *DE VI*

vitripane

A tough, transparent material used as window glass. [From the Latin *vitrum*, "glass", and "pane".] *T VII*

vitrophon

A popular musical instrument. [From the Latin *vitrum*, "glass", and the Greek *phone*, "tone" or "voice".] *ShW III*

vivest-101

A restorative medication, administered parenterally. [From the Latin *vivere*, "to live".] *SP XXIV*

VLON

"...a secret force. It comes from within, exerting irresistible thrust. It partakes of all gaiety, of the striding gallantry of the beautiful Tattenbarth nymphs, of the soul's conquest over infinity. This is VLON, which may be revealed to no one." This explanation was written by the villain Howard Alan Treesong in his notebook, *The Book of Dreams*, and included a secret symbolic design. (Vance has elaborated further on this concept in his article "The Symbol", in *Cosmopolis*, G. Mina, ed., 1988.). *BD XIV*

voitch

"A single organism, comparable to a gigantic lichen, voitch supports a black mat ten feet thick on tawny or pale gray stalks fifty feet tall. Certain growths of voitch are poisonous, others predatory and carnivorous. The benign specimens furnish food, drink, fiber, shelter and pharmaceuticals." It was commonly purple. **BD** *VIII**

volith

"...to toy idly with a matter, the implication being that the person involved is of such Jovian potency that all difficulties dwindle to contemptible triviality." [? from "volition".] **LC** *II*

voluspo

A nonsense term in the ditty sung by Mikelaus the circus performer. **M** *VIII*

vondaloy

A very durable alloy used for security gratings. [In part from "alloy".] **F** *VIII*

voulgue

An archaic hand-weapon used on the planet Thamber. **KM** *IX*

voulp

A cave-dwelling animal, not described. **MT** *IX*

vulp

"A small voracious predator, common throughout the Dalkenberg region of south-central Lune XXIII." [By shortening of "vulpine", meaning "fox-like".] **ShW** *II**

vyre

"A light weapon used for the control of rodents, the hunting of wild fowl, and like service." This firearm, as well as other complex weapons, was held to be ineffective against witches. **W** *XII**

W

walkinger
A species of insectivorous bird. *GPr VIII*

waloonch
A pejorative term; Sarp referred to Kedidah as a "hity-tity waloonch".
W V

wampoon
A species of alien creature from Argo Navis, having a whitish body;
about five hundred *wampoons* lived in an old brick warehouse in the
Parade of the Alien Quarter on Light-year Road, where they kept
shop; they disliked lights. See also *jeek* and *tinko*. *AOC II*

watak
A plant whose roots stored a gallon of potable sap, excessive drinking
of which could cause deafness. *CC III*

water-flamerian
Not described; "Shierl gazed at Guyal, dark eyes wide and liquid
as the great water-flamerian of South Almery." [From "water" and
"flame".] *DE VI*

water-puff
A popular seafood. [Compound.] *W V*

water-wefkin
See *wefkin*. *ShW XI*

wattledab
A seafood (?) gathered in bushels. [Compound.] *W XII*

wau kema
A decorative style employing leafy, aboriginal motifs in brown and
blue. *SSh*

waxweed

A wild species of weed, commonly black. [Compound.] *DTA X*

waylocks

The mind's faculties. The green elixir served in the bar of the Arkady Inn was advertised as "salubrious, clarifying of the mental waylocks, conducive to merry diversities." [Compound.] *ArS IV*

waywisp

A vagabond: "A person who arrives like a waywisp from some far corner of the universe can depart as easily without paying his bill." [Compound; and by association with "will-o'-the-wisp".] *BD XII*

wefkin

A forest-dwelling creature; also *water-wefkin* (ShW). "Wefkins are calm and stately by nature; we are solitary philosophers, as it were. Further, we are a gallant folk, proud and handsome, which conduces to fate-ridden amours both with mortals and with other halflings. We are truly magnificent beings"; and also: "...paladins of valor" (M). [? from "waif" and the diminutive suffix "-kin".] *M III, Rh I, ShW XI*

weldewiste

"A word from the lexicon of social anthropology, to sum up a complicated idea comprising the attitude with which an individual confronts his environment; his interpretation of the events of his life; his cosmic consciousness; his character and personality from the purview of comparative culture." The word is approximated by the German *Weltanschauung*. [From the German *Welt*, "world", and *wissen*, "to know".] *GPr II**

welt-cloth

A material used for clothing. [Compound.] *ShW XIII*

werd

"A man-shaped supernatural being who prowls by night and sleeps underground by day. According to Maunish folklore, it hides in the shadows, waiting to pounce on children and carry them away." [? from "weird".] *BD XII**

whangeroo
A big-shot, as "Big Boo the Whangeroo". **AOC** *VII*

Whelm
The military agency of the Alastor Cluster. [Variant usage: "to overcome or engulf".] **Tr** *Preface*

wheriot
A horned animal used to draw carriages. [? by association with "chariot".] **CS** *V-2*

whirlaway
Ildefonse's majestic flying conveyance. [Compound.] **Rh** *II*

Whitherer
A member of a group of political dissenters espousing vague goals; they held their caucuses at the Hall of Revelation in Carnevalle. [From "whither".] **TLF** *V*

willawen
A variety of supernatural creature, distinguished from fairies and various other halflings: "In a third class are merrihews, willawen and hyslop, and also, by some reckonings, quists and darklings." See also *skak*. **L** *X**

wipwark
A possibly supernatural creature associated with ghosts. **PL** *XI*

wirwove
The female partner of an *eiodark* (q.v.); the term was applied as an honorific. **Ma** *IV*

wishdream
A type of musical instrument. [Compound.] **NL** *III-2*

wisk-weasel
A common wild animal; its likeness was carved into the tent-stakes of a local tribe. **As** *VI*

wisnet

A species of wild mammal; the bucks were known for their sexual appetite. *E XII*

wittol

"One of every thousand Uldras [the gray-skinned autochthons of Koryphon] is born albino, eunuchoid, short of stature and round-headed. These are the wittols, treated with a mixture of repugnance, contempt and superstitious awe. They are credited with competence at small magic and witchcraft; occasionally they deal in spells, curses and potions. Major magic remains the prerogative of the tribal warlocks. The wittols bury dead, torture captives, and serve as emissaries between tribes. They move with safety across the Alouan, since no Uldra warrior would deign or dare to kill a wittol." *GPr I**

wobbly

The third of the artificial foods eaten on Arrabus, Wyst; it was said to "fill up the cracks" (or chinks); see also *sturge*. [Variant usage.] *W I*

wole

See *carpet wole*. *GP XV*

wolf-bane

A fungus whose ingestion induced "…cramps of the stomach, together with chills, nausea, fever, hallucinations and a ringing of the ears." It was seldom fatal. [Compound.] *L XXIII*

woohaw

An aged stick-in-the-mud of faded vitality. "I cannot deny my occasional recklessness. I am a woman who loves life! I suppose that a few old woohaws consider me unconventional. In a sense, it is a compliment!" *PoC I-7*

worminger

A handler or steward for the giant propulsive worms used to power merchant ships. [From "worm".] *CS I-2*

wortleberry
A fragrant bush whose berries were used to brew beer. [By alteration of "whortleberry".] *GPr VII*

wosker
A bloke. *ArS VI*

wracken
A marine creature preyed upon by the *gaid* (q.v.). *BD V*

wump
1. A gigantic herbivore of mild disposition indigenous to Star Home, "ponderous creatures often forty or even fifty feet long and twenty feet high. Wumps walk on six heavy legs and ingest grass by means of sinuous snouts which bring grass to the maw. The Ritters domesticate wumps and build small residences upon their broad backs." [From wump, "a heavy sound".] (Lu) 2. Slang for manufactured food, i.e. *gruff*, *deedle* and *wobbly* (q.v.); it was served in a *wumper*, or cafeteria. (W) *Lu IV-5, W III*

wurgle
A large, vicious, usually mouse-colored dog used for hunting. Its hooting was "a mournful throbbing sound". *W X*

wysen-imp
A den-dwelling creature. *CS V-2*

X

xenode detector
A type of electronic surveillance device used aboard spaceships; see also *macroscope*. [? from the Greek *xenos*, "foreign", and "node".] **BD** *XIII*

xheng
"Untranslatable; a dark and peculiar emotion which might most succinctly be translated *horror-lust*: a generalized desire to inflict torments and agonies, a fervent dedication to the achievement of sadistic excesses." **GPr** *XV**

Xoma
A stage in the quasi-religious philosophical system "Gnosis". "... each human being lived over and over again in the same body, either perfecting itself through careful practice of the Ameliorations, and eventually moving upward or failing, whereupon it must attempt the same life again, over and over until satisfactory adjustments had been made, so that it might enter a new 'Xoma', which once again must be lived in exact accord with propriety. In general, Gnosis was considered a cheerful and optimistic doxology, since the worst that could happen to a transgressor was that he or she might backslide a Xoma or two." **Th** *Glossary*

Xtl
"... (pronounced 'kstull'): the polite honorific in use on Cassander, ultimately derived from the word *stletto* or 'pirate captain'." **FT** *II**

xyxyl
A sacred bird, whose union with the sea-demon Rhadamth was said to have originated mankind. **Pn** *VII*

Y

yaga
The number seven in the Dirdir language. **D X**

yaga-yagas
A cult of Sweetfleur on Fiametta. "They set off along an avenue, which first passed a field devoted to the asseveration of spiritual verities, and another where the same beliefs were ridiculed and refuted. Special cults: meta-men, paramystics, futurians, vegetarians, yaga-yagas, each convening in a private sector, where each sect celebrated its own style of reality." **PoC VIII-1**

yaha
Garlet's word for unconscious or imaginative processes; an external manifestation of free will. "In simple words, it is the play of independent free will among choices. The ordinary mind does not control or even affect yaha, and this is the basis of the force. The conscious mind puts the question; yaha searches among the options and indicates a 'yes' or a 'no'." **NL XIX-1**

Yellow
"A time of freedom and carelessness, marking the transition between youth and maturity. When their time arrives, the young men and women of Thaery and Glentlin become wayfarers and wander the thirteen counties. They travel by footpath and take shelter at wayside inns or camp in the meadows. As they go they maintain the landscape; planting trees, repairing trails, clearing thickets of dead bramble, quelling spider-grass, the odious *hariah* [q.v.], and thorn. If anyone shirks, he becomes notorious, and the epithet *chraus* ('languid', 'small-souled', 'dishonorable') is apt to persist for the rest of his life." [? by combination of "youth" and "callow".] **MT I*, MT** *Glossary*

yapnut

A common variety of tree. [Compound.] *An V*

yarlap

A type of wild beast, not described; "...and fences to keep out the *banjees* [q.v.] and *yarlaps*". *Th I*

yetch

Slang for an outlander. *BD VIII*

yewl-stone

A precious gem. *SK IX*

yonupa

A species of tall tree inhabited by lethally playful tree-waifs. *Th II*

yoot

"...a bulky animal, hybrid of mandoril and rat (mandoril hybrids are widespread across all of Cadwal), lethargic of habit, wandering the beach, sucking up [butterfly] grubs through a long proboscis. A repellent creature, semiaquatic, with hide mottled pink and black, the yoot exudes a noxious odor, as do many other creatures of Cadwal." And: "A two-legged mandoril-rat hybrid, four feet tall, with a rudimentary intelligence. The creatures are peculiar to the Lutwen Islands, and are intensely vicious." *ArS I*, V*

yorbane

A type of wax applied by maidens to the chins of male visitors: "a quaint survival of the olden times when the Maseach were notorious for their immoderate pleasures." *BFM V*

yu-sapphire

A dark precious stone. *DE VI*

Z

zachinko
"…a small sound-box studded with keys, played with the right hand. Pressure on the keys forced air through reeds in the keys themselves, producing a concertina-like tone." It was used only during more formal social intercourse. **MM**

Zaelday
A day of the week. **BFM** *X*

zagazig
1. A stage routine which requires luring daredevils from the audience, proposed by Moncrief as a sequence in his Trevanian program. [There is an Egyptian town of this name.] (Lu) 2. A species of plant, commonly pale blue and used for the decoration of urban roads. (MT) **Lu** *V-4*, **MT** *X*

zamander
Precious blue gemstone quarried from beneath the *Shivering Trillows* (q.v.), and comprising part of Uthaw's treasure. **CS** *V-2*

zant
See *byzantaur*. **SO** *V*

Zeno
A class of spaceship. **SvW** *XIII*

zhaktum
The Koton word meaning "reckless fellow"; Paddy Blackthorne used it as a euphemistic translation of "rascal". **SP** *V*

zhna-dih
In the Dirdir language, "individual initiative …a great dashing leap, trailing lightning-like sparks." **D** *IV*

zikko

A form of gold coin, demanded of Rhialto by Um-Foad. **Rh** II

zinfonella

A popular musical instrument played aboard the ship *Miraldra's Enchantment*. **ShW** IX

zink

"...a coin representative of a man-minute, the hundredth part of an SLU [Standard Labor-value Unit, the monetary unit of the Gaean Reach]. Gaean time is based upon the standard day of Earth, subdivided into twenty-four hours, after ancient tradition." (The SLU was defined as "the value of an hour of unskilled labor under standard conditions.") **DTA** VI*

zipangote

An odd-looking beast: "They were narrow-shouldered and high in the back; they had six powerful legs and a narrow untrustworthy-looking head — a composite of camel, horse, goat, dog, lizard." The *zipangote* was driven as a pack animal. **BP** IV

zizyl-beast

An odd creature: "...you constitute a distraction, a zizyl-beast in a ballroom." **SvW** II

Zoga'ar zum Fulkash am

In the Dirdir language, a route whose name meant, "Literally: the way of death's-heads with purple-gleaming eye-sockets." **D** IV*

zogma

A noisome species of herb. **ShW** III

Zoriani nac Thair nac Thairi

Matriarchs of the Sisterhood: "In loose translation: Female Agents of Desperate Deeds." They derived power from their "...ability to defile the temple or any particular Chilite. There were six degrees of defilement, the first being a touch of a female finger, the sixth a drenching with a bucketful of unmentionable substances. The Sister, or Sisters, who executed the defilements were volunteers, usually old, sick, and quite willing to end their lives dramatically by poison wads ingested immediately after achieving their goals." *An III**

zovelle
A musical instrument having a chiming tone and played in the Carnevalle. *TLF I*

zs'hanh
A Dirdir term referring to the virtue of "…contemptuous indifference to the activity of others. There are twenty-eight castes of Dirdir … and four castes of Dirdirmen: the Immaculates, the Intensives, the Estranes, the Cluts. *Zs'hanh* is reckoned an attribute of the fourth through the thirteenth Dirdir grades. The Immaculates also practice *zs'hanh*. It is a noble doctrine." *D IV*

zumbold
A classical musical instrument, usually included in the Valdemar Kutte Grand Salon Orchestra. *BD XII*

zut
A wily creature: "…he is crafty as a zut." *SvW XIII*

zuweshekar
["Played" would be] "a feeble rendering of the Shant verb zuweshekar: to use a musical instrument with such passion that the music takes on a life of its own." *An I**

zuzhma kastchai
"The contraction of a phrase: the ancient and secret world-folk derived from dark rock and mother-soil"; i.e., the Pnume. *Pn III**

zyche
A substance whose tincture was sometimes used in wizard's potions. *EO VII*

zygage
A potent, psychedelic drug, taken as smoke, potion or nosesalve, and having debilitating effects. *BP VII*

Made in the USA
Charleston, SC
23 March 2016